His, Hers, Ours

Maya Crosby-Emery

Maya Crosby-Emery

ISBN-13: 978-1-9829-5772-8

DEDICATION

To my Mum, Karoline, my sister Ty, Sue and anyone else who helped me in this process. I'm forever grateful.

ACKNOWLEDGMENTS

Thank you to all my readers on Wattpad.
I couldn't have done it without you.
xoxox

CHAPTER ONE

Everleigh:

It's been a couple weeks, maybe around two months, since I've moved to America with my boyfriend, Dan, and if I'm honest, I wish I didn't go.

My days start at six am, I slowly get out of bed, to make sure I do not wake up Dan because I fear of what he would do. But because of his hung-over state, I'm safe this morning. I walk up to Rose's room to wake her up. I get her ready quietly and make her a quick breakfast, then I drop her off at my neighbours' house.

My neighbours don't know what goes on at home, if you can call it that. I haven't gotten the chance to make any friends since I have been here.

Every day I cover up the cuts and bruises from the day before with makeup as best as I can, like today.
I got dressed and ran to my work in the little coffee shop a couple blocks away from the apartment.
I've been working at 'The Sugarplum' for three weeks now and I also worked at a restaurant for three nights a week just to make ends meet at the end of the month.

It never used to be like that.

 I arrived to put my apron on and started my shift. The morning went on like usual, nothing that exciting happened until lunchtime.
It was always the busiest time of the day, I was running

around serving and taking orders left, right and center.

I was serving a table with two parents and their two children. I couldn't help but smile at them. They were so adorable and all seemed happy and you could feel the love coming from them. I wish I had that. I have it with my daughter I love her to bits, and I would do anything for her to be safe and happy.

I walked up to them with a smile, putting the same act as I do every customer.

"Hello and welcome to The Sugarplum, I'm Everleigh. What can I get for you?"

I spoke, writing down their order. The kids were laughing while the parents gave me their order.

"I'll get some crayons for the kids to draw with. I know the wait can be long for them." I suggested.

"Thank you, that's very thoughtful of you. Do you have kids?" the mother asked, pleased with my idea.

"Yes, I do. A little girl named Rose."

"How lovely! How old?"

"She's turning three in five months."

But before she could say something back I was called by my manager, Mary, who wanted me to wait for another table.

"I'm sorry, duty calls! I'll be back with the crayons and your drinks."

And I left.

****

Ash Mortimer:

The boys and I, just finished getting money from some low life of man that decided to spend all his money on drugs and being in debt to me rather than putting food on the table for his family.

"Ash... I'm hungry..." Paul started.

"Me too..." Louis added.

"Me three... can we get some food?" Carter batted his eyelashes at me like some girl since he was sat next to me as I drove.

"Stop whining the three of you!" I snapped making them whine even more.

"But please!"

"Ok ok! Stop it! If we go get something to eat will you stop whining?" I pleaded.

"Yes!"

All three of them said in unison, content that I had succumbed to their hunger.

Those are my men, my most trusted ones: Carter, Louis and Paul but one of them was not with us at the moment, our newest addition, Ray.

We stopped at the first diner shop. We came in and sat at one of the tables. I am feared in this city so when we came in everything went silent, stares following us as we took our seats.

That's when I saw her. A beautiful angel, with her flowing blond locks and her piercing green eyes, her smile that lights up the room. I feel like I've seen her before, she seemed so familiar.

"Hello, gentlemen! What can I get for you today?"

My thoughts were taken by this beautiful creature and her angelic voice.

"I'll get the fries, burger, chocolate milkshake, oh and the chocolate Sundae."

Paul said and the boys continued asking all that was on the menu.

"All right and for you sir?" her smile looked so beautiful.

"Just a black coffee."

"Ok, black coffee. Nothing else for you?"

"No."

"I'll add a chocolate brownie too."

"No."

"You'll thank me after."

And she just left before I could tell her otherwise.

"I like her boss, she's not scared of you,"

"Shut up."

"Could I have your brownie since you don't want it..."

"No, you ain't having it, Paul!" I growled.

"I'm back with your orders gentlemen. Enjoy." She called out after a while, balancing our orders on the trays she was holding.

I need to know more about her, she's something else. That's when I had set in my mind to make her mine, and there was nothing she could do about it.
I was enjoying my brownie when I got a phone call

"WHAT?! .... Um... yes..... I'm on my way." I hang up the phone and stood up slipping my jacket back on.

 "Let's go." I nodded over to the door, the guys following my actions.

The boys and I got up and left. I left a huge tip for her and paid the bill.

CHAPTER TWO

Everleigh:

After serving the big muscular guys, I felt happier than I have the days before. Throughout the week they had come in every day and always asked for me to serve them. It had become our little tradition that seemed to have stuck for another two weeks. Each time leaving me huge amounts of money for tips.

I felt really embarrassed each time and asked the man that seemed to be their leader to take the money back but he never let me. Always saying 'take the money Angel, you deserve it.' It felt weird to have someone take care of me, even if I saw him an hour at lunch time, he was always so nice to me.

He often came with the same three guys, only on the one occasion did he come with a fourth one. They were all very nice and welcoming to me. The brown headed one with the matching eyes, I think his name was Carter, seemed to be the nicest one, helping me clear the tables each time.

They felt safe. They became familiar, it was our daily routine and it made me feel a little better at each passing day. Their presence was not enough to make me forget the life at home, but at least I would come home remembering those mesmerizing blue eyes of that leather jacket wearing man with the gorgeous smile and dimples to match.

My heart beats a little faster every time the bell of the diner rings and he walks in as if he owns the place. I freeze and let the silent room surround me as our eyes meet, every single time.

You have a boyfriend Everleigh. I chant over and over in my mind but he just makes me forget all that is wrong in my life.

 My shift was coming to an end and I was walking home. I picked up Rose on the way, and I was preparing myself to see what state I would find Dan in this evening. She kept on babbling about what she had done that day, being my ray of sunshine.

I walked through the door and put Rose down when I saw Dan with a bottle of whiskey in his hand. I wonder how we came to this, to the drinking, the fights, the hits... I don't think he will ever change.

"Go to your room baby."

I told Rose and she looked at me and ran to the stairs. But before she could get up, Dan held her arm and she started crying and screaming.

"Let her go, Dan!" I yelled putting my bag down to the side.

"And why would I do that? Huh! Where the fuck were you?" He growled, swinging the bottle letting its content spill onto the carpeted living room floor.

"Language! I was at work! Now let her go!" My voice firm.

Rose kept on screaming and calling for me. He only held her arm tighter and shook her violently. My heart breaking at each moment.

"Will you shut up?" He shook her harder.

"Let her go!" I pleaded, tears coming to my eyes.

My daughter shouldn't see this, she should never live through this and now she's paying for my stupid mistakes.

I couldn't take it anymore. I walked up to him and slapped him as hard as I could. He let go of her and walked me up against the wall, caging me with his body, the bottle of whiskey long forgotten.

"You shouldn't have done that, you bitch."

"Run baby to your room." I ordered Rose, who was frozen in her spot, tears streaming down her cheeks.

"But mummy–" she sniffed, wiping her eyes clean of the tears.

"I'll be ok, baby." I gave her a sad smile which seemed to work as she ran up the stairs.

Who am I kidding? It won't be ok.

I felt my cheek sting and I knew that my daily hell would start.
He pushed to the ground. His sick smile came on and he bent down to me and grabbed me by my hair and whispered in my ear.

"You naughty girl... ts ts ts. You should know better than to hit me. You know what I can do."

I cringed and the smell of his breath that smelled of alcohol and his bloodshot eyes. They seemed different than the other times.

Was he high on something?

He hit me again and again, my head hitting the floor. I put my hand on my head I looked down at my fingers. Blood, what a surprise (note the sarcasm). He kicked me in my ribs as I held in the tears. I needed to be stronger than this, my father taught me better than to be weak in front of the enemy.

But how can my own boyfriend become the enemy? I thought he loved me. Who does that to the person they love?

He hit me again a couple times in the face and by that time I had a black eye, a bust lip and a cut on my head that was bleeding. I think my ribs are bruised, nothing that I haven't been through before. He took a knife and was coming closer to me when his phone rang. *Thank god for that!*

"Hello, yes. I'm coming, save my order."

He hung up and crouched down to me and lifted my shirt, he took the knife and ran it by my hip and made me bleed with the small cut. I didn't even fight him anymore.

"You got lucky this time babe. But when I come back I'll finish this. It's going to be fun."

He kissed my cheek and with that, he left. I waited for the door to close and hear the car drive off before getting up. Once it was safe to go, I got up and went to clean my wounds, luckily they weren't too deep, so no need to go to the hospital to get stitches this time.

Once I was done I went to check on my baby who was crying her eyes out once she saw me.

"Mama!" she sobbed.

She ran to me jumping into my arms as I hugged her tight. We can't stay here anymore. I can't let my baby see me like this anymore. I know there is nowhere for us to go but we deserve better than Dan. I deserve better and I know that now. He never treated me right, it took a handsome man to walk into my life to realise that he was no good for me.

With this new fire in me, I ran to my room and got a big duffle bag and put some clothes of mine and ran back to Rose's room and put her stuff in there too as well as a few toys and the money I had been secretly saving in one of her stuffed toys. I had finally gotten enough and that was thanks to the mysterious man from the diner and his massive tips every lunch time for three weeks.

I changed before leaving, took Rose and the bag and left the house. I didn't have much to change into either so I slipped on an old pair of shorts and changed shirt and called it a day.

I was walking down the streets of New York at night with a two year old in my arms, fighting the sleep away.

I didn't know where I was, or where I was going, I just hoped something would come to mind when I was walking.

We approached this little alley and heard someone scream. I walked over to try and see who it was, my curiosity will get the best of me one day. I heard talking and recognised Dan's voice. Between all of them.

"Pl-please Mr. Mortimer. I'll get your money I p-promise." he stuttered in fear.

"Dan... You should have paid me two weeks ago. You had more than enough time to get me my money."

He had a deep voice that sent shivers down my spine. I heard it before.

"Pl-please, I have a wife and a kid."

"Louis, punch him"

I couldn't help but let out a little laugh and scoff at him saying I was his wife. I'll never be his!

I didn't realise that they heard me. I was pushed up to the tall muscular man, who I'm guessing is the one waiting for his money.

"Hey don't push me!"

****
Ash Mortimer:

"Hey don't push me!"

That voice. I turned around and saw my angel with a mini version of herself in her arms. The same golden hair and she looked at me, she had beautiful blue eyes.

"Mummy, I scared" the little girl squeaked out, fear swimming in her blue orbs.
I never want to see fear in her eyes again.

"I'm here baby." she held her closer to her chest, kissing the top of her head.

She looked straight into my eyes, questioning me with her

gaze until her eyes widened.

"You're the guy from lunch." her voice was almost a whisper but loud enough for me to hear her.

I couldn't help but smirk, she remembered me. I mean she should because I have been seeing her every day for the past three weeks straight. But that smirk soon faded when I hear that dicks voice.

"Everleigh! What the fuck are you doing out here? And with Rose? What's with the bag?"

Ahh, Everleigh that's her name. Beautiful. I thought.

She was wearing shorts and a simple white tank top and a baby pink jumper. She must be freezing in this weather!

"Language! I'm getting away from you! You sick fudge tart!" her frail voice growled back at him.

"Hooo! It seems it's not your lucky night!" of course, Paul had to make a comment.

"Like hell you are! You're mine!" Dan shot back, venom dripping from his voice.

I looked at her and she looked so scared of him, the same fear in Rose's eyes. It wasn't before I saw that she had a huge black eye, her busted lip and bruises all around her neck that everything started added up.

I turned and punched him, hearing her gasp at the action but I was seeing red.

"She's mine! You lost her the minute you laid a hand on

her!"

****
Everleigh:

"She's mine! You lost her the minute you laid a hand on her!"

I stood there in shock. I couldn't believe I'm listening to that.

Is he standing up for me? But why? And why the hell would he? I don't even know his name and yet here he is, claiming me.

"Get him to the base, I'm not done with him yet." the blue eyed man growled out to the other guys that were there making them take Dan away kicking and screaming.

He walked past me and I held Rose closer to me, afraid that Dan could reach us. Rose was shivering in my arms, in my haste the leave the house I didn't really consider the weather outside in doing so. I put the bag down and took my jumper off and put it on her to warm her up, rubbing up and down her back to create more warmth.
However, now I was the one who was cold. But if it meant that she wasn't then so be it.

What I didn't realise was the blue eyed man was walking towards me, shrugging his leather jacket off and putting it around my shoulders. The weight of it taking me by surprise but it immediately gave me warmth and it smelt real good.

"You're cold, here." he called out softly to me, readjusting the jacket so that it didn't slip off.

I looked down and stuttered a thank you. He lifted my chin so that I could look him in the eyes, his touch making me feel all hot.

This is not going to end well.

"No need to thank me, angel. Come with me."

I couldn't help but blush at him.
Why the hell am I acting like a freaking school girl who is talking to her crush?

"O-ok. But don't hurt my daughter please." was my weak excuse but I felt drawn to him.

"Don't worry Angel I won't hurt my little princess" his hand now cupping my left cheek, rubbing small circles.

What just happened?

CHAPTER THREE

Everleigh:

My mind can't process all that is happening right now. I don't know what to think of all this. I should leave, everything points to danger. He is danger and yet here I am following him like a lost puppy back to his car.

He led us to a black range rover, and sat me and Rose at the back. Rose had already fallen asleep in my arms and I was feeling my eyes getting heavier, but I felt like I needed to stay awake. I mean I cannot just close my eyes on these people, I don't know them. For all I know they could kill me and not batter an eyelid about it. I know the sort of people they are, the sort of man he is. I know this under world better than anyone else.

"Go to sleep Angel. You're safe now." his voice soothed me, melting my heart and making me blindly follow his orders.

I don't even know that man's name and yet I feel at ease with him. Yet, he has been nice so far, he was always caring at the diner, trustworthy. My mind was screaming at me to run as far away as I could, I promised myself I wouldn't go down that road again but I couldn't stop myself. Without even realising I had fallen asleep in the car.

Suddenly, the car came to a stop, I woke up to the sound of his voice whispering in my ear, the cold January winds greeting my exposed skin from the open door where he was standing.

"We are here Angel."

He helped me to get out, holding his hand out for me to take but since I had Rose in my arms he took my bag and put it on his shoulder instead.
I looked up to see the mansion in front of me, it was huge and this only made my thoughts on him being in a gang of some sort be more believable.

"Wow, it's really beautiful! You live here?"

Gosh, I feel stupid now, of course, he lives here if not we wouldn't be here!

"I do, as well as a few of my most trusted men. The rest of them live in their own homes or at the warehouse." he informed me.

I didn't trust myself to say anything so I nodded. He came closer to me and tucked a piece of hair behind my ear, staring deeply into my eyes.

"Don't worry Angel, you're safe here with me. And so is the little princess. I may be in a gang, I'm sure you realised that by now but I promise I won't let anything happen to you." his words seemed to hold sincerity to them, I slowly felt my trust grow for him.

And with that, he took my hand and led me to the house and I couldn't help but blush and feel electric shocks through my hand. I tried shaking the feeling off and pulling my hand out of his but he had a firm grip but not enough to hurt me, just enough that I wouldn't slip through his fingers.

We walked in to be greeted by a man, the third man that was at the diner every time. I think this one was Carter, but I couldn't be one hundred percent sure, I'm terrible at remembering names.

"Boss! Paul and Louis told me a bit about what happ– Oh hello there!"

He smiled as he looked at me and saw that I had Rose in my arms too. I guess the two other goons are Paul and Louis.

"I'm Carter." he smiled warmly at me, his brown eyes shining with mischief.

"Yes, you take your burger with extra pickles and no mayo, right?" I may not remember names but I sure as hell remember their orders.

"You're the girl from the dinner!" he exclaimed, faking surprise which didn't go unnoticed by me.

"Yep, I'm Everleigh and this little munchkin in my arms is Rose."

He looked over at the blue eyed man and smiled like the Cheshire cat, making me a bit nervous.

"Let her be, Carter. We'll have a meeting tomorrow, but for now, it's late so, go to bed."

"Yes boss, it was nice meeting you Everleigh." making sure to whisper seeing Rose sleeping.

"You too Carter." I gave a small smile back. He was nice.

I didn't even realise that I was still holding hands with the man and I still don't know his name. I took my hand out of his and put it under Rose for extra support, she may be little but she sure is heavy!

"Well let me take you to my room." he said clearing his throat.

"Sorry? Your room?" I questioned, making sure I had heard him correctly.

"Yes." he affirmed but when he saw the look on my face he changed his answer.

"Um I mean no. no. I'll take you to a spare room. Let me just see if there is one." he rubbed the back of his neck.

"Right ok, well thank you for everything but I don't want to impose..." I trailed off following him as he started his search for an empty guest room, and trust me, there are a lot of rooms in this house.

"You are not imposing, if not I wouldn't have brought you here with me. I want you to be safe and judging by earlier events you no longer have anywhere to go." he pointed out finally finding a room for me.

He pushed the door wider showing me the beautifully simple room with a queen size bed, a chest of drawers and other pieces of furniture that I weren't quite sure what they were called. I mean I just wanted the bed.

"Umm, sorry but what's your name, you never said." I nervously spoke up.

"Ash. Ash Mortimer." he confidently stated.

"Well thank you Ash, for all this. I really appreciate it. But you really don't have to get into all this trouble I could have slept on the couch." I blushed, casting my gaze to the ground.

"It's alright. Just to warn you, this room is under renovation that's why there's all sorts of tool boxes and paint stuff around the room, so the door over there leads straight into my room which is next door to yours. On top of that we have a communicating bathroom. I hope that's alright?" he rubbed the back of his neck, the tip of his ears turning pink.

I hadn't even realised the pots of paint scattered around the room, now that I looked at it a little better, it did seem unfinished.

"What will this room become?" I found myself asking.

"Well, this is sort of my room. I was planning on opening this wall up and making it a huge master bedroom. I was sleeping in here until the paint work and flooring next door was done but it's fine, I can sleep somewhere else." he shrugged.

"What? No. I can't take your bed. Show me to another room or a sofa or something, you can sleep here." I rushed out, trying to make my way out of the room.

He stopped me by holding my shoulder, my eyes meeting his again.

"Hey, it's ok. You can sleep here, I'll take the couch. There aren't any other rooms available. I bought this place a few weeks ago and it needed to have some changes made to it, so all the other rooms aren't really finished yet. Those that are, Carter and all that are sleeping in them."

"But, I can't sleep here. I can get a hotel or something. This is too much." I started panicking again, I don't like to be in debt to anyone.

"It's fine honestly. I'll only come in to use the shower and get changed, that's it. We'll figure something out later, for you and Rose. Okay?" his eyes searching mine.

"But–" I started but got cut off by him stepping closer, leaning down to whisper in my ear.

"No buts Angel, its final." and with that, he walked into the bathroom, leaving me stunned in place.

I was too tired to fight any longer anyway, I might as well enjoy this.

While he was in there I put Rose down on the bed making sure she was warm enough and had enough space. I took the bag and started looking for my pj's but like the idiot I am, I forgot to put some in my bag.

"Shit." I mumbled under my breath, searching frantically for something decent to wear.

"Are you alright Angel?" his deep voice called out to me making me jump in surprise.

I turned to see a topless Ash leaning against the bathroom door, looking so freaking sexy! He has the classic six pack, the 'happy trail', tattoos on his chest, arms... he looked so good. I was so checking him out I didn't even realise he was up close and personal. His hand were on my waist and he was looking down to me. I could get used to seeing this every day. I sighed to myself before I shook back to reality.

What am I saying?

"What's the matter, Angel?" he cooed, cupping my cheek and inspecting my face, running his thumb gently over the bruise gracing my eye.

"Umm... I.... umm... forgot my pj's. Do-do you have

something I can sleep in?" I stuttered out, affected by his touch.

God! You just had to stutter! I scowled myself for feeling this way. I couldn't help it. I had seen this man every day of my life for three weeks, I felt like I knew him.

He chuckled and said "Sure angel, be right back."

He left to go to his closet and came back out with a pair of Calvin Klein boxers and I'm guessing one of his t-shirts.

"Here." he handed the clothing over to me.

"Thanks. Well, goodnight then. And thank you for everything." I spoke up again.

"You don't need to thank me, Angel. You deserve to be treated like a queen."

"Well, thanks." I blushed.

I love it when he calls me Angel.

He kissed me on the top of my head and left me and with my thoughts.
His kiss, his touches, his voice, him, all was getting to me. My emotions were all over the place to I decided to get ready for the night and let future Everleigh deal with all this.

I went to the bathroom to check my wounds and to change.

It felt nice being in his clothes, they smelt like him.
With that I went to bed, feeling safe and somewhat loved
and protected. I held my daughter close and smiled to
myself.

Maybe this won't be that bad after all.

CHAPTER FOUR

Everleigh:

I have been here for a few weeks coming up to a little over four weeks now leading us to be mid-February and so far all has been going well. Ash has been staying on the sofa and as he said he only came to get dressed. The works that needed to be done on the house were coming along nicely but Ash's room still wasn't ready.

 I haven't really seen any other of the men that live around this house, I have been keeping to myself and keeping Rose by my side. I know there's only about five of Ash's men that do actually live here.

At every free moment Ash has been playing with Rose and I have been grateful for that. Hearing her giggles resonate in the house have brought a smile to my face. It felt as if he had been here for years and it showed in how I acted toward Ash. It was like playing house, he was the husband, I was the wife and Rose was our daughter.

Every now and then he would find a way to touch me, not in a creepy way, but in the romantic way. He continued calling me Angel, kissing my forehead before he left the house or anytime he saw me. He would read Rose bedtime stories while I was in the shower, he would always make sure I was well taken care off. We didn't feel like strangers anymore.

"Mummy, mummy, mama"

"Mm... I'm awake Rose." I moaned pushing her little hands away from my face.

And so my day begins. I stretched and opened my eyes to see my little sunshine sitting on my belly.
I couldn't help but smile at her, I love her so much and even if I had her at a young age I don't regret it. I kiss her nose as she giggles and look at the time. Six am, right on time like every morning.

"Come on then poppet, up we get." I cheerfully sang.

I got her dressed in simple flower joggings with a dark grey hoodie leaving her baby-grow under as a t-shirt. I have several little outfits like that for her because they are so easy to clean and they look cute on her.
I didn't bother getting dressed yet because she was getting hungry and you don't want a hungry toddler at six in the morning screaming for food.

So, I carefully opened the door and walked down the stairs holding Rose's hand as she took her time to get down them. This house is massive so I got a bit lost looking for the kitchen. I walked into the living room seeing Ash peacefully sleeping and I felt bad for letting him sleep on the sofa. I wish the rooms would be ready so that he could get his room back.
I heard some commotion and walked towards the noise hoping that I didn't wake anybody.
It turns out that I was the kitchen and there was a man that I

hadn't seen before that was standing there.

"Umm... hey there." I nervously called out.

He turned around and he had these dark brown eyes with messy blond hair, wearing nothing but a pair of shorts.

"And who might you be?" he questioned, crossing his arms over his chest amused.

"Everleigh. You?" I placed a hand on my hip, a new found confidence taking over my body.

Before he could answer I felt a pair of arms wrap around my waist and a head nuzzled in my neck. It felt so good, so normal.

"Mine!"

Ash growled out.

"Umm excuse me? Can you let me go?" I asked him, even though deep down I did not want him to.

"No!" he groaned like a child, his grip tightening.

"I'll leave you guys to sort yourselves out, it's Ray by the way." the cocky fair haired man piped up, watching how Ash and I interacted together.

"Morning Ray! Sorry about him." I gave an apologetic smile.

He smiled and left. Rose was getting agitated and started pulling on my arm.

"Mama Food! Me hungry!"

"Yes baby, mummy's on it." I sighed.

Ash let me go and picked up Rose putting her on a chair on his lap making sure she didn't fall. He kissed her cheek and she didn't say anything. She normally doesn't like to be picked up by anybody else but me. She never let Dan pick her up, even before he became violent.

I started looking for something I could make her and decided to make French toast, all the ingredients were there and it was simple enough.

"I can't believe she let you pick her up, let alone sit on your lap without making a fit." I mused.

I turned to him and he simply smiled, man he looks hot.

"I guess she likes me then. And I have spent a lot of time with her too. I guess that helped."

****

Ash Mortimer:

I was sleeping on the couch when I heard little footsteps come into the living room and I knew that was my angel and princess. Since they have been here my life has been a lot better.

I have gotten closer to both girls and all I want to do is smother them with hugs and kisses and buy them all they have ever dreamed of. They filled this void in me, the missing puzzle piece to my life. Since they have been here it's like they have been here all my life and I wouldn't want it another way.

The only thing I struggle with is not being able to hold Everleigh tight in my arms and kiss her, show her how much she deserves all this affection. I want her to get used to being here, so far all this going good. I want to show her that she is safe here with me and there is no need to run away.

I will surely try my best to make her life and the life of my little princess the best life they can ever dream of.

I woke up and walked to the kitchen to find her talking to Ray. I didn't like it, she was mine and I was are to make that clear to everyone that lived here. I walked up behind her and wrapped my arms around her waist and nuzzled my face into her neck.

"Mine!" I growled claiming what is mine.

"Umm excuse me? Can you let me go?"

"No!" I stubbornly added.

"I'll leave you guys to sort yourselves out, it's Ray by the way." the idiot spoke.

"Morning Ray! Sorry about him."

I glared at Ray but he simply smiled back at me. God all the guys are acting the same, I'm never going to hear the end of this.

I was still holding her when my princess started pulling on her mom's arm.

"Mama Food! Me hungry."

"Yes baby, mummy's on it." she sighed.

I knew I had to do something so I picked Rose up and sat her on my lap ready to eat her food on the kitchen counter. Once we were sat I kissed her cheek and started checking my angel out. She was still in my clothes and damn! She looked sexy, I could just take her right here right now but kids are looking and it would be too fast so I can't... I was taken back to reality by her sweet Australian accent.

"I can't believe she let you pick her up, let alone, sit on your lap without making a fit."

I looked down at my princess who was playing with my fingers and smiled.

"I guess she likes me then. And I have spent a lot of time with her too. I guess that helped."

"Daddy! Food!"

Rose said pointing at Everleigh who had placed a plate with

her breakfast on it. She and I hadn't realised what Rose had just said.

"Baby what did you just say?" Everleigh questioned her daughter.

"Daddy." she said leaning back into my chest, a little pout on her lips because she couldn't reach the food.

Everleigh stood there in shock and just looked at me trying to analyse my reaction. I was so happy for some reason, her calling me daddy felt normal, that little girl had stolen my heart and if she saw me as her daddy that that's what I will be.

"That's my girl! Daddy's here now. You're daddy's never letting you go." I kissed the top of her head and saw Everleigh with tears in her eyes.

"Are you sure it's ok she calls you like that? She never called anybody like that before... I-I didn't even know she knew that word. I mean– like– she just called you daddy." Everleigh babbled on, not quite sure how to react to this.

I walked up to Everleigh with Rose on my left hip, giving her her toast. Once I was in front of Everleigh I placed a strand of hair behind her ear, I wiped away a tear off her cheek and kissed her forehead.

"I'm here now baby, don't cry." I whispered tenderly in her ear.

She wrapped her arms around me and held me tight. My free hand was around her waist while Rose was eating her French toast not quite understanding what is going on.

****

Everleigh:

I wasn't expecting Rose to call Ash 'daddy' and it brought me to tears because I've been dreaming of a moment like this my whole life! And now I have it... even if it probably isn't real. Yet, I'm not surprised Rose called him 'daddy' because he has been acting like a dad towards her since we have been here.
I was still in his arms looking at how happy Rose who was eating her food away.

"Do you want me to make you some?" I said pointing to her plate of food.

"Yes please Angel..."

He placed a kiss on my cheek and I couldn't help but blush. He sat back down with Rose and the rest of the boys came in the kitchen.

"Mm mm what is that smell?" I think this one is Paul.

"Good morning boys! Have a seat I'll make you some."

Once I was done cooking for all of them I left Rose with Ash because she didn't want to let him go. All three of us walked up to his room since he needed to get dressed and to get ready same as me. He got in the shower first and got dressed while I was taking care of Rose. He came out only with a towel around his waist and water dripping from his hair onto his defined chest.

"See something you like, baby?"

Mm, that new nickname drives me nuts! Resist Everleigh!

"Ummm, don't you need to get dressed?"

Was the only thing that came out of my mouth.

Way to look stupid Everleigh! Thanks, brain for the support (note the sarcasm).

He came up to me and kissed my forehead and did the same to Rose.

I'm melting right now, like seriously. I can't believe that I am letting him do that to me, be so tactile when I have hardly been here, even if it has been weeks, but I can't help it, I feel as if we have been together for years, maybe that's why I'm letting things go so fast.

"I'm off in the shower can you keep an eye on her?" I asked Ash that was getting dressed in his walk-in closet.

"Sure Angel go ahead!"

It was now my turn to go. I for once took my time to get

ready not that I need that much time, but it felt nice to get ready without worrying about what Dan could be doing to Rose.

I was wearing the same shorts when he found me and my white lace bra/ brallette with large straps. The reason was that I didn't want to be walking around in a bra in a house full of boys. I took one of Ash's jumpers/shirts and tied a knot so that it would fit me better. I let my hair down and brushed it, cleaned my face and shaved the necessary areas, brushed my teeth and put on a bit of mascara as well as the foundation on my bruises to cover them up a bit. They were healing nicely for the most part but there was still a small trace of my black eye.

Once I walked out of the bathroom, Ash and Rose were no longer there.
I walked out of the room and followed the giggling. I came to a new room and walked in seeing Ash playing with Rose and the other guys playing with her too.

I think we are in a sort of meeting room because there was a lot of people and they were all looking at me and whispering. Then my eyes met with Ash's gorgeous blue eyes.

He stood up and Rose ran to me yelling.

"Mummy!"

I gave her a hug and picked her up not liking the fact that we are surrounded by men all looking at us. Ash walked over and placed an arm around my waist whispering in my ear.

"You look good in my clothes Angel."

With that, he kissed my earlobe and making me hot and bothered at the same time. Our moment was interrupted by his men.

"Boss, are you going to present the Mrs.?" followed by 'yeah' from the rest of the men.

"This is Everleigh, she's mine and you shall treat her and OUR daughter with respect, you are to protect them. And this little princess as most of you know is Rose."

I blushed and smiled when he said 'our' daughter, I know it's too early for him to say such things but Rose started calling him daddy today, plus they have been building this strong father/daughter relationship since the beginning. I placed my head on his chest as he had his other hand helping me hold Rose on my hip.

He pulled away and took Rose in his arms.

"You are going shopping today with Annie, to get you and my princess new clothes."

He called Annie over and she was a beautiful tall brunette with matching brown eyes and she was fit, in way better shape than me.

"Hey!" she said.

"Hi!" I smiled back.

"So here is the credit card and don't worry about money. Get what you want."

"But I can't, I don't-."

He looked at me and put Rose down, he came closer and cupped my face with his warm hands. He looked me straight in the eyes, cutting me off mid-sentence.

"You deserve the world and more Angel. Don't let anybody tell you otherwise." he kissed my nose and I nodded.

"Awwwww, aren't they cute!" I heard a lot of the men say.

"Shut up!" he growled back to them.

"Ok I'll go but what about Rose?"

"I'll keep her. Go have fun!"

I nodded and kissed Ash's cheek and gave a kiss to Rose too saying bye, and I left with Annie to go to the mall.

CHAPTER FIVE

Everleigh:

Since I went shopping with Annie and I bought clothes for myself. Though, I did not buy a lot of clothes, I also bought toys for Rose and some underwear for Ash.

Why? *I don't know.*

Maybe, because I felt bad for taking his? Anyway, Annie dragged me from shop to another and bought me things behind my back. Saying that, and I quote 'you'll thank me later.'

So we drove back home and I dropped the bags at the entrance, took my shoes off and walked into the living room and what I saw really made my heart melt.

Rose was sleeping on Ash's chest in his arms. I just had to snap a picture, Ash was sleeping too holding Rose very protectively.

I walked up to them and sat next to Ash making sure not the wake them. I put my head on his shoulder and closed my eyes letting the darkness take over me.

****

Ash Mortimer:

I had fallen asleep on the sofa with Rose after lunch, after the meeting. I had sent most of my men off to make deals, to do trades at the docks, send more men to get the money people owed me, and so on.

 I've grown very fond of Rose and her mother. Rose resembles her mother, on how beautiful she is and other little things like the way she acts. But, I have this feeling that I have met Everleigh before.

 After a couple of hours, I heard the door open, instantly knew that Everleigh was back from her shopping. I was awake but I kept my eyes closed, waiting for what she would do next. And, to surprise, she sat next to me and placed her head on my shoulder. And with that, we both fell asleep once more. During our nap, she had curled up to me and I had placed my arm around her waist pulling her closer whilst still holding Rose on my chest.

I was hearing 'oohs' and 'awww' as well as camera clicks and 'look at boss and Mrs. Boss.' I could get used to her being Mrs. Boss, but I decided to scare them a bit

"What the hell do you think you are doing?" I opened my eyes taking my hand off Rose and rubbing my eyes.

 Shortly, I heard the two girls groan and wake up too.

"Dada…"

 Rose snuggled closer to me, and I put my hand on her back once more rubbing circles to wake her up gently, like my mother did when I was a baby.

"Mm mm… Ash. Why is everyone around us?"

 That's when her beautiful green eyes met mine. I kissed her forehead and told her.

"I'll sort this out, Angel."

She sat up next to me, still with my arm around her waist.

"You heard her, why are you all around her like that?"

"Well... boss." Louis started rubbing his neck as Paul continued.

"There was a problem at the docks. Nothing major, we got attacked by the Red Eagles. We got rid of most of them, and some are in the basement ready to be questioned."

Then Carter added, "And the room is done, don't forget the banquet tonight. It starts at seven."

"What's the time?"

"Five pm, boss."

"Shit!" I mumbled under my breath, yet Everleigh heard.

"Language!" all the boys laughed, afterward, I gave them a sign to leave us alone.

Rose was now fully awake, and so was Everleigh. She gave me a questioning look, wanting to ask what this was all about. Besides this, I had to show her Rose's room. I also had to ask her to be my date.

As she looked up at me with those beautiful eyes, "I know it's a bit late to ask but will you be my date to the banquet?"

****
Everleigh:

"I know it's a bit late, but will you be my date to the banquet?"

Did he just ask me to be his date?!
He did!
I am dreaming!
I'm sure of it!
Dan never took me out anywhere, like ever and we had been dating basically since Rose was born.

And now, Ash does it only after weeks of knowing me, says long about how my relationship was with Dan.

"Yes! Yes! I will!" he had a huge smile on his face and kissed my cheek.

"But I have nothing to wear."

I looked away from him not feeling up to his standards, but he brought me closer to him so that we whispered in my ear.

"Don't worry baby, I asked Annie to get you more stuff when you were out."

I nodded and put my head on his chest plus looking at my little ray of sunshine, who now was in my arms.

"Come on let's get up, we need to get ready but before I need to show you something." he got up leaving me feeling cold without his warmth around me.

I put Rose down and took her hand following Ash up the stairs to a door that had Rose's name on it. I looked at him curious about what he did whilst I was out. When he opened the door my mouth dropped open to what I saw before me.

Her room had white walls and white furniture with baby pink accents all around. She had her own bed and a little teepee play area. It was simple but so lovely at the same time. It must have taken him time and money to do this. Rose ran straight to her bed and started jumping on it.

"Oh wow... I don't know what to say.... Thank you, it's beautiful."

I couldn't even get words out to explain how grateful I am for all this.

"You don't need to thank me, anything for my girls. And besides, I said I would get her a bed of her own even if I spent the whole week on it."

He winked looking down at me.

"You spent the whole week? You shouldn't have, this is too much... First, you let us stay with us, complete strangers, the shopping and now this? You can't possibly do this for someone you barely know and care about."

I frowned a little, it was true what was I thinking to believe that we will end up a happy family just by snapping my fingers.

"It's never too much when it comes to you two. It will never be too much even if I buy you a house, an island or whatever that is on this earth that I can buy will be too much for you. We might not have known each other for long but I don't care, I care for you and that little girl, call me creepy or whatever but I feel like I have been waiting for you all my life and I don't want you to hold back from me." he held my hands in his and looked deeply in my eyes.

"Come on we need to get ready," he spoke up after a few moments of looking at each other.

"Ok, but who is going to keep an eye on her?" I said looking at my daughter.

"Paul and Louis. Carter and Ray are coming with us for security."

I nodded as we walked away Ash called Paul to stay in her room while we got ready.
We walked into the room and I went to the shower first. I did all that I needed to do apart from hair and makeup. I'll do my make up once I'm dressed. I walked out only in my towel wrapped around me. Once I came out I felt his stares pierce holes right through me.

"Damn Angel, you look good enough to eat! Get dressed before I jump on you and take you right here right now."

His eyes were full of lust and I was burning red and I felt hot all of a sudden, I won't lie, he was shirtless and him looking at me the way we did turn me on so much. I can't, not right now, I barely know the guy! And I'm no slut! I just let him walk off to the bathroom and I went into the closet to find all the things I had bought set in one half of it. My eyes fell on the perfect dress for tonight.

It was a long navy blue evening gown with a sweetheart neckline with a mermaid fit and a skirt with ruffles at the bottom. I was scared that I would not be able to fit in it, that it would get stuck by the hips since Rose I was a lot curvier. I slipped it on and so far so good, but my arms were too short to zip it up. I needed help so I went out of the closet and knocked on the bathroom door.

"Ash, I need your help. Can you open up please?"

The door unlocked and out came a shirtless Ash dripping once again with water, only a towel around his waist.

Deja vu anybody?

I turned around to show him with what I needed help with praying that it would close. I felt his warm fingers trace my back and stop where one of my tattoos is on the lower right side of my back and I felt him bend down and kiss it. I felt his warm breath on my neck again.

"You naughty girl, having a tattoo. I didn't know you had any. It's sexy."

The tattoo was one of a red rose, I got it after she was born.

"I have another one." was the only thing I could say.

He let out a low groan, was this turning him on?

"Mm, and where?"

"That's for you to find out another day."

Where did this sudden confidence come from?

He let out a little chuckle and started kissing my neck, nipping it along the way. I couldn't hold back my moans. That only made him kiss harder. I let him have more access to my neck, enjoying the moment.

While he was doing that he zipped my dress up and thank the lords it closed. His hands traveled to my waist, turning me around to face him. He continued to kiss my neck then we made eye contact. We stared at each other for a while, until his lips came crashing onto mine.

I didn't realise what was going on, my body took over and I kissed him back. Our lips were moving in sync and I put my arms around his neck tugging on his hair a bit. He let out a groan and licked my lips asking for entrance which, I gladly gave. Our kiss was hot and passionate like we needed this to live. I couldn't help but moan at his tongue roaming in my mouth. It was heavenly. But all good things come to an end, we pulled away.

"Wow…"

"Amazing…" he answered back.

"We need to finish getting ready."

"Yeah, you're right" he answered back, but before I closed the bathroom door he told me,

"Baby, I want people to know you are mine, so stay by my side tonight." I blushed and nodded in agreement.

I put on a light layer of makeup not overdoing it and curled my hair and put it in a braid that I turned into a low loose bun. Then, I put on a pair of matching navy blue heels and headed down the stairs.

Ash was waiting for me with Rose in his arms. He looked super sexy with his navy blue suit with a white shirt and a matching blue tie. Rose was in her pj's ready for bed. I walked down and all the eye were on me. I felt quite self-confident and once I was down the stairs I was holding my arm looking everywhere but in their eyes.

"Mama, beautiful!" Rose screamed wiggling out of Ash's arms to come to me.

I picked her up and placed her on my hip.

"Thank you munchkin." I kissed her cheek and she giggled. I looked her to Ash hiding a bit behind Rose.

"She's right you know, you look beautiful, even breathtaking."

We walked up, and he suddenly gave me a quick kiss. I was not expecting that to happen!
The men that were there, all gave a sound of agreement.
Both Ash and I kissed Rose goodbye. We told her to behave and listen to Paul and Louis, while Mummy and Daddy (gosh that feels weird to say) were out.

And with that, Ash placed his hand on the small of my back and walked me out to the car. He opened the door for me and we drove off to the banquet.

CHAPTER SIX

Everleigh:

The car ride was silent. But a comfortable silence. His car was super comfortable too and a little music played in the background, nothing too loud. Another black car was following us, I'm guessing it's the boys.
We arrived at this beautiful castle typesetting and it was now getting dark. He parked the car and opened the door for me.

What a gentleman!

We walked inside but before Ash gave orders to his men to make sure the perimeter is safe. I need to feel less surprised because he is a gang leader.

All I was thinking about was Rose. It's the first time I left her alone with people I didn't know that well. The first time without me, if you exclude my work days when she is at the caretakers. My mind was worrying and I was getting fidgety. I think Ash saw that.

"Hey Angel, you ok?" his deep husky voice came through me as he whispers in my ear. I snapped out of my thoughts to answer.

"Umm... y-yeah. I'm fine don't worry."

I tried walking off into the main room where everyone is but he stopped me by grabbing my wrist. He spun me around to that I was facing him pulling me closer and with his other, he lifted my chin up so that I was looking at him in the eyes.

"Baby. Tell me what's wrong." his eyes make me melt and his touch soft against my skin.

"Everleigh, speak to me. Please baby, tell me what's wrong..." his voice was stern at first by seeing me with watery eyes his next sentence was a lot softer.

I built up the courage to tell him what was on my mind.

"I'm scared... about Rose."

I merely say just above a whisper.

"Angel, Rose is safe and protected by my men. Heck if someone wants to get to her we will need to pass all my security and that's not happening anytime soon, you don't need to worry."

I sigh and cuddle up to his chest. He is stiff at first but I feel his arms wrap around me and I feel his warmth again. He kisses the top of my head.

"We need to go in now. Are you ready?"

I nod in response when the boys come back and tell us that it's safe for us to walk in.

Once we do all eyes are on us and some even gasp seeing us walk in like that. Ash has his arm around my waist, I look up at him and I see that he has his 'you look at her, I'm going to kill you' face on and I feel protected but a little intimidated at the same time. I wouldn't want to cross him.

He led us to our table and I sat there looking around and all looked super fancy, there was a chandelier in the center of the room over the dance floor. A band was on stage playing classical music, waiters serving champagne flutes and appetizers. A couple people were dancing, some others were talking. I felt out of place, there was a lot of beautiful women in the arms of I suppose influential men, maybe other gang leaders? I do not know. I kept looking around analyzing the people around me. Most young women are with older men and they are dressed as sluts, probably gold diggers or escorts. The elder women are probably their mothers or cougars for the young men or their wife. I just guessing all this I don't know what else to do Ash is talking with a guy at our table making phone calls.

I leaned over to Ash that was on his phone

"What exactly are we doing here?"

He looked up from his phone to look at me.

"What do you mean?" he knitted his eyebrows in confusion.

"Well, what are we doing here? Why did we come? Nothing is happening."

He took my hand in his and gave me that smirk of his.

"It hasn't started yet. This is like a business dinner." this time it was my turn to be confused.

"Are these people all gang leaders?"

I whispered the last part, feeling unsure all of a sudden about all this. I was scared that my dad would be here along with my mother.

Don't get me wrong I love my father, I like my mother a lot less because of past events that are not relevant now. But I don't want Ash to know that my father is a powerful gang leader in Australia. That's why I'm not scared to be with him and I'm not scared about the fact that they all have guns. That does not mean I trust them either though.
I'm worried about what Ash might do if he finds out who my Dad is. I don't know if they are on good terms or not.
A million questions run through my mind as my breathing becomes uneven.

"Most of them yes...Hey Angel, are you alright?"

He startled me as I tried to calm my breathing and focus back on him and not the millions of questions.

"Yes, I'm fine. Just admiring how beautiful it is here."

I looked into his blue eyes trying to see if I was convincing. The worry that was plastered on his face was gone and

replaced with a small smile.
He pecked me on the lips and helped me stand up.

"Come. I'll need to introduce you to some people."

We walked to a group of men that all had beautiful women in their arms, I felt like I wasn't good enough. As we came closer, a couple saw us and left which left us with the last couple. As we arrived I just stood there in shock.

I knew that man. He had made deals with my dad before and I grew up with his daughter. His name was...

"Sergei Romanov."

CHAPTER SEVEN

Everleigh:

"Sergei Romanov"

Ash greeted him with a handshake than introduced me.

"This is Everleigh, my date for tonight."

I couldn't help but feel a little hurt by 'my date', well we aren't official, heck! I hardly know the guy but I just feel like I've known him forever.

The man also known as my godfather spoke up. In a thick Russian accent that I came accustomed to.

"Hello Mr. Asher Mortimer," huh, so Asher is what Ash is short for.

Interesting...

"And what a lovely young lady you have there by your side..." ok, now I am uncomfortable. He was eyeing me from top to bottom, analyzing all my features.

He knows me like the back of his hand, I'm like a second daughter to him, he didn't only make deals with my dad, but he was/is (not sure anymore) my dad's best friend. I haven't spoken to him since the accident.

He still looked at me making small talk with Ash while I was just praying to be able to retreat to a hole and hide there. The talk came back to me, I think Sergei is eager to get to know me better, and I think he already recognized me but still needs the confirmation.

"So Ms. Everleigh...." he paused waiting for me to tell him my family name.

"It's Graham. Everleigh Graham." I didn't dare to look him in the eye, my gaze held strong onto the floor.

"Ms. Graham, where are you from? You don't sound American."

"You are right, I was born in Britain, but grew up in Australia and then moved back to Britain in my early twenties, and now here I am."

I decided to answer truthfully, he nodded his head and started tapping on his glass that was in his right hand with his index finger. I was listening to the tapping and realized it was Morse code. He had taught me that with Victoria (his daughter, my best friend) when we were younger, so I decrypted it and he said 'busted snowdrop'.

Snowdrop is how my brother calls me and he does the same. It is because I was born on a snowy day of December. I looked up at Ash who didn't seem to have understood why Sergei was tapping on his glass. I looked at him with pleading eyes trying to make him understand, that I didn't want him to tell Ash that we know each other.

After a couple minutes of small talk, Ash and I walked away bidding our goodbyes to Sergei as we walked off to see other people.

If I'm honest this was a very boring evening, I didn't say much I was just listening to Ash make business talk and talking numbers so I was calculating everything and thinking about the deals he could make to have a better profit on things, but I didn't say anything.

I have a degree in business management and accounting. So I know what he is talking about and I say, he is handling himself quite well.

All evening I have felt eyes on me and I know exactly who they belong to.
After what felt like the millionth person he spoke to, I decided to go to the loo and call Paul and/or Louis to ask them if all is good with Rose.

Ash gave me his phone since he took mine away and I walked towards the lady's restroom knowing that soon Sergei would follow because I knew that we had things to discuss.
I rang up Paul first and was waiting for him to pick up, he did after three rings.

"Hey boss. What's up?"

He answered in a serious tone.

"Hi Paul! It's Everleigh. "

I chirped.

"Hey you! How's it going at the banquet?"

His voice became sweet when he realized it was me.

"Boring, Ash is making deals and stuff and I'm just there as his arm candy...."

I trailed off. But was soon brought back by Paul's voice.

"Don't worry Leigh, you are more than arm candy to him. Trust me, he has Never, and I mean Never seen him treat a girl like he does you and that little princess."

I smiled to myself thinking about the last few days that I've been spending with Ash and the boys.

"Anyways, why did you call? Apart from listening to my beautiful voice."

I could hear the smirk in his tone.

"Yeah, um... how is Rose doing?" I questioned, remembering why I called in the first place.

"Ha-ha, she's doing fine, we put her to bed over an hour ago and she fell asleep straight away."

"That's good, she wasn't too much of a hassle?" I asked biting my lip.

'Nah! A real angel, a bit fussy with food and man can that girl run! She has little legs! How can she do that?"

I was laughing at the other end, knowing full on how much of a fussy eater she is.

"All right then, thanks again for taking care of her. I don't know when we will be back though..." I trailed off.

"No worries babe, anyway I'll leave you to your evening and see you later. Bye!"

"Bye Paul and say hi and thank you to Louis too! Bye!"

I hang up and was about to walk towards the bathroom but I was held back by an arm.
I turned around to meet with those deep blue eyes, and those eyes belong to the one and only Sergei Romanov.

"What do you want?" I whisper/ hissed.

"Now, that isn't a way to greet your godfather."

He pulled me into a hug that I returned. I must admit I missed him. He's like another father to me. He was always there.
I pulled away and looked him into the eyes.

"So, who were you talking to, and who is Rose?" he looked at me with a questioning look.

My face turned pale, he doesn't know that I was pregnant at the time of the accident. I started fiddling with my fingers.

"Snowdrop, tell Me." he placed his hand on my shoulder.

"The man I was talking to was one of Asher's men. And Rose... Rose is my daughter." I looked up to him, trying to see his reaction.

His face was blank, his eyes empty of emotion.

"Say something, pl-please."

I reached for his hand and took it in mine giving it a squeeze.

"How old is she?"

I released a breath I didn't know I was holding.

"She's turning three in May."

"Who's the father?"

God, I knew that question was coming up. I hate that question. I feel so embarrassed.

"Ummm.... don't be mad. You remember the night of the international gang meeting…"

"Yes... what does it have to do with it?"

"Well... I got into a fight with Daddy, so I ran to the bar, got drunk out of my mind and met this guy, I think he was in one of the visiting gangs, and one thing led to another.... and I found out I was pregnant a few months later... I was just coming up to six months at the time of the accident..."

I couldn't face him. I looked towards my feet, well, the bottom of my dress that covered my feet.
I heard him take a loud breath. He took both my hands in his.

"Snowdrop, I didn't know. Your father never said anything when you left."

"I know he didn't say anything, it's shameful for him to have his only heir, the one to take over his empire being pregnant from a one night stand by a guy she doesn't even remember..."

It hurt, remembering all this and actually telling someone about all this, a person I consider family, not even Dan knew the whole story.

"I'm sorry snowdrop. I could have helped." I could see the hurt in his eyes.

Deep down Sergei is a real teddy bear with great taste in vodka and head of the Russian mafia.
I cleared my throat wanting to get away from this

conversation.

"I-I need to go back to Ash"

I gave him a small smile attempting to walk away, but Sergei's voice called out to me.

"Everleigh, does he treat you well?"

I nodded before giving my answer

"Yes, and he is the best with Rose. She even calls him 'daddy'." I gave a little chuckle and walked away again.

"I want to meet her, Rose, your daughter."

I nodded again and gave him a response.

"I would like that, but Ash doesn't know who I am. He doesn't know I'm the daughter of Sean Graham, leader of the most dangerous gang in Australia and is world-renowned for its gun trade. Yeah maybe not right now." I clapped back sarcastically before continuing.

"But Rose's birthday is the thirteenth of May. So if you want to see her then I would need to tell him everything."

I'm scared shitless, I really am. I'm so scared to tell him about me. But he has to know at some point.

"Well, tell him soon, I want to see the offspring of my snowdrop."

This time I really walked away. And once I spotted Ash he was talking to Ray and Carter. So I walked behind him placing my hand on the back of his neck trailing down to his shoulder and placing a kiss on his cheek.

I felt him tense at first but once he saw it was me, his arm snaked around my waist pulling me closer to him.

"So, how are the boys doing with the princess?" his smirk just makes me melt every time.
I smiled back at him.

"They are doing well, Paul told me that she was in bed."

He nodded and told the guys to get the car because we were heading home.

Thank god for that! My feet are killing me in these heels!

Ash walked me to the car, opening the door for me, such a gentleman.
I didn't even feel myself close my eyes and before I knew it I was taken over by darkness, the car came to a stop and I felt two muscular arms take me in them.
I was put on a bed, and then I heard that familiar deep husky voice.

"Goodnight Angel."

I smiled as I was now sort of awake.

"Night handsome."

I sat up kissing him, and he immediately returned the kiss. I pulled away and stood up before it could go any further.

"I'm going to get out of this dress, take my makeup and shoes off."

"Okay Angel."

I walked into the bathroom and took everything off, there was one of Ash's button-up white shirts so I decided to have that a pajamas.
I do tend to forget to get my stuff in the closet beforehand... *Oops?* I came out with a clean face, my hair in a messy bun, with a couple buttons of the shirt undone only wearing my lace underwear underneath.

"Mm mm Angel, you look sexy in my clothes." and there was Ash, laying on the bed, only in a pair of trackies, no top, messy hair, his beautiful blue eyes boring into mine that smile of his and that body!

"Are you done staring baby?" he let out a deep chuckle.

"Ummm... I'll be off now!" I turned away to hide my blush and headed for the door. But before I could reach it a pair of arms came around my waist blocking me to his hard chest. He leaned to my ear placing soft kisses on my neck.

"Where do you think you are going?"

"To the couch." I said in a 'duh' tone.

"Nah baby, you staying with me tonight."

I didn't even have time to protest that I was carried to the bed and was held by his strong arms tightly wrapped around me.
I gave up and snuggled up to his chest, pecking his lips before letting sleep take over me once more.

CHAPTER EIGHT

Ash Mortimer:

I turned around on the bed hoping to hold my angel in my arms and feel her warmth but to my surprise, she wasn't there.
I sat up and rubbed my eyes turning the night lamp on and adjusting to the light.
I looked around the room, she wasn't there.

Maybe she went to the bathroom? At least that's what I thought.

I went and knocked on the door opening it in the process and she wasn't there.
I went out the room going to the kitchen and living room still not there. And to be honest I started panicking.

Where the hell is she?

As I was walking back up the stairs, I heard her voice. I followed it and it leads me to my little princess's room. The door was left ajar, so I pushed it more open and leaned against the door frame.

She was sat on Rose's bed, with her in her arms, Rose fast asleep and Everleigh stroking her hair humming a lullaby, rocking her ever so slightly.

A million feelings ran through me, something I'm not used to, but something I can't help but feel when I'm around Everleigh. And her love and protection towards Rose are unbelievable.

I was lost in my thoughts, smiling to myself looking at my girls.

"Are you done staring?"

I shook my head snapping me back to reality. I positioned myself on the door frame before whispering back

"I can never stop staring at you, you are so beautiful to me." I couldn't help but give a goofy smile to her.

She was blushing, so cute.

What?! Dude? Cute? CUTE? Snap out of it, you're a gang leader, you don't say 'cute'.

"Anyway, why are you in her room?" I asked questioned. She looked down at Rose than back up to me.

"She had a nightmare and she was crying."

I furrowed my brows.

"How did you hear her cry, I didn't. We have soundproof walls and her room is three doors down from ours." curiosity laced my voice.

How on earth can she hear her cry? That's not possible!

She looked up at me again, walking towards me and pushing me out of the door making sure to make as little noise as possible. Before closing the door she gave one last glance towards Rose and shutting the door she faced me.

"I can hear her breathing with all doors locked and soundproof walls. I guess it's a mum thing." she shrugged walking off.

Not satisfied with the answer I grabbed her by the wrist pulling her to face me once more.

"That's impossible."

"Well believe it."

"And how come you can hear so well, I mean could you do that before?"

I'm really curious to know. The only people I know that can do that are professional assassins or sentinels.
She paused for a moment, thinking about how to respond.

****

Everleigh:

"When I was living with Dan, I always made sure I could hear her because I was always scared the times Dan didn't go to bed that he would go to Rose's room to harm her and I was scared that if I didn't listen in, that I couldn't ever stop him."

That and the fact that I'm a trained sniper and was thought to always be aware of my surroundings, so I had practice. But he doesn't need to know that right now.
Looking back up at him, I could see the hurt and anger rushing through him. I placed my arms around his torso laying my head on his chest breathing in his sent. His arms immediately can around me and held me close to him.

"I'll never let that happen ever again, nobody will hurt you or our little princess. Never." he promised, whispering in my ear and placing a soft kiss on my head.

"Come let's go back to bed."

He tried to pull away but I stood my ground.

"Come on Angel, let's go to bed." he tried dragging me but I would not budge.

I looked up and him, my chin resting on his chest. Doing my best puppy eyes and pout lip I asked I the sweetest voice I could.

"Carry me please, baby."

His chest vibrated followed by a chuckle on his behalf.

"Come on then, hop up."

I smiled, jumping to wrap my legs around his waist, placing my arms around his neck, kissing him on the lips as a thank you.

The kiss got more passionate, he walked us to the room not once breaking the kiss while he kicked the door open and closing it with one foot.

He walked me to the bed, placing me softly on it.
We finally broke our kiss as he was hovering over me kissing my neck, heading down to my chest. A moan escaped my lips which only made him groan in response.
I pushing him off me, so that things wouldn't escalate too quickly, seductively whispering to him.

"Not now. There's no time." I said turning my head to the clock. It was already four am and I knew that I would be awake by six am. And also the fact that we came back from the banquet at a little past midnight.

I need my sleep if I want to function properly with a two-year-old!

He groaned rolling to his side of the bed. Pulling ourselves under the covers. I snuggled up to him placing my head in the crook of his neck placing small kisses. He in return placed a soft kiss on my forehead and played with the ends of my hair making me fall into a deep sleep once more.

I woke up at six am like every morning, it like installed in me. I turned over to look at Ash, still sleeping so I got out of bed, went to the loo did a face wash, sort out my hair putting it into a high ponytail and put on some trackies tucking the front of Ash's shirt into them.

I left the room in silence walking over to Rose's room to see her awake and playing in her tipi.
We both went downstairs making sure not to wake up anybody.

I make pancakes for the whole house, and I had breakfast with Rose. After that I let her play in the living room with the TV on as a background.

I'm lucky she is not one to be glued in front of the TV but she doesn't like staying in silence so, for now, the TV was good. I watched the news, and I cleaned the kitchen. Went to the laundry room and did a laundry. Hung it outside, said hello to the guards that are stationed outside, make them coffee and had a little chat before I came back in. Rose still drawing with the pens and paper I found in Ash's office.

I did all that in an hour. So by now, it's seven am.

I found a room filled with stuff and I managed to find a radio. I set it up, turned the TV off and hacked the station to get more channels.

I started sweeping the floor, dancing along to the music and Rose was dancing in her own little way. Fluffing the pillows in the living room one of my favorite songs came on 'ain't no mountain high enough'.

I took Rose by the hand and we started dancing and singing. Well, I was singing, Rose was making up words but having a super fun time!

*"Listen, baby, ain't no mountain high,
Ain't no valley low, ain't no river wide enough;
Baby if you need me call me no matter where you are..."*

We were dancing like crazy having fun laughing our heads off.
I didn't realize that we were being watched.

****

Ash Mortimer:

I woke up to find the bed empty. I looked at the time: 7:30 am. I guess she woke up for Rose.
I walked down the stairs to find all my men standing by the kitchen door smiling and music in the background.
I walked up closer pushing the guys and once I saw what the show was about I couldn't help but smile too.
My girls dancing and singing to 'ain't no mountain high enough'.

They seemed to be having a hell of a lot of fun.

She turned around and realized that we were all here, watching her, Everleigh stopped and turned the radio off.

"Hey!" she smiled at us.

"I didn't know we had an audience. Did you see that Rose?" Rose got all shy and blotted herself in Everleigh's neck, being her shy self.

"Awwwww…" all the men cooed. Sometimes I wonder how we are the most feared gang in North America when they react like this.

She walked closer to me, still holding Rose in her arms. She placed one hand on my neck playing with my hair. And she greeted me with a soft long kiss that I gladly returned placing one hand on her waist bringing her closer and the other to help keep up Rose.

"Cough, cough… boss virgin eyes… they're burning!" of course, Paul had to break the moment.

"Morning."she breathed out, her lips slightly swollen.

We had a deep staring contest but it was broken by cries. Our heads both snapped to Rose, crying her eyes out and screaming.

"Baby girl, what's the matter?" Everleigh looked at her with confusion lacing her face.

"I-I didn't g-get… a k-kiss…" she said between sobs.

Both my Angel and I smiled at her and gave her a kiss on each cheek.

"Better princess?"

"Y-yes Daddy." she wiped away her tears with her teddy bear.

I can't get enough of her calling me 'daddy' it makes me feel... I don't know... complete?

"Well, I'm off to get ready before I'm late. I'll leave you with Rose." she passed me over the child and kissed my cheek walking off. She was about to pass the boys.

"Late for what?" I turned to her looking confused. I put Rose down.

"For work." she said in a 'duh' tone.

"No, you're not."

"Umm yes, I am. I've missed too much work." she said crossing her arms over her chest, pushing her boobs up. *Gosh, why is she making it hard?*

"You don't need to work anymore."

"I do." she said walking closer, arms still crossed.

"Oohhhh boss and lady boss are having their first fight... I bet twenty dollars lady boss will win." Ray put his hand out to the guys shaking hands with some saying that the bet was on.

"Shut up Ray." Everleigh and I said at the same time.

"Uh! Language!" Paul gasped placing his hands over Rose's ears.

We all burst out laughing.

CHAPTER NINE

Ash Mortimer:

It's been two weeks since the banquet. I've been interrogating Dan, more like beating him up for the things that he has been doing to my angel and to my princess.
I've also been super stressed out lately, letters have been sent to the front door, letters addressed to me, threats against my girls.

I've sent men on the hunt for whoever is writing those.

"I want it dealt with, fast. I want more guards at and around the house. Cameras around the house and 24/7 security around Everleigh and Rose. Paul and Louis, you stay with Rose I trust you to protect her with your life."

"Yes, boss." they both say I nod and turn to Simon and Ray.

"Simon, Ray, you are in charge of Everleigh. You touch her or harm her or let anything happen to her you are as good as dead. Clear?"my tone was void of emotions.

"Crystal." was the only thing they dared to say back.

I continued on with the meeting when I was interrupted by a knock on the door.

"Come in." I said a bit harshly.

"Hey." my eye shot up when I saw my beautiful angel at the door. It was pushed open by my little princess, running towards me screaming.

"Daddy! Daddy!"

I took her in my arms and placed her on my lap.

"Sorry to disturb your meeting babe but I'm making lunch and I was wondering a: what do you want to eat and b: how many people am I making it for?"

She leaned against the door frame, with no care in the world and when she calls me 'babe', mmmm I can't get enough.

"You are never disturbing me, Angel. For the food make whatever is easier for you. Make for ten people, but you have time. Because we still have things to accomplish here. I'll be about another hour."

She nodded.

"Anything I can help with?" her eyes bored into mine, I could look at them forever and never get tired of looking.

"Nah Angel, all is good."
I smiled back at her.

"Okay dokey, well we'll be off then. Come on Rose let's leave daddy to work." she put her hand out waiting for Rose to run to her and take it to leave but she started crying and screaming.

"No! I want my daaaddddddddyyyyyy!"

"Rose come on, daddy's working. Let's make lunch." her voice was soft but stern.

"Noooooooooooooo." she continued to yell.

Everleigh huffed and walked over to Rose trying to get her off me, but damn! That kid has got a hell of a grip!
She was still crying and screaming and even I tried to tell her to go and that she'll see me later but nothing worked.

"Rose, will you stop crying if you stayed with me?""I sat her back on my lap.

She snuggled closer looking up at me and smiled nodding her head. Man, she's got me right where she wants me, wrapped around her little finger.

"Ok, but you have to be very good, no more yelling and when it's time to have lunch, we go have lunch. Ok, no more crying and yelling." I did the pointy finger at her and gave her my best soft authoritative voice. I can't do it as well as Everleigh, I'm still new to this fatherhood thing.

She nodded and cuddled up to me. Her little hands gripping my t-shirt.
I looked up at Everleigh giving her a look saying that it was fine. She gave me back the 'are you sure?' look and I nodded back in response.

The thing I love about her is that we don't even need words to communicate, our eyes said it all.
Before she left she kissed me and said bye to the men in the meeting.

The meeting was coming to an end, I looked down towards Rose. She was sound asleep her head on my chest listening to my heartbeat. She looks so much like Everleigh it's unbelievable.
I dismissed by men and headed over to Rose's room, changed her into her pyjamas and put her to bed.
I know we haven't had lunch yet but I had made the rookie mistake of waking her up to eat and it did not end well...

Everleigh nearly ripped my head off yelling: 'you idiot! You never wake up a baby and you never wake up a toddler except if you want to die!' She was a little on the dramatic side on that one and that was like our first 'real' fight. Well, it wasn't a fight really but she did yell at me for over an hour because Rose was upset and that made her upset.
The worst part was that nothing, not even food, could calm the princess down.

So I left her room posting two guards by her door, two outside her window and I had placed a baby monitor with a camera and sound so that I have 24-hour footage.
I walked to the kitchen to find Carter, Louis, Paul and Ray all sat down around the kitchen island eating up their BLT's while Leigh was still finishing up cleaning.
I walked up behind her and placed my hands on her waist kissing her cheek. She squealed and turned around smacking

me in the arm.

"You scared me!" she said pouting her plump lips. I kissed her and led her to the counter without a word.

The guys were smiling at us still eating. I grabbed us a plate and put sandwiches on for the both of us. I scooped her up and placed her on my lap once I was sat on the Barstool. We both started eating and she asked where Rose was, I told her that she had fallen asleep, she simply nodded and continued eating.
Once we were done, she looked up at me turning her neck so that our eyes could meet.

"Why are there more men posted around the house? Is something wrong?" her eyes filled with worry as she tried to search my face for anything that would give anything up.

I stayed emotionless and replied.

"Nothing for you to worry about, angel, just being careful that's all." I ended with a small smile a kiss on her temple.

"You sure?" she questioned again.

"Positive."

If only she knew that I was worried about something happening to her or Rose.

CHAPTER TEN

Ash Mortimer:

I was sitting at my desk sorting out paperwork and sent my men to do deals, trade drugs and weapons and most importantly look for the person sending these threats.
I tried to spend as much time with my girls but I've been so stressed about all this that I distanced myself so that I wouldn't blow up at them.
I was interrupted by a knock on the door.

"Come in." Ray rushed in with a paper in his hands.

"Boss, we found out who is sending the threats." I stood up and took the paper from him.

"Get some men ready, about five. I'll be going to get that dick and ask him who he's working for."

"Yes, boss."

"Also, meeting in ten." with that, he left the room. I got back to my desk and took out of the drawer my gun and put it in my waistband grabbing the necessary things for my meeting.

After that was done, it was about eight am, I walked down the stairs into the living room pointing to my men to get out of the house and get the cars ready. We were about four to go.

I saw my angel and princess painting and laughing together. I'll never get sick of that sight. They are my light in this world of darkness. And I'll do anything to protect them.

I was about to leave when I got called back.

****

Everleigh:

"Hey, Ash? Where are you going? Why are there so many guys around?" I asked confused, standing up wiping my hands with a cloth and walking over to Ash.

"Nothing, I'm just handling some business." he shrugged. I placed myself in front of him, my hands both sides of his face, my thumbs rubbing circles on this temples.

I knew that calmed him down. He's been pretty stressed out and I think I know why. I've been sneaking into his office and I found the letters that he has been receiving and I am not stupid. I know that's what's troubling him.

I don't know who they are from but once I find out they are going to regret the day they were ever born.

I looked up at him in the eyes, his hands were now places around my waist, resting on my hips.

"You sure it's nothing?" I lifted a brow.

He kissed my forehead.

"Yes, nothing I can't fix." he fake smiled.

I hugged him like my life depended on it, I'm scared he's going to get himself in trouble I just feel it deep down.
He hugged me back and once I pulled out a bit I kissed him. We had a mini make-out session and by the time we pulled back to get some air we were both breathing heavily.

"I have to go now, Angel. I'll be back soon." and with that, he left.

I just stood there, knowing something bad would happen. I just have that gut feeling that he's not coming back anytime soon.

It's been almost 73 hours that he has been gone and I have had Simon and Ray follow my every move and it has been getting on my nerves like hell.
I've been pacing around the house, I left Paul and Louis to play with Rose because I feel like I'm going to kill someone if I don't get any answers soon.
I saw Rob, one of the men that went with Ash limp in the house.

"Oh my lord! What happened to you?" I gasped seeing he with cuts all over, bruises, what I think is a broken leg.

I ran up to him trying my best to bring him to the sofa while yelling for the guys that stayed at the house to come help me.

"Get me the first aid kit, a bottle of vodka and a sharp knife stat," I yelled waving my hand to the guy that came up to me.

"Thank you, Leigh," Rob said barely above a whisper.

Once the dude gave me the things to work with I started cleaning his wounds and took the bullet that was lodged out of his arm making an incision with the knife and passing the bottle of vodka to him and poured some on the wound. He hissed at the pain and I mouthed a 'sorry'.

"So, tell me what happened, where is Ash? Why isn't he back too? Where are the others?" I started panicking but tried my hardest to stay calm.

"They sent me back to communicate a message, but in reality, it was an ambush, they are trying to break Boss down and use you and Rose as targets to get to him and they also said something about taking Shadow down? I didn't quite understand what they meant by 'Shadow?'"

Ohhhhhh shit! I know what they meant by 'Shadow'. That's me. Well, assassin me. It's like my code name so that my real name stays secret. I guess they found me but how? And what did he just say about Rose and I being targeted?

"I'm sorry what? Are we targets? Since when?" I was getting more aggravated and confused as to why this was happening. Even if I had read the letters I didn't think that it would go to such an extent.

"Yeah, Boss received threats regarding both your safety and

that's why he went there. It was to fix the problem and make sure you were safe." he breathed out. It wasn't the best time to bombard a severely injured man like I was now but I need answers.

I nodded my head and told the guy that brought me the things to clean Rob's wounds to help him to the doctors' office so that he can get proper help.
I was fuming that no one told me anything, I was left in the dark and the worst part is that I don't know who it is and that if they had hurt Rob like that I can only imagine what state Asher might be in.
I ran upstairs into Ash's office because I knew Carter would be there.

I burst into the office no longer in the sweet mummy mode that I grew to be but in my killer, gang leader girl mode. The one my father always wanted me to be.
I walked straight to Carter who was on the phone, I presume to get Ash back. He turned to see me and let me tell you we were star struck. And he was even more starstruck when I punched him square in the face.
He stumbled back a bit, hanging up the phone in the process before mumbling something into it.

"What the hell was that for?" he hissed at me whipping the bit of blood from his bust lip.

I smirked my evil smirk before answering back.

"That was for keeping me in the blue about the shit that was been going on for weeks now! And don't lie to me I know about the letters and Rob told me most of what I wanted to know!"

I was beyond mad at this point.

"You know what? Forget it, I'm taking over. I'm sick of this bullshit." Carter just stood there completely in shock.

"Call a meeting in the living room, I want everybody that you have on hand NOW!" he just nodded without asking any questions.

Eight minutes later everyone was there, Rose was sat on the floor with headphones on watching a Disney movie on the tablet because I didn't want her listening to what I was about to say.

Everybody was now seated and I was standing there with Carter in front looking at me confused and ready for Answers.
I took a deep breath and looked at all of them before starting.

"Look, I know you are wondering why I called a meeting and maybe why I hit Carter. I know what is happening and I have decided that in order to bring Ash back I need to be honest with you guys."

Here we go...

"My name is Everleigh Graham, daughter of Sean Graham and I am the next in line to the throne of the Gold Thorn and the head of the Russian mafia. I'm also known under the name of Shadow." gasps filled the room and some looked at me in utter shock, others had that 'yeah right' face on and I could see a weird emotion coming from Carter, Paul and Louis.

"I know it may seem hard to believe but here is proof."

I lifted my shirt up showing the side of my rib cage and turned to them so that they could see. I have the mark of the leader. It's a tattoo you get once you are declared leader and I had mine at eighteen. It's written 'gold thorn' in cursive and is circled by thorns and has a crown on the top left corner on the 'G' and a small rose on the bottom right side.

More gasps came into the room and filled the silence... I couldn't help but give a small sad look towards them. I did feel guilty for lying but they lied to me too.

"Moving on. All the questions that I know you have will have to wait but right now, my main priority is that we stay together as a team to get our men back. And for that, we need a plan that I have already thought about."

Before I could utter another word Carter stepped up and spoke.

"Yeah, and what were you thinking we should do Boss?" he winked and gave me a smile that said it all. He let me take charge and was waiting for his directions.

They all hollered "yeah Boss, what's the plan?"

CHAPTER ELEVEN

Everleigh:

I had spent about two-three hours getting everyone ready to get my man back.

Lucky for me they have a gun trade with my dad so they have my guns, and even luckier they have some that I designed so bonus for me!

Carter has been super helpful with the ones that didn't listen to my orders after I confessed to who I am.

I sent Paul to stay and protect Rose and if there was an attack or any sort of emergency to call Sergei.

I know this may be overboard and that I'm preparing a lot but if those people can hold a notorious gang leader for 48 hours without him escaping then they are to be taken down and fast.

I was full on leader mode and I needed to get Ash back by my side because I somehow feel like I have something to do with it. I miss his kisses and his hugs, even if I don't really know what we are or where we stand.

"Are the guys ready?" I asked Carter who was giving orders to some other of the men.

He nodded "yes they are ready when you are."

"Good. I want everyone by the cars for the last run over on the plan in five minutes. If any person is late they will be limping back with a bullet lodged in the leg. I hate tardies."

"Yes, boss." I waved him off.

I had already changed into my 'kick-ass' outfit as Paul likes to call it.

It was composed of a tight leather shorts that came mid-thigh, I grabbed one of Ash's t-shirts and tucked it in the skirt and paired it with a signature leather jacket. I had a pair of Louboutin heels on with their signature red soles. Man did I love those shoes!

I placed a garter on my thigh that had knives strapped to it. Two guns in my skirt waistband and I had a rifle waiting for me in the car as well as my gun for long distance shooting. I walked up to Rose who was playing with Paul in the living room. All the commotion didn't seem to faze her. She looks so much like me at her age I was exactly the same. She was being her cute self-giggling and talking gibberish to Paul.

"Hey princess." I kissed the top of her head and took her in my arms.

"Mummy!" she squealed and hugged me back.

"Listen, baby, momma has got to go for a bit to get daddy. You be good now and do as uncle Paully says. Ok baby?" I brushed a strand of hair out her face while she was playing with the zipper of my jacket.

"Okay, mama."

"Good girl. Love you baby." I held her close. God knows what is awaiting me. And I hated to leave her to do something that was attached to my old self before I became a mum.

I placed her back down and gave a sign to Paul to follow me. We stepped away from Rose still keeping an eye on her.

"You protect her with your life or suffer the consequences.' I sternly said to him.

He placed his hands in surrender, sometimes I wonder how he is a scary gang member.

"All clear, you know you are scarier than the boss."

"Thank you, I know." I smirked.

He laughed at my statement before I continued.

"I've already told you but if something happens, call Sergei Romanov and tell him snowdrop needs help. Got it?"

"Got it." he nodded.

"Alright. I'm off to kick ass!" I left towards the cars for the quick briefing.

"Right." I clapped my hands once and loud enough to get their attention.

"So the plan is we get in, get out as fast as we can. I give it fifteen minutes tops. Shoot all that moves apart from us, obviously. I want the placed surrounded." they nodded.

"You curly." I pointed to the blond guy with curly hair.

"Got the guns ready and all the ammo?" I raised my eyebrow at him.

"Yes, boss."

"Good. Glasses I want you to get me the building plans and tell me in what room he is in."

"I-I..." he was so nervous poor guy.

"I'm sorry, did I talk in gibberish?" I turned to him and crossed my arms, glaring at him.

"N-no boss." his head hung low. I do like this power I must admit.

"Good. Cars now." and with that, we all were in four different black vans heading to where they are keeping Ash.

"You are scary you know that. I think you made him piss his pants." I let Carter drive me because I was too mad to focus on that task.

"Yeah, I know. But I can't be all sweet and loving when giving orders. If it doesn't work on a two-year-old it for sure won't work on a grown adult. They should fear the angry mummy voice."

We both started laughing even though he knew I was dead serious. I don't tolerate to not be respected and if they fear me it's a bonus. My father always told me that I should be a nightmare dressed as a daydream, at least in this business. Before I knew it we were at the old abandoned place that I'm guessing is their warehouse.

We parked a bit further away. Once we were all out I gave them their last orders and I took Carter with me to find my man.

I know I shouldn't be calling him that when I don't even know where we stand. I mean are we a couple? Roommates? Sort of co-parents? I don't know?

I was prepping my gun making sure that it was ready for use. Glasses had given me a blueprint of the house and the rest were surrounding the place.

Carter was the only one that was going to follow me in. I do not need other men captured or dead. Once we get Ash out there are only three more men to get out if they are still alive since they left being five in total. When we find the guys we send a signal to the rest of the team and get them out of there fast and blow up the place.

Cart and I were a few feet away from the front gate. I was positioning myself to shoot the guards that were in front sending the message to the rest to shoot the ones that were outside.

I shoot the two guards right in the head. God, I missed using a gun.

"Nice shot." Cart patted my back.

"Why thank you." I mocked bowed.

"Let's go." I marched still with my rifle in hand shooting anyone that came towards us and I knew Cart had my back as well as the rest.

It was surprisingly easy to get in the house and I was walking straight towards the basement door where you could clearly hear screams of agony and suddenly my heart clenched.
I slowly opened the door and walked down the set of stairs coming closer to where all the screaming was coming from. I hid behind the wall looking at the scene that was in front of me. Ash was sat on a chair covered in blood and the three others were in the same state chained to the floor on one side of the room. A tall man (not as tall as Asher though) was standing before him with a knife in hand.

He was laughing evilly at Ash waving the knife in front of him.

"Ohh, Asher... I need to teach you a lesson and after I'm done with you-you can kiss goodbye to your girlies because you ain't going to be seeing them again..."

You could hear the sickly smirk he had in his voice. I needed

Maya Crosby-Emery

to intervene before he made any more damage.

"I have to disagree with you Herbert or is it Jerry oh wait no it's Ken." he turned around shocked and threw the knife towards me, I caught it inches from my face.

"Ts ts…" I waved my head side to side admiring the knife and running my index finger across the blade not making eye contact with the man.

"You first mistake was to think you could ever get to me or my daughter." I walked further towards him and I visibly saw him cower back. I looked at Ash who had a questioning look not quite understanding what was going on.

'Your second mistake was to throw this knife at me." I threw the knife to him making it land on his shoulder keeping him stuck flat against the wall. He desperately tried to get the knife out before I could get any closer.

The only thing you could hear was his heaving breathing and the click of my heels on the concrete floor.

"Your third mistake is to believe you can get away with this." I stabbed another knife in this other shoulder.

I looked straight at him knowing the fear I placed in him.

"Get them out of here." I ordered Carter.

"Boss it's time we need to leave." I nodded my head, walking back to the stairs.

96

"Call someone to help you out, I'll get med teams ready for them. I want to get that prick back at your base, I haven't finished with him." and with that, I walked out like the boss I am.

****

Ash Mortimer:

I've lost count of the hours or even days I've been locked in this place. My men and I have been starved and beaten but it's nothing I haven't been through already.
All I could think about was my sweet angel and my princess. Their smile and laughter was the only thing holding me up still. I hold on to the hope I would hold them again and tell them how much I care for them, heck how much I love them.

I love them.

My Angel, my princess.

I love them.

I was once again on the torture chair with this dick in front of me. I don't even know how he managed to get us. There is no way he could have done this by himself.
I zoned out what he was saying when I heard that voice I've been longing for. At first, I thought I was dreaming. But no. She was there, like really there dressed in all black looking super sexy. Damn, I can't wait to tap that! Stupid dick brain taking control.

He threw the blade to her head, my heart suddenly stopped but to my surprise, she stopped it like a pro.
She spoke to him, I couldn't quite get everything she was saying because of the hits I got I was hearing a buzzing sound in my head.
Next thing I know he was pinned to the wall with two knives in each shoulder. *Did she do that all by herself?*

Soon she gave orders to Carter and walked out with her head held high. Shit, she's hot when she is all badass. Carter untied me and help me shift my weight to him.

"Shit, she's scary." I mumbled to him.

"Tell me about it! She made the computer geek Kilian shat himself!"

I chuckle at that but ended up coughing.

"Come on man, let's get you back before she blows this place up." he nervously chuckled but I felt deep down that the Everleigh that was here today would be capable of that.

"Yeah let's go."

CHAPTER TWELVE

Everleigh:

During the car ride, I was at the back with Ash who had passed out once Carter had brought him out. The three other men were in the other vans.
Asher's head was on my lap, his breathing was stable even if it came out a bit rocky. I was stroking his hair, smiling to myself that he was there, back in my arms.

"We're here." Carter turned to the back of the car. I nodded to him. I trailed my finger on his jaw, taking care to not touch all the cuts and bruises that covered his bloody face.

"Asher, babe. Wake up so that I can clean your cuts." I stroked his hair out of his face placing a kiss behind his ear.

"Mmmmm." he shifted on my lap slowly waking up. He sat up holding his head.

"Gosh my head hurts but that was one of the best sleep I've had" he smiled looking down at me.

"Come on, big guy we need to get you cleaned up."

I helped him walk in the house, it was about eight in the evening so I knew Rose was already in bed and I was glad she was because I didn't want her to see his face in that state and I, covered in his blood.

I dragged him to the live-in doctor's office to get him fully checked before cleaning up. While I was waiting for him to finish up I rounded up everyone that went with me to get them back for a meeting.

"Alright people. Tonight rest up I do not want to see you before lunchtime. Rest you deserve it. I'll have another meeting with you tomorrow."

They all nodded and said 'yes boss'.

"Go home and rest guys." I smiled at them and they left. I was taking my shoes off when a strong arm came around my waist.

I squealed when I was lifted from the ground and brought up the stairs to our room.

"Ash! Put me down! You're in no condition to pick me up." he put me down and I scolded him.

"If it's you than I can take everything. Bullets, chains, knives. Anything." he pecked my lips.

"Come on you, we need to fix that face." I took his hand and led him to the bathroom.

He sat me on the sink counter with the first aid kit next to me as I started cleaning his wounds.

"Sooo..."

"Sooo?" I copied.

"You were pretty feisty back there. Care to explain how you can be that person when the girl I met that night in the alley was afraid of the man that hurt her?"'"

He raised his eyebrow placing his hands either side of me blocking me from leaving.
I looked down not wanting to face him. I just couldn't. I feel like I've lied to him about who I am.

"That was me then and that's me now. I can shoot and throw knives but I can't do hand to hand combat. I have a pretty mean right hook but that's all." I still couldn't look at him.

"Baby look at me." his voice was soft as he took my chin in his hand.

"How come you can't fight but can do the rest?" his left hand was now on my thigh rubbing up and down waiting for me to continue.

"My dad never taught me how. It sounds stupid but he always said that I wouldn't need to learn that when I took over." I slapped my hand over my mouth I felt like I've said too much already.

"Listen can we talk about this after we both take a shower and after we had a good night sleep, please. I'll tell you everything tomorrow but right now I just want to cuddle and be with you without the complications of my life."

I looked at him with pleading eyes. He sighed and kissed my forehead. I leaned over so that my head was against his chest.

"Thank you." I whispered out.

We both pulled away and did what we had to do. Once I was finished with my shower I slipped on a pair of leggings and a tank top leaving my hair loose. I climbed into bed and snuggled up to a shirtless Ash. Every time I looked at his lightly bruised face covered in cuts my heart hurts. I don't like seeing him in pain like that. I trailed my fingers onto his defined chest, over his tattoos, his old and new scars, memorising all his features every little detail of him.

He pulled me closer to his chest, playing with the ends of my hair with one hand while the other was drawing invisible things on my thigh.

"Go to sleep Angel, it's been a long day. For all of us." he placed a long kiss on the top of my head.

I closed my eyes and let sleep take over me with a smile wrapped in his arms and with these sweet words.

"Goodnight my angel, I'm falling for you."

CHAPTER THIRTEEN

Everleigh:

It has been a week since I have got Asher back and I have told him the full story like I did the rest of the gang members.

And to be honest I was so scared of how he would react. He was mad that I hadn't told him first and he didn't speak to me for two days.

I couldn't blame him but he came back and forgave me. I'm glad he did because those two days without him talking to me were hard, very hard.

So here I am now planning Rose's birthday party that will include all the gang and Ash's mother is even making the trip from Miami to Chicago just so that she can meet Rose and myself.

I'm a nervous wreck and I want, no need everything to be perfect.

Now the hard thing was coming my way: to ask Ash if I can invite Sergei to meet Rose for the first time and hopefully I can do that before her birthday.

I walked up to his office giving it a knock.

I was trying to control my breathing when his deep voice came out to me.

"Come in."

I pushed the door open and he greeted me his gorgeous smile. God, he is making this fracking difficult to control the urge to pounce him.

"Hey, Angel come here." he patted his lap and I sat on it straddling him.

"Is there anything you need?" he asked rubbing up and down my thighs.

I bit my lip to not communicate to him what he is doing to me and judging by the smirk that is plastered on his lips I know that he knows.
I lean forward cupping his face with my hands and kissing him slowly. He gladly returns it.
But my quest came back to mind and I pulled away even though I wish I could do that all the Time.

"I need to ask you something, it's a matter that is close to my heart."

He nodded his head, stabilising his breath.

"Can Sergei come over sometime this week to meet Rose and can he come to her Birthday party too? Please?" I bit my lip nervously this time waiting for his answer.

"Yes baby you can, I'm on good terms with him and I know how much this means to you."

I kiss him again as a thank you and I'm ready to hop off his lap when he holds me down.

"Now where do you think you are going?" he whispers in my ear sending an uncontrollable amount of shivers all over my body.

"Going back to planning our daughter's birthday." his smirk grew bigger as he started kissing my neck.

"I love it when you say our daughter." he starts nibbling around my collar bone making me let out a little whimper.

He starts kissing down my chest stopping at my cleavage because I have one of those tank top type things with spaghetti straps that advantages your cleavage and I was stupid enough to wear a push-up bra not helping my case either.

His hands were now placed just beneath them and he was just admiring my breast making me blush slightly.
He tilted his head to the side before adding:

"Did your boobs get bigger by any chance?"

Oohh the nerve of that horny little devil.

"Calm your Dick down they are only bigger because I've finished my monthly and ovulation period is coming up next. So enjoy them while you can."

His smile only grew more and he attacked my boobs with kisses once more.

"Asher stop it… it tickles!" I giggled out but that only made him continue more. His hand are now under my top and he has lifted it off.
I tried wiggling out of His lap but without realising it I was grinding him.

"Mm mm Angel you might want to stop moving." he groaned out and that's when I was met with his little big friend poking me by my thigh.

"Where would the fun be if I stopped now?" I pouted and said in the sweetest voice I could.

He growled in response and smashed his lips to mine, it was a kiss full of passion, want and lust. I started unbuttoning his shirt and running my hands down his chest to the buckle of his belt. His tongue tangled with mine and things would have escalated if a certain someone wouldn't have broken that moment.

 "Sorry to… um… interrupt the baby making but we need you, boss at the docks." he cleared his throat.

Ash immediately covers me with his arms trying to block me from, what I'm guessing by the voice is Louis, he sighs and nodded to him.

"I'll be ready in say… twenty minutes."

"Yes, boss." and with that, he left and closed the door behind him.

"I need to let you go, but I don't want to..." I look at my hands and start playing with my fingers.

He brushes away stray hair that fell on my face and made me look at him.

"Be ready by seven pm, we'll go out to dinner just you and me and then we will come back and finish what was rudely interrupted by Louis. How does that sound?

I kissed him and smiled back at him.

"That sounds amazing. What do I need to wear?"

He put his hand under his chin and was pondering on what he was going to say.

"Ummm. How about you slip on something sexy and forget about any underwear because we won't be needing that." I gasped and gave him a little hit on his shoulder.
He only chuckled back at me.

"I'm only joking chill." I sighed in relief.

"Or am I?" I scoffed and got off him to retrieve my top and slipped it back on heading off to the door.

"Ohh Angel come on. I know you like It." he was buttoning up his shirt again.

I turned to him and put on the sexiest smile I could and said before leaving:

"Maybe I will do as you asked maybe I won't. You have to wait and find out tonight.' I winked and he groaned in frustration and anticipation.

Ha! Serves him right. A little torture won't hurt him.

CHAPTER FOURTEEN

Everleigh:

The day went on without any major incidents and I hadn't seen Ash since our heated moment this morning. I don't really know how tonight is going to turn out, I'm super nervous.

I decided to snuggle up with Rose in front of one of her favourite movies also known as 101 Dalmatians. She had already fallen asleep when Annie came right in front of the TV blocking my view.

"What do you think you are doing?" she gave me a pointed look placing her hands on her hips and tapping her foot.

"What do you think you are doing?" I argued back still confused about what exactly she is doing here. She huffed air before continuing.

"You are supposed to be getting ready for your dinner date with Boss tonight." I raised an eyebrow at her.

How does she know that?

"I know because he wouldn't shut up about it when he was talking with the guys, it was bound to happen at some point in time."

Did I say that out loud?

"You did." she gave me an amused look.
By that point, I was up from the sofa with Rose in my arms walking up the stairs with Annie following me up to her room to lay her down.

Once I was done putting her down for the afternoon nap that she had missed because she was out at the park with Paul and Louis.
I closed the door behind her and turned around to face her.

"And you are bugging me because…" I crossed my arms over my chest waiting for her answer.

"I'm here to get your ready silly! And we better hurry it's already coming up to five o'clock" she exclaimed out of joy. I slapped her arm playfully to tell her to quiet down since we were still in front of Rose's room.

"Ow!" I gave her the shush sign and dragged her to mine and Asher's room to let her continue her explanation.

She shut the door behind her and went straight to my closer looking and pulling clothes out. I was just standing there in utter shock. I was not expecting her to help me out. I never really had any other best friend other than Victoria and she did love bags, clothes and stuff but I was never her model, nor did I ever need to dress up for a guy because my father, brother and Sergei never let a guy approach me even when we were in meetings.

"Ummm, Annie. What exactly am I going to do while you destroy my closet?" I walked up to her and she came out with undergarments in her hand.

"You Mrs. Future Mortimer are going to have a shower and do all the necessities such as shaving and so on." she placed the lacy underwear in my hands and pushed me into the suite before I could protest.

Deciding to put my faith in her clothing style knowing that she did have a good taste in clothes since the time we went shopping and she bought all the store for clothes for me whilst I was just taking the bare minimum. I took twenty minutes to do my shower with a hair wash and all. I slipped on the red lacy bra and pantie and walked out of the bathroom with a towel on my head.

"Wow, you are one sexy mama! I mean look at that body! Guuurrrlll! No wonder the boss want to tap that. I sure would! Tell me your secret to the perfect body!" she was fanning herself to add more dramatic effects.

 I blushed a bit at her comments and put on a silk robe that was hung by the bathroom door feeling uncomfortable with her intense gaze.
She finally snapped out of it and walked me to the chair that she had placed in front of the dresser where was laid different beauty products. She sat me down and started her magic. She took a good hour maybe more to finish with my face and hair and I just wanted something discreet. She did a

warm toned eye with a deep red lipstick and a small wing liner to accentuate my and I quote 'sexy devil cat eyes'.

This girl has a very colorful vocabulary when it comes to describing me. I didn't remember her being that enthusiastic when I first hung out with her. I like her like this even if she has gone batshit crazy for just one dinner.

She chucked me a red dress and told me to put in on and I did. I came out of the closet and walked to the mirror to see the finished result. And damn did I look good. I don't remember the last time I was this dolled up. The dress was red with a deep neckline that revealed a lot of cleavage that gave my boobs a good look but led me to take off my bra since we could see it. I didn't mind much though. It was a very form fitting dress that stopped just my knee. My hair was in loose curls and I had a pair of black high heels on. I turned around to face a very happy Annie and I gave her back that smile.

"You look really beautiful Everleigh." she stood up and took my hands in hers looking deep into my eyes smiling.

"Thank you so much, Annie, I look really good all thanks to you." I took her in my arms and gave her a big hug and she gave it back.

"Look at the time it's seven! Gosh, time flies when you are having fun! Let's get that pretty little ass of yours downstairs." I nodded and we both headed towards the door and down the stairs.

At the bottom of them was waiting for a very handsome looking Ash who was in a black button up shirt with black dress pants and a matching vest, no tie and smart shoes. His hair was done in a nice quiff and he had his dazzling smile with those dimples.
I walked up to him and gave him a peck on the lips.

"You look gorgeous Angel." we both gazed into each other's eyes and I was about to compliment him back when Annie interrupted.

"Thank you I know! She's my masterpiece!" she added more drama whipping a fake tear at the corner of her eye. Ash and I both rolled our eyes at her behaviour but I still let out a small giggle when I saw the look on her face.

"Well, you guys better be off then! Go on lovebirds enjoy your night! Don't worry about Rose everything will be al–" Carter got cut off by a loud cry coming from upstairs.

Both Asher and I pushed our way through and went up to Rose's room to see what the matter was. We pushed the door open to find a very upset Rose and a very distressed Paul trying to calm her down.

"What happened?" both of them looked at me and that stopped Rose's yelling and a sigh of relief came from Paul. She ran up to me screaming 'mummy mummy' as a picked her in my arms placing her on my hip giving a murderous look at Paul for making my baby cry.

"Hey don't look at me like that. She was asking for you and

when I told her you were going out she started screaming murder! She has a good set of pipes there!" he ran his hand through his hair lightly pacing around the room.

"Maybe we should stay here, for Rose, it's best so that she doesn't get to upset." Ash placed his arms around my body from behind looking at Rose in my arms.

"I'm sorry what did you just say?" I turned in his arms placing Rose on the floor and she immediately wrapped her arms around my leg.

"Well... I thought with Rose in this state you wouldn't want to go and I completely get it if you don't want to go. We can do this another time." he smiled sweetly at me and I'm touched that he is taking my possible feelings in consideration for this but I want to go out.

"It's really sweet that you let me chose but I want to go out. I did not go through that torture with Annie and shoving my butt in this dress for no one to see it." I placed my hands on his chest waiting for in response.

"What about Rose? She will be upset" he asked with a little worry in his voice.

I smiled and bent down to Rose's level with as much grace as I could considering the tight dress that I am wearing.

"Baby girl, mummy and daddy are going out together to eat but we will be back later and you will see us again in the morning but for now you have to go to bed and listen to mummy and be a good girl for your uncles." I caressed her hair and she still had teary eyes and a pouty lip.

"But Rose wants to go with you mummy." she sniffed and I do feel bad for wanting to leave.

"Ok baby, but we did this before. Why do you want mummy to stay tonight?" I questioned her whipping the few tears that had left her eyes.

She took a deep breath and swung her arms around my neck.

"Because I scwared." I rubbed her back picking her up with me.

"Scared of what princess." Ash was to question stepping closer to us placing his hand on her back and the other on my waist.

"That mommy and daddy won't come back to me" and she let out her tears again. We did a group hug with Rose in my arms and me in Asher's.

"You know baby that won't happen. We will always come back." I tried reassuring her. I looked into Ash's eyes and he gave me the same look.

"We will stay." we said in sync. She nodded her head in my neck and did the grabby arms to her daddy and he took her.

"Um, guys I don't mean to interrupt your little family moment but I think you can still have your night out." Ray came from behind us.

"How? I don't want to leave Rose anymore. I thought I did but I changed my mind." I was quick to add.

"Don't worry I've got an idea! Just give me fifteen minutes." and he left running down the steps leaving a very confused me and Asher.

CHAPTER FIFTEEN

Everleigh:

After what felt like hours were merely fifteen minutes like Ray promised and both Ash and I were led blindfolded to the garden.

"Ready guys?" Ray asked with a hint of excitement in his voice.

"Ray hurry up to take this blindfold off I want to see!" I whined and a chuckle came from behind me wrapping his arms around my waist.

"Patience is a virtue baby. What do you think Ray? Should we let her wait a little longer?" his chest vibrated from his laugh and both the guys were laughing at my misery.

"He has his blindfold off? That's not fair!" I pouted my lip and crossed my arms and turned my head to where I'm guessing Ash is.

"Angel don't be sad. Here I'll take it off." and he did.

He slowly slid the fabric of my eyes and I was once again met with his baby blues. I smiled softly at him and reached up to kiss his lips as a thank you. We must have taken a little longer than I thought as we were interrupted by someone clearing their throat.

"Sorry to interrupt yet again but for dinner is served. If you would like to follow me to our private table specially set up for you." Louis ushered us to the table and I was just in awe of what Ray had set up for us.

He had led us to a part of the garden I had not seen because this place is massive! There was a table placed in the center of it was a bottle of wine. All around at a safe distance were candles of all shapes and sizes all lit up. Fairy lights were wrapped around the branches of the nearby trees as well as lanterns.

"Wow! You really outdid yourself, Ray. Thank you." I walked over to him and gave him a big hug and he immediately gave it back but not for long because I was snatched back by Ash.

"Mine!" he said possessively. He doesn't do this often only when I go and hug or talk a little too long to his men, or any man for that matter. Ray put his hands up in surrender.

"She's all your mate. You have made that very clear since day one." he had a slightly panicked look on his face which was quite endearing. Asher gave him the death glare and that sends him off to skedaddle. Asher started to walk me to our table where Louis, who was our waiter for the night, was waiting with the bottle of wine in his hand looking very smart with his penguin-like suit.

"Oh before I leave Rose's room is on your left when you are

at the table and look up so that she can see you and you can see her. Paul is up there too." I smiled at him again feeling very lucky to have all these guys in my life.

"All right thanks, Ray now fuck off!" Ash added with a sweetly aggravated voice. I placed my hand in his and walked him to our table before telling him to take it easy with him he was only helping and being nice.

"Yeah a little too nice in my opinion." he mumbled under his breath but I still heard.

After we ate our improvised meal that was done by Carter which consisted of spaghetti and meatballs. I felt like I was in lady and the tramp when they have that romantic dinner and end up kissing at the end of it. I watch way too many movies with Rose.

"So baby girl, there are a lot of things that I don't know about you and vice versa. For example the fact that you are the heir to the Russian mafia and one of the most powerful gangs in the world. Care to explain how that happened?"

He raised his brow at me and crossed his arms before placing them on the table and leaning in. I, on the other hand, took another sip of my marvelous red wine to give me some courage.

"Well as you know already I am the daughter of Sean Graham and my godfather is the head of the Russian mafia. So far so good. Anyway, I was the firstborn of the family thus making me the rightful heir to my father's empire." I took a breath and he nodded for me to continue.

"So, even if I had a brother that was a little less than a year younger my father saw the spark of a leader of some sort in me I guess? But my mother if you can call her that didn't agree with me taking over. She was so besotted with my brother that she would try everything to let him have it."

I frowned a little at all the memories of how awful she was to me all to have my brother have all I have worked for.

"Even if she was awful to me for his benefit, he wasn't like that with me. He always helped me and pushed me to prove her wrong that I was set to take my dad's place. He was a great brother." I felt his hand on my cheek and the other was holding my hand.

"Don't cry, Angel. I'm here now and he seemed like a good man your brother. What happened?" I didn't even realise I was crying until he mentioned it. But talking about my brother is a tough subject for me to discuss because that day I didn't only lose my brother but also my best friend.

I took a shaky breath in and tears kept running down my cheeks. I can't not right now at least.

"Hey, hey. Everleigh you don't have to talk about it now. It's fine to continue with telling me how you became what you are today alright?" his voice was soft and loving making more at ease and I was very grateful that he didn't pry anymore on that subject. I took a deep breath and whipped my tears away without destroying what is left of my makeup.

"So anyway," I let out a nervous laugh and continued "Sergei didn't like my mother and still doesn't to this day. I was very good friends with his daughter but she was very much a girly girl and he tried to keep her away from this life and since he didn't have a son or any other male relative for that matter like a nephew as such and so that's when I came into the picture."
I gave him a small smile and he gave it back giving my hand a squeeze.

"So to piss my mother off he put me next in line for his empire. And when I was eighteen I got the tattoo representing the new brand that I will create by joining both of those empires. And that's basically it after it gets complicated once I got pregnant with Rose." he nods in understanding taking a sip of his drink.

"Thank you for sharing. It makes things a little more clear. What do you say we head up and cuddle in bed." he stood up a reached for my hand and walked me back into the house.

"Thank you for tonight. It wasn't exactly like it was planned but I still loved it."

"Me too, Angel. As long as you are there than I am a happy man." he leaned down and left a long and sweet kiss on my lips.

We arrived in our room and we both started to undress. I

was in the bathroom in my underwear taking my remaining makeup off when a pair of very strong arms came around my arms. Asher started placing kisses going from my shoulder to my neck. Making me let out a sigh of delight at the contact of his bare chest against my back.

"Asher! I brushing me teef!" I tried to reason with him through brushing my teeth. But he didn't stop. I finished with my teeth and he swung me over his shoulder and plopped me on the bed making we squeal and yell his name.

"Better save those vocal cords for a little later love when you are going to be having one heck of a night."he justified himself with a cheeky grin and lust filled eyes.

I don't think I am not going to do much sleeping tonight if you know what I mean.

CHAPTER SIXTEEN

Everleigh:

The sun rays were shining through the curtain, caressing my bare skin and that's when things for last night replayed in my head once again. I smiled to myself and turned around to face a very awake and smiling Asher.

"Morning beautiful Angel. Sleep well?" his morning voice got me all tingly, he started tracing invisible patterns on the skin on my back and back up my shoulders and down my arm. I softly moaned at his touch.

"Sleep? I didn't do much of that thanks to you." I gave a knowing smile and he just pecked my lips.

"Well, you can't say you didn't have fun. I mean I didn't hear you complain. It was quite the opposite really." he smirked and I playfully slapped his arm.

"You cheeky bastard!" he simply let out a laugh, and that laugh is like angels singing. Ok that was exaggerating a bit but man, I love it and I think that it might be more than his laugh that I'm in love with.

I cuddled up more to him not caring that we are both naked because let's face it, we've both seen it all.

"Uh, Angel if you don't want another round I suggest we get up and get dressed." I blushed at what he was pointing to, a not so small friend.

"Ok, ok, you might want a cold shower now." I kissed him again getting out of bed and walking to the shower. Before I passed the door I turned around and gave him the sexiest smile I could muster.

"But I'm not against sharing the shower, you know saving the planet and all..." I couldn't finish my sentence that I was chased into the shower by a very horny Ash.

Ash was first to step out the bathroom with I was finishing cleaning my face. As I walked out I saw him walking up to the set of drawers that was placed in front of the bed. He was shirtless with only a pair of boxers on and if I'm honest I was checking the hell out of him.
I had never seen his back without a shirt on funny enough. It was full of muscles like the rest of his Greek god body. The thing that caught my eye was a tattoo that covered most of his shoulder blade linking its design to the one on his arm and chest.

A memory of the same tattoo came to mind. The one of the night I had hooked up with a complete stranger, *Rose's father*.

"Um, Ash, that tattoo you have on your back." I nervously asked putting on my underwear in the process.

"Yeah, what about it?"

"Tell me why did you get it? And what is it?"

"Um ok, I got it…" I didn't even need to let him finish that I already knew the answer.

"After the first time you/ I got shot and it's a phoenix," we said in unison.

"Yeah, how did you know that? I don't remember mentioning it to you before." he turned around looking straight at me crossing his arms over his chest making his muscles flex.

I sat on the bed fiddling with my fingers on my lap. I took a deep breath and started.

"I know because you told me…" I paused before I continued, seeing the confused look on his face.

"The night we slept together at the international gang meet up in Australia nearly four years ago."

****

Ash Mortimer:

"What?" I asked not quite understanding where she is going with this.

"Ok let me break it down. Did you go to the gang meeting?"

she looked at me with a very serious and nervous look in her eyes.

"Yes." I answered simply.

"Right did you go to the bar with the rest of the gangs after the last meeting?" she asked again.

"I guess so yeah." I shrugged sitting next to her.

"Do you remember sleeping with a girl, a drunk girl for that matter?" she raised her brow at me. I looked at her a little taken back by her question I mean I sure did sleep with a girl and she was great in bed at that but so is Everleigh.

"Um I did but I don't remember much of it I was pretty intoxicated and I'm guessing so was she." I rubbed the back of my neck and gave a quick glance towards her. Her face held shock mixed with a thousand different emotions and her face turned pale.

"You are Rose's dad." she bluntly said. I didn't get it, I am her dad. Well, she calls me that and I'm fine with it I love her as my daughter.

"Well yeah, I am." I replied with a light 'duh' tone.

"No, no Asher I mean her actual father, sperm and everything. I'm the girl you slept with that night, you told me about that tattoo that night."

I think my face turned as pale as hers. Things started to add up in my brain. Now that I think about it Rose has my eyes, my lips and ears. I think Everleigh is right. But maybe she is lying. What are the odds that you sleep with a girl that you don't know nor remember and never seen her again until a fateful night in a dark alley and it appears that she has a daughter that happens to be yours? Yeah, not much.

"I-I know you probably don't believe me. I understand if you want us to leave or call me a liar. We can do a DNA test if that makes you feel better, I... I 'm sorry." she whispered the last part and I could see her tears falling onto her lap and quickly whipping her tears away.

"I should go." she stood up and the way she was talking was just breaking my heart. I know I'm not responding like she would have hoped but how would you when you find out that you are a father.

"Hey, hey, hey. Look at me, Angel." I ran in front of her placing both my hands on her shoulders blocking her from going anywhere.

"You and my daughter aren't going anywhere. I don't think you are a liar but I would like a test to be done so that I can prove that she is mine in papers etc. I love you and her too. I mean it."

Her eyes were glazed with tears threatening to fall, I kissed both her cheeks.

"R-really? You love us?" her voice was barely above a whisper but just enough for me to hear. I kissed her nose and smiled at her.

"I love you. I love Rose just as much, her being my daughter or not. I love you."

Her tears were now falling freely and she kissed me with so much passion.

"I love you too." and she kissed me again. She makes me so happy. I can't believe she loves me. I love her so much, more than she will ever know.

CHAPTER SEVENTEEN

Everleigh:

"I love you too."

That was the only thing that played in my mind as I was standing there facing a very hot and shirtless Ash. I can't believe I actually said that, and that he said it back too.

We stepped to one another, he placed his hands on my hips and connected our foreheads.

"I love you, everything about you. I love that little girl, mine or not." he breathed out and before I could say anything else there was a loud knock and the sound of footsteps entering our room.

"Boss. Mr. Romanov is here. Said you were expecting him."

Carter said a little out of breath and confused as to why he was here and frankly, me too. Ash let out a breath and pulled away from me and gave a slight smile looking at my confused face.

"Surprise."

It took me a few seconds to compute what was going on,

sure I knew that at some point before Rose's birthday we would meet but I wasn't expecting this early. I just smiled the biggest smile I could do, kissed him and ran straight past Carter and down the stairs to the living room and up the entrance.

"Papa!"

I yelled and he turned around and his look softened once he saw me. I ran up into his arms. He picked me up and I placed my legs around his waist like when I was little. The last time I saw him was at the Gala and I was a bit shell-shocked to see him and I was worried that he hated me or something after I left without saying goodbye.
He was carrying me like a baby as if a weighed nothing, my head on his shoulder as he was rocking me back and forth. And if it wasn't for someone clearing their throat I would have probably fallen back asleep.

"Sergei." Ash's voice meant business.

"Asher. Nice of you to let me see my little snowdrop." his thick Russian accent could be recognised in an instant, to me at least.

He put me back on the ground and looked me up and down and that's when I realised I was only in a bright pink underwear and one of Ash's t-shirts. And the second thing I realised is that there were quite a few guys around me. All Asher's and Sergei's guys. I flushed bright red and hid behind a very mad Ash at the fact that besides him, Sergei and Carter, everyone was looking at me in a lustful way that made me uneasy.

That's when my knight in shining armor, or more like my wonder woman, Annie, walked in with a pair of joggers and threw them to me. I mouthed a thank you and slipped them on.

"You look at her like that one more time and it will be the last thing you will see."

 Asher snapped at his men and Sergei did the same to his men but in Russian and he didn't seem pleased at all about this. I came out from behind Ash and took both his and Papa's hand and dragged them into the kitchen. There was a silence and I could sense a certain tension. About what? I couldn't say. I suppose there is more to this visit than just seeing me and meeting my little girl.

Luckily the pitter patter of little footsteps could be heard. And there entering the living room was a rather sleepy looking Rose with her teddy in one hand and the other rubbing her eyes to get the sleep out. Ash stood up and walked to her taking her in his arms like I was in Sergei's just moments before. Only with her, it was a lot cuter because Ash was shirtless and he was holding little Rose all dressed in pink princess pyjamas.

Doesn't a guy look sexier when he holds a baby in his arms? Nope? Just me? *Alright...*

She moaned a grumpy morning moan when she was shifting to get more comfortable in his arms. I finished with all the coffees and placed them on the central kitchen island, then walked up to give my daughter a good morning kiss.

"How did you sleep baby girl?" I cooed as she blotted herself closer to Asher's chest. Now that I see them with each other the resemblance between the both of them shows even though she looks the most like me.

"Good mama. Food please now mummy." I nodded and started with breakfast.

"Do you want anything papa?" I turned to look at Sergei who looked completely compelled by Rose. I had forgotten that he had never met her before. It just felt so normal for me to have him back with me that the basic things slipped my mind.

"Who that mummy?" Rose spoke up leaning towards Sergei, tilting her head to the side.

He smiled at her and put his hand out for her to shake.

"Hello there Princess. My name is Sergei. I'm your mummy's godfather, but you can call me pop-pop."

She looked a bit taken back by his voice. She had never heard someone with that thick of an accent before today. All of a sudden she became shy and hid her face in Ash's neck. He chuckled softly at her movement and placed her more comfortably on his lap. But even though she hid her face she still shook his hand giving him her award-winning smile that makes everyone melt and that look in her eyes. It does the trick.

"She is exactly like you at the same age. Acts all shy and adorable but still gets you under her spell. You did the same when you were little, with all the other mafia and gang leaders because you would never leave your father's or my office when there would be meetings. You had all the most feared men in the palm of your hand, and she is doing the same."

Asher was quick to agree with his statement, making my cheeks turn a shade of pink.
We all ate in relative silence apart from the times where Rose would talk about her dollies or the fact that her birthday was soon and that she wanted a pony.
After that, all three of us excused ourselves to get dressed while Sergei waited in the living room with Carter discussing some gang business.

I decided to wear all black because we were going to go to the basement and start questioning the guy that kept Asher captive. My outfit consisted of black jeans that made my bum look really good, a black top that stuck to my body like a second skin with a 'v' neck covered by a crisscross pattern in the front of it and finally my signature shoes: the Louboutin red sole, black high heels. I must say I looked hot. I curled my hair and made little horns on the top of my head just for style and added effect.

I turned around and Ash was in a designer suit like one he wore when we first met. It was all black with a pristine white shirt under the vest. His hair was slicked back and he placed his gun in his waistband and fixed his tie in the mirror.

Once we were done, the both of us walked down the stairs back into the living room, where Papa was waiting for us. Soon after Rose was running down the stairs in a light brown dress that twirled when she turned. Her hair was up in a messy bun as she ran towards us. I knew that Annie had helped her get ready while I was getting dressed.

To my surprise, she ran straight into Sergei's arms giggling and his face just made my heart melt. I wiped away the single tear that left my eye, his look reminded me so much of Veronica's cheerful blue eyes.

"You alright Angel?" Asher's voice brought me back to reality, his arms around my waist and his warm breath fanning at the back of my neck.

"Yeah, I'm just glad that he is back in my life and that Ro likes him so much." I answered honestly.

****

Asher Mortimer:

"Tell us you bastard!" I yell at the guy that tortured me.

After talking a little while with Sergei getting to know Rose and himself better, Everleigh, him and I all went down to interrogate the man that held me in that cell and ask for whom he works for.

I had been at it for a good hour and he still hadn't said anything. Sergei was standing there being intimidating and

Everleigh was just admiring the set of knives that were set on the left side of the room.
I've noticed that she has a thing for knives and long shotguns.

"Leigh, I think it's your turn to have fun. Don't you think Asher?" Sergei's voice ran out in the mostly empty room bringing all the attention to him.

I simply nodded not wanting to upset him, because to be honest, he is one of the most powerful mobsters in the world. I turned to the man who visibly gulped when he saw my angel stalk towards him with a very sharp dagger in her hand.
I stepped back giving her full access and stood next to Sergei. She walked up to him and was standing right in front of him and next thing I know he is screaming his name.

"Well, Roger Filley. You are going to tell me who your boss is." she said walking around him. He had the dagger logged into his ribs on the right side.

"I don't have one." he spat back.

"Ohh really. A man such as you can't possibly be able to keep a man as strong and smart as my man for no reason and on your own. To me, it seems like your boss let you take all the blame and he is probably living the life."

She looks so scary yet sexy. I've got mixed feelings about all this. I love the side of her that is sweet and fragile in a way, makes her angelic and so pure. And yet, on the other hand, she has this dark side attached to her past that keeps haunting her and even though she is good in what she does there are still aspects that I can't yet grasp.

That side of darkness, I have it too, maybe worse that she has. And I am not proud of the things I have done and the man that I have been. And I just hope she will not be faced with the old me. God and the boys know, especially Carter, know in what dark hole I was in until I met her that fateful night. Even if it took me four years and a totally unexpected encounter at a dinner to finally realise that she was the one to bring me back to the man I am and still aspire to be not only for her and myself but for that little princess that has changed my life for the best.

And no dick head will come in the way. I will protect them and make anyone pay forever making one of them cry, or hurt them in any way. And Roger will suffer greatly.

CHAPTER EIGHTEEN

Everleigh:

This week went by very, very slowly. I've been like a mad woman running around the house to finalize everything for upcoming events and on top of all that Rose got sick.
Thus making half of the house sick too. Luckily for Ash and I, and our strong immune systems, we (for the moment) aren't sick.

But just my luck, of course, this morning I had to wake up feeling like crap. And to add to it I slept in Rose's bed because she was feeling poorly last night so when I woke she was wrapped in my arms, her face in the crook of my neck, snoring softly.

I put my hand on her forehead to see if she had a temperature and she didn't seem to have one.
I slipped out of her bed making sure not to wake her since she hadn't slept a lot the past week nights.
I quietly walked out of her room and headed straight to my room to see if Ash was awake and to possibly fall back asleep.

But as I was walking down the hall I was hit with a sudden feeling of being light-headed, that made me stumble. Before I could make a glorious face plant in the ground, a pair of arms caught me before I fell.
I looked up to see my savior thinking it was Asher bur

something about his touch felt odd. I was met with a pair of hazel eyes, not my baby blues, and a dimple-free face. Ray was the one who caught me.

"Hey, you alright there Leigh?" he asked concern clear in his voice.

I nodded regaining my balance but stumbled again into his arms.

"Careful! I'm bringing you back to bed!" not feeling strong enough to tell him that I was fine and that it was probably nothing, he helped me walk back to my bedroom but not before getting his phone out and calling Asher that was in his office.

Ray laid me on my bed and covered me with the quilt.

"I'll get you a cup of coffee or something. Be right back. The boss should be–"

"How are you?" Asher came barging in nearly knocking Ray off his feet.

"Here soon." he sighed and left us alone in our room.

Ash came up to me and kneeled down by the bed and started looking for any injuries.

"I'm fine. Just lost my balance." I place his face in my hands so that he was looking at me. I gave him a weak smile. He placed a kiss on my forehead and got back up and headed to his drawer.

"Arms up." he asked as he came back to the bed with one of his hoodies in his hands.

I obeyed him and sat up so that it would be easier for him to put the hoodie on. Once that was done he came and laid down beside me and I snuggled up close to him enjoying his warmth already feeling a lot better than I was a few minutes back.
A knock was heard and Ray appeared once more with a tray filled with all sorts of different breakfast foods. All looked amazing but when he came closer one smell was just god damn awful. He set the tray on the nightstand beside me and that made me gag. I couldn't stand it anymore I ran out of the bed with a little whimper after losing Asher's warmth and headed straight to the on suite.
I spilt my guts out not really caring that both boys were in the room next door to me.

Soon enough the familiar touch of Ash came back. He was rubbing circles on my back in a comforting manner telling me to let it all out and that all would be fine.
Once I was done I started crying all that I knew. I really hate feeling this vulnerable and weak.

"Hey there baby girl, don't cry. You're alright." he held me tightly in his arms so that my face was in his chest and his chin rested on top of my head.

"Let's get you cleaned up shall we?" I nodded my head as he picked me up and undressed me placing me under the warm water in the shower.

After we bathed together I had gained I bit more strength and was able to dress, much to Asher's dismay, and brush my teeth and hair.

He placed me back in bed and cuddled up to me. Next thing was darkness and empty dreams.

****

Asher Mortimer:

After I got the call from Ray about my Angel I dropped all that I was doing and rushed straight to her. She was in bed looking very pale and tired.
When Ray came back with the food I was glad because nothing like a good meal could help when you feel like crap. But that didn't go as planned either. She rushed to the bathroom and next thing you hear was the sound of someone spilling their guts.

I ordered Ray to check on Rose and keep me updated on her situation as of the rest of our crew that got sick. Most recovered fast and were back to work but I still had to finish some paperwork and other things like my mom coming over for Rose's birthday the day after tomorrow.

Once Everleigh fell asleep and I was sure she was fine enough I left to finish what I was doing before all this happened.

As I took a break to have something to drink and eat and I'll go check on my angel on the way down the stairs.
I walked to the door and into our room to see her spread out on the bed fast asleep. I couldn't help the little chuckle that escaped my lips. She shifted in her sleep so I immediately stopped and came close to her and kissed her forehead and whispered ' I love you' and left her to sleep a little longer. She needs it.

I was in the kitchen and Rose wanted something to eat. So I started cooking something and she was blotted in my arms with her blanket/ teddy type thing that she never leaves out of her sight.
I turned around to the sound of a phone click indicating someone took a picture. And there she was standing behind the kitchen island, in one of my hoodies, messy hair and a bare face. She looked to natural, so pure and that's how I like her.

"Sleeping beauty has awoken," I smirked at her as she came closer to us.

"Mummy!" Rose squealed and opened her arms to her mom.

"Hello my baby girl. You feeling better?" she asked her brushing stray hairs out of her face. Rose was quick to nod and cuddle closer to her mother.

"Look at the picture me took." she took her phone out of her pocket and showed me what she took when she came into the kitchen.

I smiled at the sight and kissed both of my girl's heads and went back to what I was cooking. I managed to get Everleigh to eat a little, more like a lot. Her appetite grew since this morning.

A little later she felt weird again and so we decided to cuddle on the sofa and watch reruns of friends because that's her favourite series, while Rose was playing on the carpet in front of us.

Suddenly the doorbell rang and next thing you know a very familiar voice to me yells.

"Where is my grand baby?" I shot up alerted by that voice and I gave a look to Everleigh and stood up walking towards the front door.

"Mom?" I asked shocked.

****

Everleigh:

"Mom?!"

Hold on a minute. Mum?! His mum is here! She wasn't supposed to arrive until tomorrow! I look like utter shit!
I picked up Ash's phone to look at my reflection of his phone and fixed my hair a bit and to look if I looked ok for the first meeting with the most important woman in his life.
Rose sat there completely oblivious to my panicking and the fact that someone was at the door. She was talking to herself

in her imaginary play world.

I stood up and started walking up to Ash and his mother that were now moved to the living room. Ash looked happy, surprised and confused at the same time but happy nonetheless. I shut the TV off and came up to them. She caught my eyes and smiled a big smile and embarrassed me in a bone-crushing hug.

"I waited forever to meet the woman that changed my boy for the best. I'm glad it's someone like you and not one of his whores."

I breathed out a 'pleasure' before she pulled away to hit her son on the arm.

"You didn't tell me she was this beautiful!" I suppressed a laugh. I think I'll like her very much.

"Ohh, honey! I'm Clair! I'm sorry I didn't introduce myself before. But my son here was bombarding me with questions." they playfully glared at each other and that's when I saw the similarities between both of them.

She was a petite woman, white hairs that framed her but not the type that makes her look old but the type that fits well. She had sparkling grey eyes and a matching bright smile.

"Now where is that grand baby of mine?" she clapped her hands and that got my daughter's attention she looked up from her toys and asked

"Who that mama?" tilting her head to the side.

Clair gasped and the sight of Rose who she just realised was in the room. She walked up to me and I picked her up so that she was face to face with Clair.
Clair had tears in her eyes looking at my princess, her hand in front of her mouth not believing what she had in front of her.

"Hello, there little one. I'm your grandmother. Clair." she smiled at Rose.

Rose looked at me and then to her daddy not quite getting all that was going on.

"Nan?" she asked her little British accent coming out that she picked up from Dan and his mother. I melt every time when she talks it's just so cute.

"Yes, your nan princess. My mommy."

 Asher spoke up. And that's when the realisation hit her. She smiled widely and put her arms out so that her grandmother could take her in her arms.
That moment was just beautiful. Clair's tears finally fell as she held her only grandchild in her arms and I just started crying too. *Jesus! What is going on me with! So many emotions.*

Asher took me in his arms while I was drying my tears and smiling at all this little family together. MY family.

And I won't let anyone or anything compromise this happiness.

CHAPTER NINETEEN

Everleigh:

Today is the day. It's my baby girl's third birthday and it's her first birthday with her dad. Her real dad. I received the test results yesterday and I still haven't told Asher. I want to surprise him later on today.

I'm feeling a little better than I have been the last couple of days. I'm still throwing up every now and then but I can keep it under control. Clair has been a real gem to me and Rose and I'm glad that Annie is here too to help me out with everything.

I'm not over keen on the other girls in the gang because they all look at me like I killed their father or something.

I woke up quite early this morning to get everything set up for her party later on this afternoon.

Ash and I both walked up to her room and kneeled down by her bed. She looks really cute when she sleeps.

"Morning birthday girl." I whispered in her ear while stroking her cheek. She shifted in her sleep, slowly opening her eyes to look at us.

"Time to wake up my princess." Asher continued and that seemed to do the trick. She put her arms out for her father to carry her and we set off to the kitchen.

The men that were already up and ready all greeted her and

wished her a happy birthday.

I started cooking breakfast that consisted of heart shaped pancakes for my girl and a full English breakfast for my man and myself.

I placed the dishes in front of them but I didn't let them start before I took a picture of my little girl the morning of her third birthday.

A placed a jug of orange juice on the table and looked up to see Asher with the DNA test results in his hand. I had placed it on his plate for it to be a surprise.

He looked at my eyes full of hope.

"Does this mean what I think it means?" his voice full of excitement.

"Yep." I nodded popping the 'p'. He stood up faster than lightning and ran to me picking me up in his arms and twirling me around.

Once my feet hit the ground once more he kissed me long and hard and went to give a kiss on Ro's cheek.

"This is the best news I've probably ever had." he pulled me back into his arms for one last kiss before we continued to eat our breakfast.

I went upstairs to get dressed for the party but I was hit with a new wave of nausea that led me to spill out all that I had eaten a couple minutes before.

This is really getting out of hand. I'll have to do something about this week but for now, I need to suck it up at least until tomorrow.

After I cleaned myself up I walked out of the bathroom to see a worried looking Asher sat on the bed. He patted the seat next to him indicating for me to sit there. Once I did he pulled me onto his lap placing one hand on my thigh and the other playing with the ends of my hair.

"Still not feeling great?" he questioned.

"No, not really. It's on and off all day. I don't know why. Sometimes I can keep it down other times I can't." I answered truthfully seeing no point in lying.

He sighed and held me closer. I love being in his arms. I feel at home whenever I'm surrounded by his warmth.

"If you don't feel well enough you don't have to go through today. Stay in bed and relax." his hand was now massaging my scalp and man did it feel good.

"No. I want to do this. She's my baby and it's her birthday. Sick or not I'll make sure she has the best day ever!"

He kissed the side of my head.

"Ok but if things get too much you tell me and you'll be off to bed. Am I clear?"

I turned my neck so that I can look into his eyes.

"Yes Daddy." I mocked giving him a sexy smirk before I stood up and walked into the closet to get dressed.

I came back out wearing a black and white dress that stopped just above my knees but the transparent fabric continued past that. It had spaghetti straps and black/grey leaf pattern on this dress. I paired it with black stilettos and pearl earrings.

I pulled my hair into a high ponytail and did a light natural makeup. Then I headed to Rose's room and helped her get dressed.

I had got her a special outfit for today that consisted of a tulle skirt, a denim button up shirt and a flower necklace, pink ballerina type shoes with a flower on each shoe and exceptionally I curled her hair a put a little lip gloss on her lips as a little birthday treat.
Once we were both done we headed downstairs to meet the first guests that arrived. I kept things simple. Just close family and friends. That basically meant the gang and the Russian mafia.

Clair was busy in the kitchen preparing all the little snacks to eat. I let Rose run to her daddy while I helped Clair out.

"You didn't have to do this Clair. I can do it. Go enjoy your son and grandchild." I smiled at her. She smiled back and responded:

"It's the least I can do."

Once we were done a felt a pair of strong arms around my waist and I kiss being placed in my neck as I placed the last of the food on the table.

"You look absolutely stunning my love." he said in my ear sending chills down my spine.

"Thank you, baby." I turned to kiss him on the lips.

"I've got a surprise for you later." and before I could ask anything about it he left me there, full of questions.

The afternoon passed with no problems whatsoever, and now it was the time for presents. We were now only close family and friends, the rest of Ash's men went back to guarding.

Clair got her a set of new princess pyjamas, Ray and Paul did a joint gift of a set of ponies for her to play with. Ponies where the new craze for her. Sergei got her tickets to see the Russian ballet that was coming around Christmas time. Asher got them matching t-shirts on his was written 'daddy' and on hers was written in pink 'daddy's girl'. Each with the number one on.

"Should I be jealous?" I asked feeling amused as I was sat on Asher's knees since the rest of the space in the living room was taken.

"Ok, now it's my turn since I've auto proclaimed myself her godfather." Carter piped up and came in front of Ro and placed in her hands a long red velvet box. He helped her open it and I gasped when I saw what it was.

Inside was the sweetest thing ever. It was a simple gold chain necklace with a gold heart and her birthstone, a green emerald.

"Oh my gosh, Carter it's beautiful. You shouldn't have." I was at the brim of tears as he was placing the delicate jewels around her neck.

I turned to Asher who had a proud look on his face. He stood up and walked to his friend and gave him one of them bro hugs. I was soon to follow.

"Guys, wait till you see what I got her for her eighteenth birthday." I wiped the tears that escaped and laughed at Carter's statement.

"Alright, I still have one more surprise. And it's outside." Asher said bringing the attention back to him.

"If it's a pony, oh so help me God, Asher you will not live to see another day." I matter of factly said. All laughed.

"It's something better and that lasts longer." he winked at me and took my hand as everyone went outside as asked.

Once I was out the once disheveled garden was filled with blooming Rose bushes and other flowers. A path was now drawn in the ground, lit candles all around. And at the end of the path was a very nervous looking Asher.
I didn't even realise that he had walked up till the end. I looked confused at Sergei that gave me a reassuring smile and gave me a slight push toward my Ash.

He took my hands in his once I was in front of him.

"Everleigh Jane Graham. You are the light in the darkness that I needed to get me out of the hell I was in. You gave me the best gift of all, our precious daughter Rose."

"Umm, Asher what are you doing?" I asked confused as to what was going on.

"I'll get there, just listen for the moment." he looked dead serious so I nodded my head and let him continue.

"I know we just got back together not long ago but I feel like we were never apart. That smile, those eyes, those lips, your body, your laugh, heck even the way you talk drives me insane. And I don't want to be far from you any longer than I have too. You have proved yourself to me and my gang. And I don't want to call you my girlfriend anymore." he stopped and my breath left me.

He took a deep breath exchanging a glance with Carter before starting again.

"I think my wife will suit you better." tears were clouding my vision as he went on one knee still with both my hands in his.

"What do you think Angel? Be mine, in sickness and health, through all the crazy that is our life. The dangers as the good days?" he kept my left hand in his as he took another red velvet box similar to the one Carter had but smaller.
He opened it and revealed the most breathtaking ring.

"Will you marry me?" he gave me puppy dog eyes. And that's when the fountain of tears broke out.

"Of course I will! YES!" he slipped the ring on my finger and took me in his arms sweeping me off my feet and twirling me around.

"SHE SAID YES!" he yelled as everyone cheered.

He put me back down and kissed me. As we pulled back he whispered in my ear.

"I love you to the moon and back." I kissed him back and answered.

"I love you the most." he smiled a real smile with dimples and all and wiped my tears away.

I felt a pair of little arms circle my legs and looked down to see my birthday girl. I picked her up and kissed her cheek.

"Mummy and daddy happy. I wove you." she kissed my cheek and her dad's and she just makes me melt every time. We both told her we loved her and walked to the group of people that watched this moment between us.

Annie and Clair were crying. Paul was close to tears but you could see that he was holding back. Sergei came and hugged me but not before giving a death threat to Asher. He kissed my cheek and told me he had to leave to handle some business.

Ray came up to me gave me a hug and whispered in my ear.

"Congrats little sis, I'm proud of you." I cried again, thinking about how I would have loved my brother to be here with me in this moment.

"Thanks, Ray."

And lastly was Carter. I playfully glared at him and crushed him in a hug.

"Congratulations Leigh. Love him till the end, be there for him even in the darkness and drama that can come. You changed him for the better, you and that princess."

"Thank you, Carter, I will."

Once I pulled away Annie came and hugged me while Asher was giving hugs and handshakes.

"Show me the ring girl!" she all but yelled in my ear. And so I obliged

"Oh my God! It's gorgeous!" she took my hand to inspect the ring closer.

A hand was placed on my shoulder making me jump a little but I calmed down when I saw that it was Clair.

"It was my grandmother's ring. It's been going down generations. Every Mortimer woman has worn that ring with pride and beauty. I'm glad that my son chose you to wear this family heirloom." I smiled once again.

The door rang, so I went to get it. Checking myself in the mirror so whoever it was didn't get scared half to death when seeing my face with my makeup smudged. But lucky for me, it wasn't too bad. I looked once again at my ring and couldn't help my smile at it feeling the love that surrounds me. Nothing can change my mood.
I opened the door and nearly fainted when I saw who greeted me.

"Hello, my dear."

"Mum? Dad?"

CHAPTER TWENTY

Everleigh:

I just stood there, frozen, trying to understand what the hell was going on.

"Well, aren't you going to let us in?" my mother's voice snapped me back to reality as I opened the door wider for them.

"What are you doing here?" was the first thing that crossed my mind.

"How did you know where I am?"

They both turned to me, my mother held a really creepy smile.

"Well my dear, it wasn't very hard to find you, just had to follow the trail of disappointment." ouch, that hurt. And I think it could be read on my face as my dad spoke up for the first time since he has been here.

"It was easy to find you. You placed an order in the gang's name for my guns and you chose only your favourite ones and you signed with an 'S' as in Shadow." I nodded slowly getting all the information in.

"That still doesn't answer the fact that you are here, after

what? Four years of not seeing or hearing of your mother, and two to three years for your dad? Why the hell are you here now?"
 the aggravation in my voice started to be heard and as if right on cue Asher came in as stood by my side, wrapping an arm around my waist.

"Well dear, we came here to see our grandchild of course."
I call bullshit!

"You must never tell a lie, mother. Isn't that what you have told me all these years? What is the real reason you are here?" I cocked an eyebrow most definitely calling out her bullshit, she has something up her sleeve and she has dragged my poor dad into it too.

"We just really wanted to see you, pumpkin and that little girl of yours. I... I mean we missed you very much. And since I saw that you were with the Black snakes now, I was just curious as to why you were with them."

I could see the longing in my dad's eyes. He meant every word he said.
To be honest I missed him too, very much. And I took it really hard when he stopped coming to see me. I think that's one of the reasons I started dating Dan, was because I needed that male love and interaction.
For a moment I had forgotten that Asher was there by my side until my mother had to clear her throat and bring him up.

"Aren't you going to introduce us?" she snarled looking at

157

Ash.

I was going to answer when he stepped forward and shook both my parent's hand.

"Asher Mortimer. Mam, Sir. I'm your daughter's fiancé and father of her child." he said full of pride and joy kissing my temple and coming back to the original position we here once in.

And the look on both their faces was priceless. The shock that was written on their faces just made my day even more. I smirked at that.

"Well, I wasn't expecting that." my father breathed out. I let out a laugh at that. And he returned a warm smile. But my mother, on the other hand, had a scowl on her face.

"Well, we had a long journey here. I guess we should head off now. We'll be back tomorrow to discuss more and to meet that child."

She had replaced her scowl with a fake smile as she walked to the front door and left without saying goodbye.
My dad, on the other hand, gave me a long hug, which I gladly returned, and a kiss on the top of my head before mumbling "I missed you so much pumpkin. More than anything" a tear escaped my eye as a responded back.

"I missed you too daddy, I love you." I held him tighter as more tears left my eyes.

"Me too baby girl me too." and with that, he left too but not before shaking Asher's hand and whispering something in his ear.

The door closed and I was immediately scooped up in my man's warm embrace. And I just lost it. A fountain of tears erupted. And this time it wasn't happy tears. They were tears of sadness, anger, loss, betrayal, longing. All the emotions that I had kept together about my parents just ran free. Ash was holding me close to his chest. Telling me sweet nothings in my ear, running one hand through my hair, the other rubbing my back soothingly. After about ten good minutes of crying I finally calmed down and my tears became hiccups and sniffles.

"Let's get you to bed angel. It's been a long day." he took my hand but I just wanted to be carried.

I pouted and put my hands up like Rose's does when she wants to be carried. He let out a chuckle before saying a "come here" and picking me up as if a weighed nothing.

He kissed the top of my head as we made our way upstairs to our bedroom.
He put me down and took his shirt off and changing into a pair of sweatpants that hung low on his hips.

"I'm going to check on Ro, my mom and placing new security around the house. I'll be back" and with a kiss, on my lips, he left.

I walked to the bathroom getting out of my dress, putting my hair in a messy bun and taking what was left of my makeup off, cleaned my face and I walked out of the bathroom only in my underwear.

I got a pair of pyjama shorts and one of Ash's hoodies and placed them on the bed. I passed by the full-length mirror and I stood in front of it.
I remembered all the nasty things my mother and Dan ever said about my body and tried to look at the good things about it. I still had some stretch marks on my boobs from when I had Rose, my mark from the mafia and my father's gang, something that I was proud of. I ran my hand over my belly and it felt different. I turned to my side and when I looked closely, a small bump could be noticed.

I ran my hand over it again, remembering that feeling I had when I had Rose. I thought to myself could I be pregnant again? Is this really happening right now?!
Then I thought about the symptoms I've been having, nausea, losing balance, feeling very tired and so on.
I couldn't think about it more because Asher came back in and gosh did he make me jump.

"Hey baby, why are you looking yourself in the mirror?" he questioned coming closer to me. I stepped back and quickly slipped on his hoodie and shorts. Before turning around giving him a kiss and hopping into bed.

"Nothing just looking at my body." I shrugged my shoulder curling up into the covers.

"Alright, babe. But next time tell me. I love to look at your body." he winked and spooned me from behind, pulling me into his warm body. It didn't take long for me to fall into a blissful sleep, even with all the questions running through my mind.

CHAPTER TWENTY-ONE

Everleigh:

Today I woke up feeling a lot better than I have the past mornings but I still feel nauseous so I booked myself an appointment at the doctors to run some tests and to put my mind at ease a little bit.
I walked down the stairs dressed in a pair of black shorts and a random shirt, a pair of trainers and my hair up in a ponytail, not really bothered with makeup this morning.

I head downstairs to the kitchen to grab something to eat. I knew that Clair was taking care of Rose and Asher was at a meeting with the rest of the boys so it was only us girls today.
I said good morning to everyone and after lunch, I went for my doctor's appointment. Taking one of Ash's cars out, I drove to the clinic. After waiting for a few minutes in the waiting room after signing up it was my turn to be called.
I was in the office, sitting patiently for the doctor to come back with my blood test results. I had an unsettled feeling in my stomach. Then she walked in results in hand.

"Congratulations Miss Graham. You are eight weeks pregnant." her warm smile reassured me a little.

But I knew that I was pregnant and now that I know for sure I don't know how to feel. Happy? Sad? Excited? Nervous? I don't know.

I guess I'm looking forward to another baby, I love being a mum to Rose and I would love to be a mum to many more kids. But we never talked about it with Ash. What if he doesn't want another baby? The irrational voice in my head started placing elements of doubt in my mind but I pushed it aside.

"Come back in a two to three weeks for the first scan. And congrats again on the baby and the engagement." I looked towards the doctor surprised.

"How do you know?" I raised an eyebrow at her.
She smiled and laughed a little before answering.

"The big rock on your finger gave it away." she shook her head pointing at my beautiful engagement ring on my left hand. I smiled at it and thanked her before leaving back to go home.

As I walked in I was greeted by a pair of little arms wrapped around my legs holding me very tight.

"Hello, mummy! I mwissed you berry much!" I pulled her into my arms and kissed her cheek.

"Hello, my little princess. Mummy missed you soooo much! How was it with Nanny Clair?" I asked wiping her stray blonde hair out of her face, walking ourselves to the living room where everyone was.

"Good afternoon everybody!" I was greeted by 'hi' and

'afternoon.' Soon enough, I was taken into a kiss by non-other than my fiancé that I love so much.

"Hello, beautiful. How was your appointment? Is everything alright." the slight worry was clear in his eyes. I smiled brightly thinking about the news I had received today and nodded.

"Everything couldn't be better." we kissed again but my statement couldn't be more wrong.

Later on that evening I was playing with Rose on the floor and I was trying to think of a cute way to tell Asher that he is going to be a Dad again. This time I won't drop the D bomb on him like I did with Ro.
The doorbell rang so I stood up and dusted myself off before opening the door.
Was standing there, my mother and behind her was my Dad.

"Why are you here?" I really don't like when they come unannounced like that.

"Why for dinner of course." my mother said smugly.

She walked in like she owned the place and didn't even bother greeting me, unlike my father, who like always, pulled me into a hug.
I followed them into the living room where Ro still was playing with her toys.

"Gosh, this house is a pigsty! Don't you ever clean it?" and here we go with the criticism! The only thing out of order was Ro's toys and she didn't have many of them. The major stack was in her room. She only had a little box that stayed downstairs.

"I do clean mother but I do have other obligations and the house is not a 'pigsty' as you so called it." I said I little more harshly than I had intended.

"It's alright pumpkin, the house looks fine." I dad piped in and thank god for that! I smiled at him gratefully as he walked over to play with Ro.

****
Asher Mortimer:

I was walking down to see what my girls are doing since I had just finished signing a couple contracts when the door rang.
My mom was out getting some shopping for tonight's dinner that she and Leigh would cook for tonight since I gave the night off to Louis, Paul, Ray and Carter because we have been working with no breaks for four days straight because of a new gang that have been breaking the accords.
I walked up to the living room but stopped before entering listening to what was being said.

"Gosh, this house is a pigsty! Don't you ever clean it?" I woman's voice that I didn't quite recognise said.

"I do clean mother but I do have other obligations and the house is not a 'pigsty' as you so called it."

So it's Everleigh's mother! How dare she say that this house is a mess! It's not Everleigh's job to clean the house 24/7 we are not in the 1950' and besides I pay people to clean this house.

But luckily her father added something to calm the growing tensions.

My mom soon walked in with the groceries and I went and helped her.

We all ended up in the kitchen as Everleigh was helping to tidy up she spotted some malteaser's that I told my mom to get her. The look on her face was so cute, she was smiling so bright and ran straight into my arms for a kiss and a hug. I knew they were her favourite and I win extra brownie points.

She thanked me and was about to start them when her mother's harsh voice interrupted again.

"Are you sure you want to eat that? I don't mean to be rude but you have put on some weight and I think you should cut off on sweet and chocolaty things."

The glimpse of happiness that I had brought her was snatched away by a person that is supposed to love her no matter what. The more she talks the more I hate that woman. Sure Leigh has a little more curves than when she first arrived but I don't mind, she's still as beautiful as the first time we met, maybe more so.

I saw her swallow hard and put the bag of chocolates away. I just stood there in shock and so was my mother. We haven't been in a situation like this. It was so tense. And I think Leigh felt it as she left claiming to go check on Ro.

I excused myself too knowing that she needed me right now. I saw her sat on the staircase with Rose in her arms letting small clear tears roll down her face. As we made eye contact she quickly wiped away the tears and gave me a smile as if all was fine, but I knew better.

"You don't have to give me a fake smile babe. I can read right through you." I sat beside her taking both my girls in my arms, kissing them both on the head.

"I know but it's a force of habit I guess. I hate being weak in front of people and my mum knows that she hit a nerve calling me fat in front of you." she let another tear leave her eyes but I kissed it away before it could go any further.

"Don't listen to her. She's just plain mean. I love you no matter what you look like. I've seen all of you and I loved every piece of it. Don't beat yourself up with what she thinks. We'll snuggle up in bed and eat them damn sweets if we want to."

She let out one of my favourite sounds: her laugh.

It wasn't very loud but it was there and that's what matters to me. The guys call me whipped and I guess I am. I really love her and she brings the old me back, not the cold me. The one I despise the most because I resemble someone I dislike even more.

"Thanks, Asher. I love you and I'm glad that you are by my side." she leaned closer to me and I held her tightly squeezing Ro in the middle too.

Dinner came along and things couldn't be more awkward. My mom was trying to make conversation between Leigh and her mom. Sean and I were talking about future shipments and Ro was in her own little world eating away. Everleigh was hardly eating but you could see that she was forcing herself and that she wasn't enjoying this evening as much as she would have been if her parents weren't have been here.

They weren't even supposed to stay for dinner but my mother found it rude if we didn't ask and they said yes. All was going sort of fine I guess you could say, right until Everleigh's mom started a very unnecessary conversation.

"So I guess the reason you are getting married Asher is that you felt bad for Everleigh being a single mum and a failure?"

She questioned talking another sip of her wine, making Leigh drop her fork with a 'clink', my mother and I choke on our food and for Sean to shoot her a very mean glare. I guess that isn't a very happy married couple.
Once I composed myself, I took my fiancée's hand and gave it a kiss before sending a glare in her mother's direction.

"I'm marrying this lovely, beautiful woman beside me because I love her. Not out of pity or guilt of any sort. The only failure in this story is me for letting her go when I did and letting the two best things that's ever happened to me slip through my fingers. And I will not stand for you to treat my future wife with so much disrespect in front of our daughter. I think it's time for you to leave."

 I stood up taking Rose out of her high chair since she was the first to finish eating and took Leigh's hand in mine and took them out of the dining room.
Her mother stomped out of the house and Sean gave us an apology, hugging his daughter goodbye.
Everleigh was in tears once the door closed and while I was putting Ro to bed my mother was taking care of Leigh. She needing a bit of motherly consolation and I knew that my mother already considered her, her daughter.

I carried my angel up to bed and changed her in one of my boxers and hoodies. I pulled her close to me running my hand through her hair until she fell asleep, in my arms where she belongs and if the safest.

CHAPTER TWENTY-TWO

Everleigh:

Ash's mother has been very supportive this last week she has spent with us. She loves Rose so much it warms my heart. She has been nothing but nice even if at first she might have had her doubts. I don't blame her, Asher is her son.
I walked into the kitchen looking for sour/ sweet things to eat. I know that cravings come later on in the pregnancy and I am only in the very early stages but that's all I want to eat.
I was walking back towards the living room with my snacks when I was greeted with such a sweet sight, I think I might get a cavity.

Ash and Rose were playing together, something that has happened before but for some reason, this time feels different. Maybe because he really is her father, maybe because of pregnancy hormones? I don't know but I just take in the moment watching the father of my children play with the eldest and her ponies.
I place my free hand on my stomach and smile down at myself. I didn't realise that I was being watched when a certain someone came and stood next to me.

"How far along are you?" her voice knocked me out of my daze.

"I'm sorry?" I turned a bit shocked towards Clair.

"How far along are you dear?" she asked again still in her sweet voice.

"B-but, how..?" I was gaping like a fish opening my mouth and closing it not knowing how to register all this. She giggled at my state and continued.

"You are currently eating pickles dipped into peanut butter. Sweet and sour treats were my favourite when I was carrying Ash."

She smiled and gave me a knowing look pointing at the jar of peanut butter full with chopped pickles and a spoon.

"That and you were smiling at your stomach. No woman does that apart if they had a glorious meal or if they are expecting. I would bet on the latter."

I couldn't help but look down and take a spoonful of this glorious mixture.

"Does he know dear?" she placed her hand on my arm bringing me a form of comfort in all this. I swallowed my spoonful before answering.

"No, he doesn't. I just found out yesterday and will all the drama with my parents going on, I didn't want to add anything extra on top of it all."

She took my hand in hers giving it a slight squeeze to which I smiled back at her.

"You are the first to know…" I smiled shyly at her and she gave me a huge grin before embracing me in her arms, rubbing my back bringing me a wave of comfort.

This is what mums are here for. Not just for teaching you lots of things but there to comfort you in times like these. I only wish my mother was like that with me but sadly that is never going to happen.

"Well isn't two of my favourite girls." Ash brought us out of our little moment. He was holding Rose in his arms, she was blotted against him, arms around his neck.

He came over and gave us each a kiss on the cheek.

"What are you girls conspiring about behind my back?"

I turned bright red and swallowed the spoonful of goodness I just took. I gave a panicked glance to Clair who softly smiled at me.

"Nothing dear, just some girl talk." she winked at me and just nodded towards Ash.

"Ok ladies, I have meetings to attend with your dad babe. I won't be back until morning." he gave me a pout as Clair dismissed herself. I walked closer to him and kissed him softly on the lips.

"It's alright baby. As long as you don't punch him and I don't end up spending the day with my mother, I'm sure I'll live."

I passed my hand through his hair cupping his cheek.

"I love you, you know that." he kissed my forehead.

"Yeah, I know. I love you." we kissed again then he passed me, Ro before he put on his jacket and left the house this Carter in tow.

"Well baby girl. It's just you, nanny and me tonight." I kissed her cheek and walked off to finish my jar of pickles and peanut butter.

CHAPTER TWENTY-THREE

Before the international gang meeting.

Asher Mortimer:

It feels like weeks since the last time I've slept. I just feel like things are falling out of hand.
My father just passed down the gang to me and just up and left, but not before creating havoc with everyone. My mom is constantly crying at night, she doesn't t talk about it. She just locked herself up in her room and comes out to cook for the guys and me.

"Boss, we need you at the docks." Carter my best man and best friend, as well as my right hand, came in my office. I've built a strong group of men that I trust. Paul, Louis, Carter and Ray.

We arrive at the docs to pick up a gun arrival from Australia. All was going smoothly till a rival gang decided to come crashing in.

"Fuck!" I groaned as we were all shooting back. Luckily it was a gun trade that we had so, it didn't take long to kill them all.
But my men know better than to kill their leader straight

away. He was kneeled down in front of me, his hands tied behind his back ready to beg for my mercy.

I have built my name in the mafia not only with the help of my father but with the fact that I will not grace anyone that has wronged me. With that, the word was out that I had no heart, and I don't. Nothing could possibly change that. All women are sluts and look for two things: Money and power. And that, they will never get out of me. I'm a hump and dump kind of guy.

"Mr. M-m-Mortimer. P-please. I have a family. I-I - I didn't m-mean to come after you. I swear." that low life of a man begged. I didn't even blink and the next thing you hear was the sound of my gun and a loud thump.

"Clean this up."

I walked off back to the house, I still had things to do like get rid of this man's family. My father always said, 'never leave a trace', and I know to live by that motto.
Soon enough I was on a plane off to Australia to the international gang and mafia meeting. It's a huge meeting with different gangs around the world to make alliances and numerous deals.

Three days later, after many hours of dealing and talking about plans and gang-related business, it was finally time for the best part: the after party.
It was held in the host's house that happens to be the gang

that I make gun trades with.

I wasn't in the mood to get laid this evening because since I've arrived all the girls that came to my site have been drooling like hungry bitches.

I was at the bar sipping a whiskey on the rocks when a fight between two people could be heard.

"Leave me the fuck alone dad! You know I can't stand the bitch and you let her boss you around like that? Seriously? I'm the next in line and you do fuck all about it!" a very feminine voice yelled.

"Don't you dare talk to me like that and don't call your mother that!"

I suppose that's girl's dad roared back.

"Oh yeah? What are you going to do about it? Hit me? Shoot me? Disown me? Oh wait, she has already done all three. If you didn't want me to take over you could have just told me and let your 'oh so beloved son' take my place!" her voice is so soft to be that mad.

"You know what forget it. I'll be in Russia with Sergei in a week and I won't see your face again." I turned around to see her come my way.

"Three shots of the expensive vodka please." she sat next to me and I couldn't help but admire her beauty. She had long blond hair, beautiful green eyes that had a fire in them that I liked. She seemed quite young but then after I'm not good with ages.

"Sorry miss but I can't." the bartender was almost shitting himself.

"What do you mean you can't? You can and you will! You are employed by my family thus making you obey what I want." she seemed to have lost it. She was rude to him, another stuck up spoilt bitch. Shame, she was pretty.

I continued to sip my drink not paying attention to her anymore and in my side vision, I could see her, gun in hand.

"Give the bottle Carl or so help me god it will be the last thing you do. And my 'daddy' won't be there to save your arse."

Ok, I must admit she looked super-hot. Until now I didn't notice that she was in a form fitted, tight in all the right places, white dress. It made her look so innocent, yet she clearly wasn't.

That Carl dude gave her the bottle and a shot glass before retreating somewhere else in the bar.

"Daddy issues?" I questioned.

"More than just daddy issues. But nothing a little vodka can't fix." she poured herself a shot and raised her glass.

"Cheers!"

And she downed the shot without even flinching.

That one shot was soon followed by much more and I joined her. Soon enough we were both every out of it and I had brought her to my hotel room. I still didn't know her name, nor did she know mine.

One thing led to another and well, let's say we got to know each other very, very well. She was so perfect. Before and after the amazing night we talked, like actually talked, no flirting, not just sex but like I told her about my tattoos and she seemed generally interested.

The next morning I woke up with a killer headache, very few memories of the night before. All that I was left with was the smell of sex in the air, a white thong on the lamp shade on the nightstand and her features in my mind.

That blonde green eyed girl has warmed something in me and I don't think that anyone can relight that flame other than her.

CHAPTER TWENTY-FOUR

Everleigh:

I've been having morning sickness more frequently and I have been trying to hide it from Ash because I don't want him to find out right now. With Clair, we have been planning a little surprise present to tell him the news. She has been very supportive all this time and I am truly grateful for her in my life.

But sadly all good things come to an end. Clair has to leave in a couple of days and I need to release the big news of my pregnancy before she leaves, so, I have organised a dinner with my parents and have the boys and Asher's mum.

I was getting things ready, Rose was in her room playing and Ash was setting the table since they would all arrive soon. Clair was out with Annie grabbing last minute things I needed for the roast dinner and the rest of the boys were taking care of gang stuff for Ash. I was in a simple pair of jeans, the only ones that still fit me might I add, and a nice blouse type top with a long cardigan. I was pottering about in the kitchen when the doorbell rang.

"I'll get it!" I yelled into the house and walked to get the door. Of course, my parents had to be here earlier than necessary to come piss me off. More so my mother than my father.

I walked them to the kitchen and continued what I was doing, chopping the carrots.

"You could have done an effort on the way you dress in the house. You never know when guests will suddenly appear. And since you have decided to marry a man like your father you might need to up your game." and there it was, that Remarque that she just had to do. I did think it was too silent to be true. I guess I was right.

As if on cue Asher came in and took the knife out of my hands and placed it on the side of the chopping board. I didn't even realise that I had cut the carrot to buggery and all that was left of it was confetti, literally. I took in a breath before turning around to get a new vegetable that I can cut up.

"What are you cooking, pumpkin?" my dad's voice rang out in the silence and I was glad for that. I smiled.

"Your favourite, roast beef with Yorkies, tones of gravy, veggies and roast potatoes" we exchanged smiles and I could see Asher in the corner of my eyes giving away a very small smile too. My mum, on the other hand, did not seem to get that this was supposed to be a happy family moment.

Noooo she just had to ruin it.

"You never could do it as good as mine. And that is a fact. Your meat was too cooked, potatoes soggy…" she went on saying what was bad about my cooking and I mumbled under my breath.

"Nothing is ever up to standards for you anyway."

"I'm sorry. What was that? I hate it when you mumble. Speak clearly." her voice was strict.

"I said, nothing is ever up to standards with you. All I do for you is bad. I try so hard to be the perfect daughter you've always wanted me to be but I never seem to come even close."

I hadn't realised that I was in tears before Asher came to me to wipe them off. I pushed out of his arms as I didn't want to be comforted at this moment.

"You never looked proud of me. You barely ever looked at me after Ben died! You have always blamed me and I have been living with the guilt for nearly five years! Five fucking years! But you hated me way before that. His death only added oil to the fire."

She was going to talk again but I was on a roll here and I wasn't about to stop now. I needed to get this off my chest.

"But you didn't give a fuck about that. You never did. All you wanted was for your precious son to take over daddy's place even if I had the rightful place. When I got pregnant that was like a godsend to you. Wasn't it? It was the perfect excuse to get rid of that horrible daughter you had. But the funny thing is, I actually thought that it would change you, becoming a grandmother. It sure as hell changed me becoming a mum. I needed your help and support and I got neither."

 I was full blown out crying and Ash just kept rubbing my back and letting me talk. He knew somehow that I needed this and he was there for me.

"And look where I am now. I am engaged to a man I love more than anything, I have a beautiful baby girl and a new family that is there for me and I am still next in line for Sergei's mafia and there is nothing you can do about it. You thought I couldn't survive without you well look at me now!"

 I felt proud of myself for all the shit I had gone through and this was only the tip of the iceberg, but of course, she had to butt in.

"You say all this darling but you are nothing. You are nothing without the man you so-called 'love'. You are nothing without your father and me. You are nothing without Sergei. And it's not a title or a piece of diamond on a band that will change the fact that you are, and will forever remain, nothing." Her words hit me like a bus.

 I still can't go over the fact that she is supposed to be my mother and that my dad has said nothing during all this. Her face remained stoic as for my father, well I couldn't see since his eyes were cast to the ground. That just built my anger more.

"And you 'dad'." I said with air quotes before continuing.

"You have been watching me take all these blows from your wife and you never said anything. Ever. You just sat there and listened to her like a lost puppy. And you still do. How ironic that the leader of the most feared gang in all the East and South Asia and Australia can't even stand up to his own wife." that's when I lost it.

My so-called mother's hand slapped me across the face.

"Don't you dare ever talk to us like that you ungrateful bitch." she spat at me.

"Leave now!" Asher's voice boomed over all the rest.

"No need babe. I'm going I can't stand being here any longer." I walked over the front door, took the first pair of keys and ran out of the house ignoring the cries from Asher and my dad for me to come back.

I clicked the keys and to my surprise, I had picked up Asher's keys to one of his lovely sports cars. I hopped in and put the key in the ignition and drove off never looking back.

CHAPTER TWENTY-FIVE

Everleigh:

I was driving without a care in the world. Driving over the speed limit on empty roads gives me this thrill of speed and freedom. And the plus was that I had Asher's sports car that could go from 0 to 100 in about five seconds. So, that was that.

After I calmed down a little and turned the music down in the car a drove down the roads of the suburbs where a lot of the housing is. I ended up in a mal famished area. I felt really stupid driving down with a very expensive car when these people struggle with everyday life. As I was driving with my windows down yelling caught my attention. I parked the car and stepped out walking to where the sound came from. It was probably a silly idea but I was up for shit decisions right now.

I came up with a sort of big house that seemed abandoned but I knew better. I was in a bad neighbourhood and this place looks like the secret hideout of a poor gang. I placed a hand on my stomach as I walked into the broken door.

In the hall was a young boy around 6 that was getting told off and by the looks of things looks like he had a hell of a beating as well. In front of him, his back to me was a man I guess a few years older than me, was the one yelling at his face telling him that what he was doing was wrong and that he was a disgrace. My heart went out to him. My mummy bear instincts kicked in and I sure as hell don't like to be brought down like that.

Funny enough there was a gun laying by the front door on a table.

Lucky me.

I checked to see if it was fully loaded and made sure the coast was clear before I made my move. The boy caught my eyes. His little brown eyes showed panic and relief at the same time. I mouthed to him that I was here to help and he slowly nodded.
But the man seemed to have caught on that they were no longer alone.

"Ohh look what we have here. What is a bitch like you doing here all on her own? Here to get fucked?" the man all but chuckled.

I smirked my assassin side coming out.

"No, I came for the boy. You see I don't like child abuse, nor any sort of abuse. For that matter. And lucky for you, I caught you in action." I cocked the gun feel very confident.

"Ohh girly put that down, you don't know how to use It." he mocked. He walked closer and I shot him in the foot.

And gosh did it feel good!

"Bitch! Allan!" he yelled for Allan again as I made a sign for the boy to come behind me. He quickly ran behind me as I placed a hand on his back to keep his close to me.
Another man ran down the stairs that were further down the back of the entrance.

"Fuck!" he muttered. It was one of Dan's old friends, well not quite a friend of his more like dude that he once had a deal with.

"Miss me?" I questioned.

"Shadow?" I smiled and nodded.

"Ohhh, Allan... What did I tell you about trafficking behind my back? About Human slavery?" I still had the gun pointed at his head as he stepped closer to me. His buddy fell unconscious.

Weak, he is out after just one bullet in his foot. I thought to myself.

He gulped.

"You said not to or next time I will be dead before I could say the word slave..." I fired a clean shot between his eyes. The little boy gripped my t-shirt. Shit! I forgot he was there. I slipped the gun into my waistband. You never know it can come in handy.

I turned and bent to the same level as the boy.

"Hey there. Don't be afraid. I'm getting you out of here. My name is Everleigh and I'm a mum to a little girl called Rose. You can play together later, yeah?" he nodded still in shock I think. I took his hand and pulled him out of that house before any other members came Back to cause any more trouble. I strapped him in the passenger seat and drove off as I looked into the rear mirror I saw a car driving behind us so now we start a wild goose chase.

I took sharp lefts and rights going down narrow streets and roads, all whilst making sure that the little boy was safe.

"What's your name love?" I asked glancing at Him then back at the mirror.

"D-Damon. I-I am five and a half. Nearly six." I caressed the top of his head and smiled tenderly at him. He didn't flinch he seemed to enjoy the touch. I guess he doesn't get this type of affection at home.

"Tell me, Damon, do you have a mummy or a daddy that I can take you back to?" I was still driving pretty fast.

"N-no, I don't have a mummy and you shot my daddy." I glanced at him and he had clear tears running down his little cheeks. I felt really bad.

Was his dad Allan? Or the other dude?

"Ohh baby I'm sorry but your daddy was not a nice man." he shrugged and whipped his tears.

"It's ok. I don't like my daddy. He was yelling at me and hitting me telling me I was nothing but a mistake. Mummy is an addict." my heart swelled at the news.

Poor kid.

My right hand was on the gear stick and I felt a little warm hand against mine. I looked to see that Damon had placed his hand on mine.

"You saved me. You are nice Beverly." awww he can't say my name properly.

"I'm glad I did buddy. You can stay with me. I promise you will be safe with me baby ok?" he nodded his little head. He is so brave.

Unfortunately, this cute moment was short lived as we came to a crossing. I had the right of passage and before I knew it we here hit in the back side of the car on Damon's side. I put my arm out to stop him going through the windshield and with my other hand, I tried to take back control of the car. The car ended its root on the side. My head was banging like if I had a whole marching band in my head.

"Damon, you alright?" I called out trying to get out of the car.

"My leg hurts." he groaned.

"Don't move I'm coming to get you out."

I limped to his side of the car and dragged him out as carefully as I could. I smelt burning when he was in my arms. I turned and saw that the gas of the car had leaked and that we had it an electric pole and both together had started a fire and if we didn't get far from this car now we would become crispy crunchy.

I ran as far as my body could take me with the boy in my arms as the explosion sounded at the back of us.

I came up with a tree to catch my breath. I sat Damon down and me after using the tree as a backrest.

"You ok buddy?" I asked worried looking at him. He had a couple extra scratches here and there but it was his leg that was in a bad state.

"My leg hurts."

"I know, baby boy, I know but we have to stay strong a little longer." I took him in my arms and held him close. I started to feel dizzy, my vision going blurry. I placed a hand on my stomach as if to see if my baby was alright. I had a feeling wash over me as if I knew that he or she was alright too.

"You ok?" he asked me but suddenly I found myself unable to answer him. I started seeing black spots.

"Mummy?!" a little voice sounded in my ears and then all black.

CHAPTER TWENTY-SIX

Everleigh:

Deep breaths and another. Keep going. You're doing fine love.

I've been repeating this over and over in my mind. I've been replaying the events of a month or so ago. I was mad, I was drunk and the both together never end up good.

BEEP BEEP BEEP BEEP

That would be the timer. I took the stick in my hand and opened the door of my bathroom to see my brother sat nervously on the bed.

"So what does it say?" I took a new breath and looked at the stick in my hands.

Positive.

I broke down in tears and soon found myself in the warmth of my brother.

"Hey, hey. Shush we will get through this, yeah? I'll be here every step of the way." he rubbed my back and held me tighter as I cried harder. I was going to be a mum and it just started sinking in that in About eight months I'll have a little baby in my arms.

The door creaked open and in came another familiar face. My best friend Victoria. Her sparkling blue eyes came into view and I felt safe once more. She sighed and gave me a hug.

"I guess it's positive then." she stated and I couldn't bring myself to speak so I nodded.

"I'm going to be an aunt!" she squealed. I couldn't help but smile at her childlessness.

"And me an uncle." my brother being hit just now that the news was indeed real.

"And me a mum." I cried again.

We did another group hug before we all sat down at the foot of the bed like the old days. I wiped my tears away placing a hand on my belly unconsciously rubbing it and smiling.

"How are you two doing? I hope my brother is treating you right!" I smiled knowingly at the both of them who were now a shade of crimson.

"He treats me like I'm the only girl in the world." she blushed harder and took his hand in hers. Ben smiled tenderly at Victoria.

"And she is the only girl in the world that I'll ever love more than myself." they were just too cute. But I needed to play my part now.

"Hey what about me?!" I pouted and crossed my arms.

"I love you too, snowdrop and that little niece of mine." I gave him a confused look.

"Niece?"

"Yeah, niece. I just have a hunch that it is a little girl that you are carrying." I knew tear escaped my eye and he was quick to sweep it away.

"Awww you two are so cute! I wish that when I have children they get as well along as the both of you." Victoria confessed.

****
Four months later.
****

I just came back from my doctor's appointment and I just found out what I was going to have. I was so excited to tell Ben that he was right.
I walked into the house and was about to yell that I was back. My parents were out on a business trip so they still didn't know I was pregnant nor that Ben was dating Victoria.

 You see my mother never approved of Ben dating a girl like Victoria. Victoria is a very sweet girl but she has a lot of authority and my mother can't stand that since we were little I was the leader of the group and Vic always bossed my brother around and that he was wrapped around her little finger. Even then he was madly in love with her and much to my mother's dismay he wasn't her little puppet to play around with anymore.

I came to the living room all smiles when I came face to face with both my parents. My eyes widened when I saw that in front of them was an ashamed looking Vic and Ben. He mouthed sorry to me.

"Well isn't the little whore home." my mother spat.

"Getting pregnant by a complete stranger. I knew you were a low life luckily your brother told me the truth about you. Get out." I flinched at her words. Tears fell from my eyes without my consent. My dad looked ashamed and Ben and Vic looked really guilty.

"I guess I learned the truth about my brother too." I left in tears feeling disappointed in him, her and myself.

"Hey, snowdrop. Wait up!"

"Leigh!" they both yelled at me. I was already up to my car about to open the door when they caught up with me.

"Let us explain. Please." my brother pleaded.

"What? Explain to me why you threw me under the bus like that?!" I snapped.

"Look Leigh. We are running away tonight and we want you to come with us. Your mother caught us prepping the Bags and she Asked us why we were doing up your bags and it just slipped. We couldn't let her know about us, not yet." I scoffed at her confession.

"Oh, so it was easier to rat me out that to get caught. Gee thanks! What A good best friend I have." I crossed my arms over my chest and resting them on my swollen Belly.

"Leigh we are truly sorry but our offer still stands. Come with us. We will help you out with the baby and start new."

Ben begged. He had inherited of granddad's looks, deep blue eyes, so dark like the depths of the ocean, dark chocolate almost black hair. He was his spitting image it was scary.

"I-I can't. Not after all this." I opened my car door and put the key in the ignition. I looked out the window to see Vic crying and Ben looking like a ghost.

"We leave at eight tonight. Come if you change your mind." with that, I drove off.

I sat in a dinner thinking over my options. Go? Not go? I knew that I couldn't forgive them right away for what they did but at the same time, I know why they did it.

I stood up from my seat left money for my order and rushed to my car.

7:55 pm. Gosh, I hope I'm not too late.

I drove off in direction of the house but there was a long cue of cars and further on flashing lights and sirens coming in the background. How odd.

I put the car in park and walked to where all the commotion was. I gasped at the sight in front of me.
I white van and a light blue mustang were only scraps of metal on the road. I recognise my brother's car and ran to where the passengers were. Tears were streaming down my cheeks as I knelt down and saw that Vic had her eyes shut, blood running down the side of her head. Ben was fighting to keep his eyes open.

"Ben hey it's me. Stay with me. Please." I placed my forehead against his bloody one.

"Its ok snowdrop." he hand reached my cheek. I blinked a few more tears away seeing that sweet smile of his.

"You were right. It's a girl. You are going to be an uncle to a niece." I rushed out seeing his eyes close.

"I knew it. I already love her so much. I love you Everleigh don't ever forget it snowdrop."

He closed his eyes once more and took one last breath.

"Ben. Ben! Ben! Wake up! Wake up please! Victoria needs you! My baby girl needs you! I ... I need you." a pair of arms came and took me away from the car. From my best friend. From my brother.

"Mam, please stop struggling. It's over." but I couldn't believe it was. I was screaming and moving about in his Arms.

"I'm so sorry... You were right. I'm so sorry...." I whispered repeatedly.

It was over. All of it. And I felt so guilty. How will I tell Sergei that his little girl won't ever come back into his arms? How am I going to tell my Parents that their beloved son died in my arms and that I just stood there crying?

"Everleigh, Everleigh baby girl wake up. Angel come back to me."

CHAPTER TWENTY-SEVEN

A little trip back in time...

Asher Mortimer:

"Don't you dare ever talk to us like that you ungrateful bitch." Everleigh's mother spat at her face after she had just slapped my Angel. How dare she touch her in that way?

"Leave now!" my voice boomed over all the rest.

"No need babe. I'm going I can't stand being here any longer."

She walked over the front door, took the first pair of keys and ran out of the house ignoring the calls from her father and me.

"Everleigh!" I yelled and chased after her but I wasn't fast enough to catch up that she was already gone.

I stomped back into the house and grabbed her mother by the arm and dragged her out of my house.

"Hey get your hands off of me!" she complained just as the boys and my mom got out their cars looking at me like I tattooed my forehead.

"Get the fuck out of my property now and don't you ever dare to come anywhere near my daughter or my wife or it will be the last thing you do. Am I clear?" I seethed.

"Crystal." she whimpered.

Ha! Not so tough now are you bitch? I mused to myself.

"Get the fuck out of here." I shoved her away from me as her husband came out from behind me and said the following:

"Don't stop me from seeing my granddaughter and my daughter. I realise the mistakes I made and I am truly sorry... Tell me when she comes home. Please? From one father to another I need to know that she comes back home safe." with that, he left yelling profanities at his wife.

"Yo dude what was that all about?" Carter came up to me with a puzzled look. I ran a hand over my face and sighed.

"Leigh's mom went full bitch mode and she couldn't stand it anymore I guess, so they went at each other's throats and things were said, a slap flew and Leigh ran out in tears. And left to god knows where with no phone." I summed up in a few words what had just happened.

"Wow, dude, rough. Where is the little boss?"

"Shit." I muttered.

The

"She's upstairs in her room. I forgot she was there. I hope she didn't hear all the shouting."

Speaking of the devil there she was all dressed in pink with her teddy bear in hand and tears in her eyes. Gosh, I hate seeing any of my girls sad like that.

"Princess, what's the matter?" I cooed and scooped her into my arms. She was fast to snuggle up with me and hide her face in my neck.

"Mummy mad and daddy yelled and I got scared. I don't want mummy and daddy fighting." she sobbed. I looked towards the guys and they all gave me a sad look.

"Baby girl, mommy and daddy were not shouting at each other. We love each other. Mommy was upset with her Mommy and daddy so they had a fight and daddy stopped it. Do you understand Rose?" she nodded in my neck and held me tighter, sniffling away.

We all sat down in the living room and it had been a few hours now that Everleigh has been out and I'm starting to get a bit agitated.

"Dude she will come back. Chill she just needs a bit of time to cool off." Paul reassured me placing a hand on my shoulder. But I just couldn't rub off the feeling that something bad happened.

"I don't know man, something feels off."

I admitted and I looked over to my precious little girl. She looks so much like her mom it amazes me. She had fallen asleep in Annie's arms and Annie was curled up to Ray on the sofa opposite me. I need to ask them if there is something going on between them or not. I'll ask Everleigh she would know.

I'm back at thinking about her. I can't stop and I won't stop till I have her back in my arms safe and sound. I'm so jumpy about it. She makes me feel so many different things that I haven't felt in what feels like forever and I just don't know what to do. I sound so much like a girl right now, what is up with me?

You are in love.

We waited a while longer and Annie had put Rose to bed, mom had made a few snacks, Carter and Paul were trying to calm my nerves by talking business with me, Ray was all flirty with Annie and I didn't even realise that Louis wasn't there till he came rushing into the room out of breath like he had just run a marathon.

"Boss. It's Everleigh." he paused and I looked at him waiting for him to continue.

"There has been an accident. She's in the hospital."

Those few words sent my world crumbling like it has never before.

CHAPTER TWENTY-EIGHT

Asher Mortimer:

I grabbed the keys to one of the vans and ran out but not before giving direct orders to everyone. I told my mom to stay with Rose until she wakes up and then brings her to the hospital later. Carter and Ray insisted to come over with me, Paul was in charge of getting as much information to what had happened with Louis and send some men over to the hospital just in case it wasn't just a random accident.

"It's going to be alright dude. I'm sure she is fine." Carter tried to calm me down because let's just say I was doing 80 on a road at 50.

I parked the car after a twenty-minute drive and ran into the lobby and straight to the front desk.

"Everleigh Graham. What room?" I went right to the point. The receptionist looked absolutely terrified once she saw who I was. I love seeing the fear in their eyes as they recognised me.

"R-r-room t-wo three zero. East wing." she stuttered out pointing in the right direction. I didn't even say thank you that I was already off to where my angel was.

I came up to the room to see what I assume was her Doctor come out the room.

"How is she? Is she alright? I swear to god if something happ–" I didn't have time to finish that the doc was already answering my questions.

"I suppose you are the husband. I'm Doctor Salvatore. She and the baby are just fine. A couple bruised ribs and a few scratches and cuts here and there but nothing alarming. She is just knocked out by the stress of the accident and the shock."

She smiled knowingly at me and that's when it hit me.

"The baby?" I all but whispered not quite believing what I was hearing.

"Yes, the baby. Your wife is pregnant, I thought you knew. Congratulations you are going to be a dad." she placed a hand on my shoulder. Everything around me was a blur.

 Everleigh was having a baby, my baby. My EVERLEIGH!

She didn't tell me and now she was in a car accident and I could have lost the both of them and I wouldn't have even known that I was having a baby?!

"Sir are you alright? Would you like to sit down?" the doctor ushered me to a seat in the sort of waiting room that was outside of the room Leigh was in, just a turn to the left past the corridor of rooms.

"Hey man. I heard what the doc said. A baby? Wow." Carter sat down next to me patting my back. I hunched over, placing my elbows on my knees and my face in my hands.

"What am I going to do man? One kid is tough enough. Protecting both girls is hard. What if I can't live up to the standards of being a good dad? What if I become just like him? What if something else bad happens? What if–"

So many questions were running through my mind and just sitting there not being able to see her was driving me mad.

"Dude chill! Everything will be alright. I'm sure Everleigh has been freaking out about it as much as you and she is the one carrying the child. Don't you think she didn't tell you because she was scared that you would react like that? Don't you think that she had a lot of things to deal with in one go, the proposal, her parents, the fights and on top of that her pregnancy and the fear that you might leave her? Don't you think she hadn't thought of all that before?" he was right. He is always right that man! I don't know how he does it.

"I know man but–"

"But what? Ash, she needs you right now and here you are shitting yourself because you are letting your mind drift to stupid things. This baby on the way is a true blessing and you should consider that. This is your chance to do what you missed with Rose. You are here now and you will still be there, you are nothing like your father and if ever, you pull a stunt like that to her, trust me Ray and I will make sure you regret doing that to our little sister. Am I clear?" he sternly said pointing a finger at me.

I have never seen Carter to authoritative towards me in all the years I've known him.

"Clear as day my friend. Thanks for that." I honestly said I stood up and he copied, we bro-hugged as Ray walked into the waiting area.

"The doc said that you can see her now."

"Go see your girl and make sure you make her feel loved and cherished. We will take care of the rest."

I nodded to Carter and ran off back to her room. As I walked in the sight in front of me had my heart stop. She was hooked up to an IV tube, a heart monitor telling me that she was still alive. The room was so cold, I rushed over to her and took her fragile hand in my rough ones. Her beautiful face was bearing a couple cuts just like the doctor had informed me. I brushed a few of her blond strands off her face.

"Everleigh, Everleigh baby wake up. Angel come back to me."

I pleaded, a single tear left my eye. I haven't ever felt like this in my whole life. Never have I felt a fear this strong to lose something so dear to you, and it scared me, she scared me, what she made me feel scared me.

"Baby girl please, wake up. I need you, we all do. Let me see those beautiful eyes of yours." I stared at her and waited another minute and nothing happened. As I was about to stand up again my hand left hers and she spoke.

"No, stay." she had gripped my hand.

"Please stay." she begged once again. I ran to her side and kissed the living daylights out of her.

"Calm down cowboy! I just woke up." she giggles as she lightly pushed me away.

Gosh, do I love to hear her laugh!

"I was so worried when Louis told me that you were in an accident." her face held shock like she had just remembered something.

"The... The... I need to tell you something." she took my hands in hers and looked straight into my eyes.

"I should have told you this before that I was pregnant but I was so scared of how you would react to the news. So many things were happening at the same time and I panicked. I'm so sorry." tears left her beautiful forest green eyes.

"It's ok. I know you were scared. To be honest I am too but I'll be here through everything." I wiped her tears away.

"There is something else–" she didn't have time to answer when the doctor waltzed in.

"Hello miss Everleigh. How are you doing?" she walked around the room and checked all the machines she was hooked up to see if all was fine.

"Nothing seems to be alarming. The baby doesn't seem to be showing any signs of distress so that's all clear. Since now you are awake we can talk about when you and your son will be discharged." she smiled sweetly at us.

"What? Wait a minute. Son?"

CHAPTER TWENTY-NINE

Everleigh:

"What? Wait a minute. Son"" Asher's voice raised.

Ahh shit!

"That's the other thing I wanted to talk to you about." I whispered.

His hand left mine and his face was full of anger.

"What? Did you get knocked up again and now you have a son? Who's the father because I sure as hell ain't!" he yelled I saw the doctor slip out of the room.

"Let me explain, he's my son because–"

"Oh, so he is your son? How old is he? Who did you fuck before or after me? Gosh, Everleigh!" he ran his hand through his hair in frustration. Tears pricked my eyes. I have never seen him this angry before and it scares me.

"Ash, let me explain it's not what you think." my voice was starting to get a little louder this time.

"What is there to explain Everleigh? How many other

bastard children are you hiding around the place? Is Rose even mine?" something in me snapped.

"How dare you insinuate that I just sleep about with other men and have children with them for any sort of benefit? How dare you call them bastards and how dare you say that Rose isn't your daughter! My son, as the Doctor said, is a boy that I found in a warehouse that belonged to an old dick face friend of Dan's. I heard yelling to I went to investigate. **My** son was being beaten black and blue and yelled at by a man that was supposed to be his father. I shot the both of them and took the boy with me. I was chased and before we got hit I asked him about his real parents and his mum was an addict that never cared for him and his dad forced him into the gang to do dirty work. Did you really think that I was just going to leave him live like that? He probably told the ambulance people that I was his mother so that he didn't have to be sent somewhere far from me. He is only a little boy."

I poured my heart out. *How dare he say all those things*! Tears were running freely from my eyes.

I saw the guilt in his eyes and I saw the regret drawn on his face. He was about to say something, I suppose it was an apology but I didn't let him speak. I was so mad at him for thinking those things and not even let me explain myself!

"Don't. Just get the doctor I need to talk to her." he sighed and walked out the door before opening it he let out.

"I'm so sorry Angel." and left the room. I cried once more

letting it all out.

****

Asher Mortimer:

Gosh, why am I so stupid?! Arrrggg! Why did I say all those things to her?

I left to go to the waiting room to see that everyone was here. Rose, my mom, Annie, Paul, Louis, Everleigh's dad, Carter and Ray obviously. Ray followed the doctor into the room as I sat down in one of the chairs the furthest away from everyone. I needed to think.
A few moments later Ray came out of her room and made a Beeline for me.

"You son of a bitch! Sorry, Clair." he came up to me and punched me square in the jaw.

"Why did you say that to her? Do you really think that low of my sister?" he was about to punch me again but was stopped by Carter.

"Dude calm down."

"I can't calm down when he said that my sister was a hoe sleeping with men and having and I quote 'bastard children'. What were you thinking? She is in there in bits because of what you told her! It's not good for the baby all this stress."

Man, what is it with them being right today!?

"I don't know alright?! I don't know why I said those things to her! I'm so stupid! I just didn't think clearly." I honestly said, there was no point in lying now.

"Then don't just stand there and go see her! You fucking moron!"

 Is this opposite day or something my men are giving me advice and giving me orders?
I ran back to her room and saw her sitting on the bed rubbing her stomach.

"Don't worry baby, mummy's here. I'm sure daddy didn't mean what he said. You will be a part of a very big loving family. Not like the one I had, you will have two older siblings, Damon and Rose. Well... Damon isn't your brother yet but soon. I love you baby and I can't wait to meet you." she continued to rub circular motions on her tummy.

"So Damon is his name." I questioned more like stated.
Her head shot up and our eyes met again.

"Yes, his name is Damon. But why do you care?" she scoffed and turned away crossing her arms.

"Baby, look at me." she didn't budge.

"Angel, look I'm sorry for what I said earlier. I'm just–" I let out a deep breath.

"I'm just terrified about all this. One child has been hard on me. Having you and that little princess in my life was a blessing but it was hard and I learnt to handle it. Carter talked to me about the new baby and I've realised how much I am looking forward to it but adding the boy to the mix... it was just too much for me to handle in one day. I'm so sorry baby. Please forgive me."

She turned to me tears in her eyes. I hate seeing her cry.

"And you think it hasn't been hard on me? You think I haven't thought about all this? I'm twenty-four for God sakes! I have a daughter, a baby on the way, a possible new son and I'm engaged! On top of that my parents are back in town and you think I'm taking this all as cool as a cucumber? No Asher no!" she burst into tears again.

I sat on the bed and took her in my arms rubbing her back.

"I'm so sorry. Please angel forgive me. I love you so much and I will love each and every one of those kids but please don't shut me out. I can't have you mad at me baby girl." she gave into the hug and looked at me through her lashes.

"Do you really mean it?" she sniffed.

"Yes, baby girl. I would need to time to adapt to everything but we'll pull through."

"I love you, Asher." she kissed my cheek.

"I love you too Angel."

We stayed on the bed cuddling for a while longer the time for Leigh to calm down. Ray is right, all this stress isn't good for the baby. I can't wait to officially start my real big family with this beautiful woman in my arms.

CHAPTER THIRTY

Everleigh:

After my cuddle time with Ash, the doctor came back in followed by Ray and Carter that came in with a very agitated Rose in their arms.

"I WANT MY MUMMY! I WANT MY MUMMY!" she yelled at the top of her lungs hitting Carter as hard as she could.

"Take her, please! She has been screaming since Asher came back into your room."

Ray begged me, I laughed at that and took Rose in my arms and she immediately calmed down and curled herself on me laying her head on my chest. Her cries became hiccups as I rubbed her back.

"Miss Everleigh sorry to interrupt but I came here to check things and to see if you would like to go see your son. He won't let anyone come near him till he knows that you are alright but since he won't let us put his leg in a cast so we can't move him to see you. Do you feel up to it?" Asher had a hand on Rose's back as I was blotted against him.

I looked at him and he nodded kissing the top of my head.

"Go, babe. Rose is asleep, hand her back to the boys and let's go meet our son." he took my hand and I melted at his words. I leaned back into him and gave my agreement to the doctor.

She led us to the room where Damon was. The door opened and I saw him in tears and staying as far away from the male nurse as he could.

"Get the hell away from my son. Don't you see that you are scaring him?"

 I placed my hands on my hips and tapped my foot. The nurse turned around and gulped before running out. I turned to look at Ash and saw that he had put his hand on his hip thus leading his jacket to be out of the way showing off his gun. I rolled my eyes and came up to sit on Damon's bed as Ash kept a little distance.

"Hey, baby."

I ran a hand through his hair and the other wiping away his tears. He came and gave me the biggest hug he could but in doing so he pushed my ribs and earned a hiss out of me. He pulled away with more tears in his eyes.

"I sorry i-i-i h-hurt you."

His lip quivered as tears left his eyes. My heart broke as I took him back in my arms rubbing his back and rocking him back and forth.

"Shhhh, shhhhh baby you didn't hurt me. I'm alright. Stop

crying now okay?" I pulled away and saw that he stopped crying and was wiping his tears away.

"Ash baby, can you pass me the tissue box behind you please." he took the box and came closer. Damon was a bit startled and try to hide in my side.

"Who's that?"

He asked me through his lashes. Ash knelt down in front of him and took one of my hands in his.

"I'm Asher. I'm your new Daddy if you will let me." he looked up at him and gave that hopeful look. Damon looked at me then at back at Asher.

"Ok, daddy. But I want to stay with mommy and protect her." I smiled at that and kissed the top of his head.

"Ok little lad. But before that, you need to get your leg fixed so that you will be strong to protect mommy, yeah?"

Damon nodded and gave a hug to Asher which we weren't expecting. My heart was pounding looking at both my boys' bonding. I don't think Asher understands how much of a good father he is and will continue to be.

After getting his leg in order I stood up but suddenly felt a little light headed. I tripped but Ash caught me before I fell.

"Wow, babe. Take it easy. Let's bring you back to the room." he called in the doctor to bring me a wheelchair and a pair of crutches for Damon.

Ash helped me back into my bed and kissed my belly and my head. Damon came in bed and made himself comfy before the both of us drifted off the sleep.

"Sleep well, my love." Asher kissed me one last time before leaving the room.

****

Asher Mortimer:

I stepped out of the room leaving my love and new son to sleep because they sure did need it.
I stepped back into the waiting room with a coffee in my hand the warmth of it keeping me awake.
My mom had left to rest, Paul had brought her back as I left him in charge because Carter and Ray were really determined to stay no matter how much I tried to get them to rest.

Sean stayed behind too because he felt that it was his fault that she was in that car accident in the first place, though I think so too, it's not fair on him to feel that way when his only child left is in the hospital.
I came and sat down next to him. Rose was soundly sleeping in his arms, I wasn't surprised after the temper tantrums that she has been pulling all day to see her mom. I ran my hand on top of her head through her blond curls that were so much like her mothers. She shifted in her sleep opening her eyes and smiling at me.

215

That smile will break some hearts one day...

It was like looking into a mirror when I looked into her eyes. The same blue that has been running in my family for generations.

"Mmmm daddy…"

She put her hands out for me to take her. I chuckled lightly as Sean handed her over to me. I placed her on my lap as her little legs straddled me and she placed her head on my chest, her ear on my beating heart. She snuggled into my chest holding her teddy bear tightly in her arms before falling asleep again.

"A father's touch is just as powerful as a mother's one." Sean snapped me out of my loving gaze set on my daughter.

"Everleigh was the same. She hated being in her mother's arms or in anybody's arms for that matter but I just had to be close enough to her that she would be yelling 'daddy, daddy' and was straight into my arms. Rose is doing the same with you."

I smiled tenderly at her once more rubbing circles on her back, she and Leigh both love it, it calms them down.

"I've decided to divorce with Everleigh's mother. I have now realised what Everleigh has been saying to me all these years. I've lost my son to this woman, my best friend stopped talking to me. I can't lose my princess, not again. She probably hates me."

He choked on a sob and put his face in his hands. I put a hand on his shoulder, patting lightly.

"She doesn't Sean. She can't, she's too much of a daddy's girl to hate you. She loves you that's why she cares so much. Stop beating yourself up."

He gave me a small nod.

"Take good care of them because when they are gone, they are gone and even if you climb a mountain and swim every ocean they won't ever come back."

Rose snuggled up closer to me and smiled in her sleep.

I'm so blessed to have her in my life. Never will I ever let anything happen to her, nor her mother, nor Damon and nor to that new baby on the way.

CHAPTER THIRTY-ONE

Everleigh:

Today was the day I could finally go home and I was really looking forward to it!
I had changed into a pair of joggers and one of Ash's hoodies.

"Ready to go, babe?" I nodded my head.

I stepped out of the room when two sets of little arms came around my legs for one and my hips for the other.

"Mummy! Mummy!"

I giggled at their cuteness as a new pair of strong arms came around my waist. His smell drives me mad and wrapped me up in comfort. His hands were softly placed on my growing tummy. He kissed my cheek and swept Rose off her feet taking one of my hands in his as I took Damon's.
Once we drove back home I showed Damon to his new room right next to Ro's. Asher had asked some of the guys to set it up for him straight away so that he felt at home.

It was a simple black, white and grey room with geometric shapes and superhero accents, it wasn't too babyish and he could grow into it.

"How do you find your room bud?" Asher asked with Damon on his hip.

"I love it! Put me down please I want to hug mummy too." he started wiggling out of Ash's arms and ran straight to me.

"Thank you, mummy." he whispered in my ear like it was a secret.

I smiled and left him in his room while Ash and I went to his office to clear some things out.

"Come sit here babe." Ash patted his knees for me to sit in his lap.

I smiled and sat on him getting comfy.
He kissed the top of my head and placed his arms around me taking my left hand in his and admiring the ring he had placed.

"I have a surprise for you, well more like a gift." he opened a desk drawer and pulled out a paper file.

"What is this Baby?" I asked opening the file.

"Adoption papers for Damon William Otool..."

I turned to Asher tears in my eyes.

"Are you for real?" I asked not quite sure if I was dreaming or not.

"For real babe." he nodded trying to hold back his smile.

"Are you really sure you are ready for a new kid?" I asked biting my lip. He pulled my lip out from my teeth and kissed me full with passion.

"I love you Angel and all three kids. I'm more than ready to take on this father role and I'm more than happy to have you by my side all the way." tears were flowing down my cheek, tears of happiness.

"I love you so much, Asher James Mortimer." I kissed him again and signed the papers.

I jumped off his lap and ran into Damon's room and hugged him so hard I think if Ash hadn't come in I would have broken him.

"Mummy? Why you hug me so tight?" his deep chocolate eyes bored in mine.

"We are your real mummy and daddy now buddy. You are Damon Mortimer now. We love you so much, baby." I cooed running my hand over his cheek.

Realisation hit him as he started crying and came into my arms his head going straight to my neck and his little arms around my neck.

"I love you, mummy."

"Hey what about me buddy?" Asher called out next to us.

Damon turned to him.

"I love you too daddy but I love mummy a little more."
Asher placed his hand on his chest in fake hurt.

"I'm going to get you." Asher did the monster face and put
his hands out to catch Damon but I picked him up and
started running away in all directions, Damon was
screaming and laughing at the same time.

So was I.

We turned a corner and I put him down so that we could run
different ways. I ran to Rose's room and told her to come
play with us too.

"Aghhh, MUMMY!! DADDY GOT ME!"
I heard Damon yell from outside the door.

Damon was laughing as Asher was holding him and tickling
him at the same time.

"Mummy!" I gave a pointed look to Ash trying to hold my
laughter back as much as I could.

"Put my son down!" I yelled out with a laugh at the end.

"Never! Only if I get a kiss." he pouted his lips.

I rolled my eyes and gave him what he wanted making sure
both kids didn't get squished in our respective arms.

"I love you all." he said aloud.

Two months later:

My baby bump was growing nicely and the kids had settled into a normal routine. Damon had gotten more and more confident around the gang members.

"Asher! We need to go!" I yelled taking the keys to his new replacement car for the one I crashed.

Once we arrived at the clinic we waited for a little till my name was called.

"Mrs. Mortimer." we both stood up hand in hand as we were led to the room.

The doctor placed the gel on my tummy as she waved the wand about. We heard the baby's heartbeat and I saw Asher's heart melt. He became so soft but his poker face came back on.

We headed back to the car with the baby pictures in our hands.

"Show me the picture again Angel." Asher begged. I showed him again.

"That's really our baby?" he questioned again. I laughed a little and nodded.

"Yes. That's our baby, Asher." I confirmed again.

"Wow. That's my baby, our baby. He or she is in there now. Like right now. And I'll be able to hold it soon yeah?" he was like a kid getting his presents in Christmas.

"Yes, Ash. Our baby will be here soon." he smiled so wide I think I would have gotten blinded.

CHAPTER THIRTY-TWO

Everleigh:

Asher has been stuck to me like glue same as Damon. Both my both my boys have been following me around like lost puppies.

Rose has been in her little world like usual. She loves to follow her father around. She is constantly in his office with him when she doesn't want to do something. She has been a little devil ever since she turned three.

"MUMMY!" here we go again.

"Yes, baby girl." I sighed.

"Where is daddy?" she was dressed in a pink tutu with a crown in her hair that wasn't quite straight and she took one of my hand bags and some of my less expensive jewelry to play with.

"I don't know princess. Let's go find him." I put my hand out for her to take as we walked to his office.

"Knock knock." I called out before opening the door but he wasn't there.

We walked down the stairs and to the kitchen. I know that at this time he gets a snack.

Nobody. Rose was up on the window seal looking out to the garden.

"Found him, mummy!" she squealed.

I came up behind her to have a look for myself and sure enough, both my boys were outside, no shirts on, play fighting.

Ash's toned chest clashed with Damon's little round baby belly. He is only five but he had a fire spirit in him. Just like his dad. It's funny how they are so much alike when they don't share the same DNA. The way they have this little concentrated face when they do things, the same smirk, those puppy dog eyes and so on.

I smile graced my lips as I saw that Asher was teaching him to fight. He has his hands up and letting Damo hit them with all his might.

"I want to see daddy." Rose pouted.

I helped her get down of the window as she ran outside into her daddy's arms. I walked up to them, a hand placed on my belly rubbing small circles.

"Mummy! Daddy was showing me how to protect you!" Damon beamed.

"I saw that buddy and I am sure you can beat daddy." I winked towards Ash who now had Rose in his arms.

"Alright, dinner is nearly ready so go get a shower and I want you back down in ten minutes tops. Ready set go!" Damon and Rose ran off. They have grown fond of each other. I find them so sweet together.

The other night Rose had a nightmare but I didn't hear her call out for us. When I went there once I heard her I found Damon and Rose cuddled up in each other's arms.

Damon had woken up and went to comfort her. Since then even if she loved her father more than the whole world, her brother is a close second in her heart now.

Once both kids were clean and in pyjamas I put dinner on the table and waited for all the guys to get their food. We were eating and Annie came in late looking under the weather.

"Are you ok Annie?" I asked concern clear in my voice. Her eyes were a little puffy but the makeup covered the redness.

Did she cry?

"Yeah. Fine." she took a plate and shoved a little food on it. Throughout dinner, the guys were talking gang stuff and the kids were eating and playing among themselves, but Annie was totally out of it.

Dinner was over and Asher was off the put the kids to bed since Clair had left the day before to go back to Miami.

I followed Annie to her room and closed the door once I came in.

"Ok spill. What is up with you?" I crossed my arms over my chest waiting for her answer but she just burst into tears.

"Ohh babes." I rushed over and hugged her tightly in my arms.

"Tell me what the matter is." I rubbed her back for a while till her sobs became hiccups.

"I-I'm pregnant Everleigh. And it's R-Ray's baby." her eyes filled with tears once more as she cried again.

I was a bit set back by the news but held her closer.

"It's going to be alright babes. Our babies will be around the same age!" I tried to lighten the mood and it worked a little.

"How long have you known?" I pulled away handing her a tissue box.

"Since you came out of the hospital. I was feeling dizzy and a nurse realised so she ran some tests and well…" I nodded my head.

"Does he know?" her eyes went to her feet as clear tears ran down her cheeks again.

"I-I told him today and–" she let out a loud sob as I gave her hand a squeeze.

"He didn't say anything. He just stood there and said 'I don't believe you' and I ran off before he could say anything else." she sniffed and wiped her eyes with a new tissue.

My blood was boiling. *How could he just say that?!*

"I'm going to chop his balls off!" I stood up but was held down by Annie.

"Please Leigh. I don't want to make matters worse." she pleaded.

"Annie... he needs to realise what he is missing. I'm sure he is just as scared as you are. I'll get Asher to talk to him about it. He'll set him straight."

"No Everleigh. He wants nothing to do with me or the baby and I'll have to deal with it I'm fine." she took a new breath in trying to keep the tears at bay but I knew that she wasn't fine.

"Annie. Let me help you. It's going to eat you up. Trust me I know what it feels like to not have your baby daddy by your side." I sighed seeing her inner battle to let me help. She finally nodded.

"Ok... tell him but if things go south I know how and who to kill." she winked at me.

She's back. I smiled at that I gave her another hug and told her to rest and relax in a nice warm bath.

CHAPTER THIRTY-THREE

Everleigh:

I walked into our room to see Asher in one of his t-shirts and joggers with his laptop on his knees working.

"Baby…" I purred coming up to him.

"Yes, Angel." he put the laptop next to him on the bed giving me his full attention.

"Can you go knock some sense into Ray for me before I go and chop his balls off?" I smiled sweetly at him.

"What did he do?"

"Annie is pregnant… he… he just had to react badly to the news then told her he didn't believe her." I didn't realise that I was crying again.

Argh, hormones!

"Hey, baby girl. I'll go talk to him. Don't cry, baby. Go take care of Annie. You two girls need rest." he kissed the top of my forehead before heading out.

****
Asher Mortimer:

I stood up and left the room. I will kill him. I thought to myself. I never admitted it but Annie was like a little sister to me. Not a lot of people know it but Carter and Annie are siblings. Shocking I know right. They look nothing alike and they don't like it to be known because Carter hates his mother for cheating on his father and leaving him only to come back with a baby Annie and left again leaving his Dad to take care of a baby that wasn't even his.

I came up to the game room to see Paul and Ray playing on the PlayStation 4.

"Paul can you leave us please I would like to talk to Ray alone." he nodded then left closing the door behind him.

"What the fuck is going on why you." I said aggravation clear in my voice.

"Dude, what do you mea–"

"Cut the crap, Ray. I know about the baby Annie is carrying, your baby. You gave me advice when I freaked out about having another kid well let me give you a little of mine." He bent over placing his elbows on his lap.

"She left before I could finish what I wanted to say. She is so stubborn mate. I think I love her and we had fun but a baby? I don't think I can stop having fun and settle down, not yet." I sighed and sat next to him.

"Listen, mate. I know having a kid is hard and fucking scary but you just told her that she was a liar. She was brave enough to tell you and you blew her off."

"I know... I know... I do want kids but now is too early." he whined.

"Dude you still have nine months to go before the baby is actually here you do realise. That leaves you plenty time to grow a pair and be ready to be a dad. And once you heard that baby's heartbeat on the monitor your life changes for the best that I can assure you."

I mind drifted to the first ultrasound of the baby that moment when I saw that baby on the screen with the beating heart in the background was one of the best moments of my life.

"I only wish I was there for when Everleigh was pregnant with Rose. I missed all these little moments and I regret not being there. And I don't want you to regret this decision later. I was lucky enough to find her again but Annie is a lot more stubborn than her it might not be that easy to get her back." he sighed and nodded his head agreeing with my words.

"Your right man. I can't lose her. Not like that." I smiled at him and gave him a pat on the back.

He ran out of the room to go to Annie and I followed him in. Everleigh was with her and they were talking baby stuff.

"Annie." he breathed out. And the look on her face was not the best. Leigh came up to me and gave me a side hug, I knew she wanted to stay, she loves a bit of drama.

"What do you want Ray? Get out before my brother comes and beats you up." a flash of fear came in his eyes but was covered by his determination.

"Let him. I know I have been a jerk and I realise now that I don't want to lose you or this little baby growing inside you." he went up to her.

"Please let me be there." he knelt down and kissed her stomach. I heard a sniff next to me to see that Everleigh was crying, again. Her and her hormones, thank god the doctor warned me about all her emotions going all over the place.

"Get the fuck away from my sister you dipshit!" of course, Carter had to show up at this moment.

"Keep your voices down MY kids are sleeping!" Everleigh snapped and all listened. I must admit she did scare me at times.

"Carter, I'm sorry. I realise I was stupid and I want to be here for her. I will always be there for her. I promise." I saw Carter huff and a few tears leave both the girls eyes.

"Welcome to the family. And if ever you hurt one of them be prepared to die a slow and horrible death." Carter warmed before taking both his sister and Ray for a big bear hug.

I held Leigh closer in my arms kissing the top of her head.

"Let's leave them and get you to bed angel ok?" I whispered in her ear. She nodded.

I took her hand and walked her back to her room. We stopped in front of Damon's room only to see him reading a story to a very sleepy Rose who was cuddled up to him with her teddy bear in one arm.

"There are no monsters here Ro. I'm here to protect you and mummy. I won't let anyone hurt you." he cuddled to her too and closed the book before turning the light off and dozing off.

"He is a great big brother." Leigh whispered as we came back to our room.

"That he is."

I'm truly blessed to have all these people in my life.

CHAPTER THIRTY-FOUR

Everleigh:

These past few weeks have been so calm, maybe a little too calm. The kids were still as fond of each other, Ray and Annie have been stuck together like glue, Carter has been watching everyone like a hawk because he is becoming an uncle not just once but twice, Asher has been working his arse off. Something is up but I like the calm for now.

I'm coming up to my fifth month and this baby has me crying or yelling every five freaking minutes. I've been having the weirdest cravings and since we are in the heat of summer I'm literally melting. If I could walk around naked I would.

I'm so hot I live in booty shorts and tank tops. I've fallen in love with cloudy lemonade and things full of sugar but Ash only lets me have fruits since they are naturally full of sugar.

"What's the plan for today?" Paul asked me since we were all around the kitchen table, but Asher, who has been locked up in his office with Carter for a few days now.

"I don't know. I might relax, my back is killing me and the heat isn't helping." I said sitting down with my bowl of grapes.

"Well Ray and I have an appointment at the doctors for this

little guy here so we'll be off soon and we might put in some baby shopping in too." Annie nodded toward Ray.

"Mmm ok. Well, Ash and Carter don't seem to be coming out anytime soon." I sighed. The kids came running in trying to get my attention.

"Mummy! Mummy!" they yelled in sync.

"Yes, my loves what do you want?"

"Can we go to the park please?" Damon batted his eyelashes.

Damn that boy will break hearts.

"My loves mummy is tired today. Maybe tomorrow. You can play in the garden I'll ask daddy if you can have some outdoor toys to play with." the look on their face broke my heart.

"But I want go park!" Rose yelled stomping her foot.

"Mummy said another day Rose." I stroked some of her curls out of her face. Damon just stood there thinking.

"What if daddy takes us?" he questioned. My heart broke a little more.

"Baby boy... daddy has a lot of work to do. He can't take you." his little smile turned into a frown. I hate that frown.

"I'll take them!" Louis piped up.

"Are you sure? Both kids, by yourself?" I asked unsurely. He had been a little off since I have been back from the hospital and that was months ago.

"Yeah. They are good kids and the park will be a good place for me to bond with these little ones. And you'll be able to get a good rest." he had a point.

"Do you want to go to the park with Louis?" the kids' eyes lit up again.

"Yeah! Thank you, mummy!" they hopped into my arms and gave me lots of hugs and kisses.

"Ok then get dressed and mummy will get a bag ready and after lunch, you can go to the park." I told the kids and they didn't need to be told twice.

"Thank you, Louis. It means a lot that you're doing this today." I stood up and took the dirty dishes and brought them to the sink.

"No problem Leigh." I gave him a side hug before heading up and getting the kids' bag ready.

"Be good for Louis kids ok?" I told the kids who nodded eagerly.

I kissed both of their heads and placed caps on their head

since the sun is banging outside and sun cream won't fully protect them.

"Alright so here is their bag with the bottle of sun cream, a change of clothes, two bottles of water and a few snacks and toys as well as some money if needed. Don't let them out of your site. If not enjoy your afternoon I want them back for four pm." he nodded and left with the two kids to the family car.

I sighed and closed the door. I trust Louis but this is the first time I left them to go out of the house without me and I'm quite nervous an about it.

It's almost five o'clock and there still is no sign of Louis and the kids. I've been pacing the floor and Asher has been trying to get hold of Louis.

Maybe they got stuck in traffic. I mean we are in summer there are a lot of people. Or maybe they are out for an ice cream. Or that they are having so much fun that they haven't seen the time past. Yeah, that's it!

Asher hung up the phone and huffed.

"Angel... I think you need to sit down." he came up to me and guided me to one of the sofas.

"Asher what is going on? Where are my kids?" he took my hands in his as he sat so that we were facing each other.

"Angel listen to me. The kids... the... Louis.... gosh there is no easy way to say this." he turned his head.

"The kids have been taken." my eyes that were now full of tears widened.

"What do you mean by 'taken'?" my heartbeat picked up as I placed a hand protectively on the remaining child I had.

"They were kidnapped, Leigh. Louis got hit on the head pretty badly and he is in the hospital to get stitched up."

My mind went to a blur. My kids were gone god knows where and the only person who could know what happened is not in any shape to do so.

"I won't see my babies or have them in my arms tonight?" tears were falling like a river now.

Asher took me into his arms as I was crying all that I knew.

"I'll get them back. I promise I will. The person behind this will die. I'll do everything to get them back." Asher's voice broke at the end but the determination in his voice took over.

I just want my kids back in my arms. This is all my fault...

CHAPTER THIRTY-FIVE

Everleigh:

"We will find them, Angel. We will get them back." Asher cooed in my ear trying to calm my cries but that only made them worse.

"You don't understand Ash. It's my fault they are gone... It's all my fault." I sobbed harder on his shoulder.

"It's not your fault. It's nobody's but my fault. I should have protected them. I-I didn't…" his voice cracked making me cry harder once more. I pulled away from his shoulder and cupped his face.

"Asher. It's mine. I should have sent some more guys to go with the kids and Louis. I knew going out with the kids all by himself wouldn't work but I did it anyway. If I were a better mother and thought things through, they would still be here. If I wouldn't have been tired and selfish I would have both my babies in my arms and we wouldn't be in this situation right now! I'm the one to blame!"

I yelled standing up and putting distance in between Ash and I. The hurt and confusion painted on his face was clear. I wouldn't be surprised if he blamed me, I already blame myself.

"They should be here, with us, with me. Protected. And they are not and it's because of me." I couldn't face him anymore. The tear fountain couldn't stop now and I was beating myself up. A pair of strong arms came around me and I was surrounded by the familiar smell of him.

"Angel. Don't say that. It's not our fault and especially not yours. The people that have them, they're to blame for taking them, not us, ever. Do you hear me? It's not your fault. And it never will be." he kissed the top of my head before taking me back to sit down.

"You need to calm down and get your head straight. I need you with me to find them. And all this stressing isn't good for the baby." I nodded my head whipping my tears away with the tissues that Asher had given me.

"Carter and Paul are already on it trying to know what happens to the kids at the park and are trying to figure out a location to where they might be." I nodded and got my phone out of my pocket.

"Hello."

"Papa, its snowdrop. I need your help. Call dad and be at the house ASAP." with that, I hung up the phone and got up waddling to Asher's office.

There was a knock on the door and I knew straight away who it was.

"Sergei! Daddy!" I walked as fast as I could to go and greet them.

"Princess what is the matter?" Sergei asked concern lacing his voice as he cupped my cheeks. Tears were burning my eyes again as I told him and my dad the situation at hand. I knew we couldn't do it without their help. They have done it before and they can do it again, I trust them. If they could save me then they could save my children.

****

A few hours before.

Louis:

I took the kids to the park furthest from the house. The kids were singing in the car all the way long! Urgh sometimes I wonder how I have put up with them this long but I have my reasons.

Once at the park I let them run free and sat on one of the benches still keeping an eye on them. My phone rang, I looked at the caller ID and knew straight away who it was.

"Hello, son." the voice rang out.

"What do you want?' I gritted out.

"That's not a way to greet your old–"

"Don't say it." I cut him off.

"I said what do you want?" I sighed frustrated.

"Have you see what I have done? Shame she came out it one piece, the car didn't." the pieces fitted together.

"You caused the car accident!" I growled into the phone. A sickening laugh erupted throughout the phone.

"Ohh silly little Louis. Of course, I did. That boy needs to learn! But don't worry I have something else up my sleeve. Might want to keep a close eye on them." with that, the phone call ended. I put the phone away and scanned the playground till I saw the kids happily playing on the swings.

"Is this seat taken?" I looked up to see a beautiful woman dressed in a flower print sundress with one of them big straw hats. She had midnight black hair and eyes just as dark.

"No, not at all." I gestured to the spot next to me. She started off the conversation while I kept my eyes on the children.

"So you have kids?" she questioned. I turned to her and pointed to where the little ones were playing.

"They are not mine. Just taking them out for a run." I turned to look at her again.

"You?" she nodded and pointed to a place behind me. I turned my head once more but I couldn't see anything.

"Where is–" next thing I know I was on the ground, my vision getting blurry covered in black dots. The screams of help from Damon and the piercing cries of Rose mixed to the buzzing in my ears was all I could make out.

I tried getting back up only to be hit in the head again and this time I felt a prick on my neck.

"I don't have kids, in fact, I hate them." the woman had bent down to my level before knocking me out cold.

"Louis! Save us! Mummy! Daddy! Louis!"

CHAPTER THIRTY-SIX

Everleigh:

It's been four days, a total ninety-six hours since my babies have been taken. We have been looking high and low for them and who could possibly be behind all this. Louis is still not in any condition to help us and nothing from the park is helping us pinpoint a location.

I am slowly going mad, the heat is never a helping factor and everyone is walking on daisies around me and not trying to stress me out. The only person that is keeping me up to beat is Ray and that's because if not he has two very pregnant and hormonal females ready to beat his arse and that terrifies him. Nobody helping out has had proper sleep and it's starting to take its toll on all of us.

I knock on Asher's office door with a cup of tea in my hand.

"Baby?"

 I questioned pushing the door open after not hearing any response. I walked in to see him surrounded by piles of paper, his laptop was the only source of light that shone on his face. His office smelt like grown men (not the best smell in the world) and he was half asleep in his chair, you could see his head starting to drop because of lack of sleep.

"Baby, get some rest." I placed to cuppa on a coaster on his desk and brushed the fallen hair out of his eyes.
I was met with those blues eyes he shares with our daughter and I tried hard to hold back the tears when I saw all the sadness locked in them.

"Go to bed, rest." I whispered to him. He shook his head taking my hand that was in his hair out and into his hand.

"I can't. Not until I find them and bring them back home." he yawned.

"Asher you need to sleep. You being tired will not help us find them. Take a few hours break to sleep. Sean and Sergei have loads of men on the case, well-trained men that will, find something, anything to bring them back. Sleep. Please."

Our foreheads were now touching as he had brought me to sit on his lap. My belly was the only thing keeping us from being close to him. Even under this heat, I wanted to feel his warmth. I wanted to be in his arms and wake up and find out that all this was just a bad dream. But alas, it isn't...

"Asher, go to bed." I pleaded once more before he gave up and nodded standing up and pulling me with him.

"Ok. But no more than a few hours, four at most. And I want to be woken if there is any improvement, got it?" I nodded and kissed his lips before taking his hand and leading him back to our room.

Once he was knocked out I set myself free from his grip and

waddled out of the room, slowly closing the door behind me as I left.

Where are you Damon and Rose?

****

Damon:

My eyes slowly opened as I was hearing some weird noises coming from next to me.

I turned my head to see Rose with tears running down her rosy cheeks as she was holding her teddy bear closer to her. Once she saw that I was awake she scooted closer to me.

"Damo... I scared." she whimpered as I took her into my arms. I looked around us and saw that we were in a weird and cold room. The walls were grey and there was just one window but it wasn't like at home. It was a very small window that was right at the top of the wall near the big door. The sun was still out but I didn't know where we are.

Soon the door came open and scary looking men came into the room.

"Ahhh look the mutts are up." the one in the middle spoke up as he came and crouched down in front of us. I held Rose closer to me because daddy told me to protect her, always. He took my arm and pulled me away from Rose.

"Get off me!" I yelled trying to get out of his grip. I turned to Rose and saw her cry again as one of the other men came and snatched her teddy from her arms.

"Don't touch her!" I shouted again only to be thrown on one side of the room.

"DAMON!" Rose cried as he ran up to me and curled up to my side. The third man left a tray on the table that was on the other end of the room.

"Wait till my daddy comes and gets you." I growled to the men as they were leaving. The taller one, the man that grabbed my arm came back to me and grabbed my jaw in his hands holding very hard.

"Listen here you piece of shit. I–" the man was cut off by the man that took the tray in.

"Let him be. Remember no harm should come to the kids. If not the boss will have your head." he warned the other. He let go of my jaw and stood up.

"You got lucky this time kid." he spat then walked out with the two others.

The man that called the mean one away told us before they left.

"Eat up. And don't waste anything."

The big door closed and the locking sound could be heard. I sat up and took Rose back into my arms as I let a few tears fall before standing up with a bit of a struggle. I walked over to the table and picked up the bread and sat back down next to my little sister.

I broke the bread loaf open as hard as I could and once a tore a piece off, I was met with a plastic looking thing poking out.

"What's that Damo?" Rose asked as I handed her the piece of bread. I took the plastic thing out, a phone.

"It's a phone RoRo!" I turned it on and did what mummy always did with her phone when she calls pop-pop.

"Hello? Who is this?"

"Mummy?"

CHAPTER THIRTY-SEVEN

Everleigh:

I was sitting on the sofa rubbing my belly cradled in Asher's arms as the baby was giving us his/her first kicks. Asher had woken up a few hours ago and there still wasn't any info.

"Where could they be Asher? It feels like weeks since we have seen them." I pouted as Ash placed his hand on the side of my belly only to be kicked.

"I know baby." he sighed.

"What if–" I couldn't finish my sentence as the ringtone of my phone was heard.

I reached out for it looking at the caller ID: unknown.

I sat up looking worriedly at Asher as he made a sign to Ray and Paul that were walking by to come to us. Luckily Paul had a laptop in hand and plugged the phone into the computer to track the call. I took a deep breath and pressed the green button putting the phone on speaker.

"Hello? Who is this?"

"Mummy?" my breath hitched in my throat as a tear escaped my eyes.

"**Mummy is that you?**" Damon's little voice rang out as I saw I wave of relief pass in all of us in the room.

"Yes, baby it's momma. Are you ok? Is your sister ok? Are you hurt?" I rushed my questions out.

"**Mummy I'm scared.**"

"I know buddy, I know, you are a brave boy." I told him hoping to bring a little comfort.

"**Mummy, RoRo and I are ok. But the scary men will be back soon, mummy I'm so scared.**" I smiled at the little nickname he had found for Rose but at the mention of 'scary men' I sat up straighter.

"Tell me where you are, what does it look like?" Paul motioned for me to keep talking as he hadn't pinpointed their location yet.

"**It's cold and dark here mummy. There are a big door and a tiny window right at the top of the wall.**" I turned to Asher as I mouthed me ' Basement' and I nodded.

"You are doing great buddy. Can you tell me anything about what the scary men looked like?" I tried to keep my voice as upbeat and happy as I could so that I wouldn't scare him further.

"**They had big tattoos like daddy and they looked like the hulk. All in black. There was one that was really mean to** me mummy and another that took RoRo's teddy." I could almost see him pout and crease his forehead through the phone.

'When are you and daddy coming to get us?" I snapped out of my reverie and let out a shaky breath.

"Soon baby boy. Mummy and daddy and all your uncles and pop-pop are doing all they can to come and get the both of you." I heard shuffling in the background before I couldn't hear Damon anymore.

"Mu-mu---my. Are --- y--- here?" the line kept cutting as my heartbeat accelerated. The line can't cut, not now!

"Damon?! I'm here buddy! Mummy's here!"
Silence.

"DAMON? DAMON!" then the line went dead.

"Please tell me you have something." I put the phone down on the table suppressing the urge to throw it.

"In a matter of fact, I do." Paul smirked and turned the laptop our way. Asher's jaw clenched as his knuckles became white.

"Asher. What's the matter?" I cocked my head to the side and placed one of his hands on my belly and the other one holding his. When the baby gave a kick he snapped out of his trance and turned to me his jaw still clenched.

"I know who took them. Get everyone ready."

"Leigh, Angel. I think you should stay home where it's safe."

His eyes were pleading but my babies are gone and he just expects me to sit and stay home? Yeah, not going to happen. I grabbed him by the collar of his shirt so that he was at the same level as me and at that point, I was already on edge.

"Listen here. I'm five months pregnant, hormones flying around the place, my kids are locked up scared in some crappy place. And you want me to just sit at home and wait for you to come back? Are you really sure about what you want?"

I had passed the point of no return. I was already dressed and good to go. By the look on his face he was clearly scared and so he should be. Mama bear is out and has a thirst for blood and to kill the dick that took my kids away from me. He visibly gulped as I kept a strong glare.

"I take your silence as a yes. Let's face it, you weren't going to win anyway." I kissed him and let him go, giving him a sweet smile and walked off to the car where all the weapons were at.

"Hey shorty! Could you give me the–" I couldn't even finish my sentence that Shorty butted in.

"Pat."

"I'm sorry. What?" I crossed my arms over my chest resting them on my swollen belly.

"My name is Pat, short for Patrick, not shorty." he too, crossed his arms over his chest.

"Yeah so, just give me guns and knives and we can all get on with our day." I scoffed.

Irritation was dripping from my voice. My mood was unchanged and shorty over here was just pushing it with me not knowing his name.

"Ok *Shorty*. I don't have time to lose learning your name. I have other things to do and I have nicknames for all of the guys and I don't hear them complaining." I just looked at my nails, clearly annoyed of this situation.

"They don't say anything to you, but behind your back. And I have the balls to stand up to you. My name is Patrick. Not shorty get that in that little brain of yours." he said through gritted teeth coming dangerously close to me. I may call him shorty but he still towers over me.

I turned around and spotted Ray. I whistled and he threw me his gun whilst still talking to Simon. We had set in a code and he would either give me a gun, a knife or a riffle and so on depending on the whistle. I would test him in the house under any circumstances so that he is ready for an attack because I don't go walking around the house armed. So once

I had caught it, no questions asked, I turned back around to face shorty and shot him in the leg. He went down with a groan/ grunt type noise.

"You shot me you bitch!" he yelled at me holding his bleeding leg.

I took a step closer to him and looked down at him, and that was a bit of a struggle considering my belly was starting to block the view of things on the floor. I placed my hands on my hips still with the gun in hand.

"What did you just call me?" I raised an eyebrow at him.

"A bitch! You are a bitch! Why did you shoot me?!" I shot him again, this time in the shoulder.

"ARRRRHHH! WHAT THE HELL! You shot me again!" I shrugged when a pair of arms wrapped around me and turned me around to face them. I knew straight away it was Ash.

"Angel what is going on? Why did you shoot him? Are you ok?" he looked up and down to search if I had any injuries on me. He relaxed when he saw nothing.

"He just got on my nerves calling me a bitch and getting mad for me not knowing his name."

I gave a little pout and placed one of my hands on his chest. I saw anger flash through his eyes but before he could say anything the sound of a gun cocking caught my attention. I saw shorty in the reflection of Asher's eyes and before anything else could be done I turned and shot the hand that was holding the gun.

"Right! I have had enough! I have wasted three perfectly good bullets on a little shit like you and I am extremely tempted to sacrifice a fourth one to go in between your eyes."

If I were to be in a cartoon I think smoke would be coming out of my ears. I looked over my shoulder to a shocked Asher to let him decide what he wanted to do to him since it's his gang.

"What do you think? Torture him?" I asked faking innocence.

"Let me handle this Angel." he took the gun out of my hands and shot him right between the eyes.

"Anybody has anything else to add? Just know the next person that disrespects my girl or anyone else that is in a higher rank than you for a crappy reason will finish like him or worse." his voice held so much power it sent chills down my spine.

 None of his men dared to say anything back.

"Clean this mess." he ordered to one of his men.

"Let's get our kids back." he took my hand and led me to his car.

Not long to wait my loves. Mummy and daddy are on their way to get you back home, safe and sound.

CHAPTER THIRTY-EIGHT

Everleigh:

The car ride was silent, only our breaths and hammering hearts could be heard.
I started fidgeting and analysing all my surroundings.
Asher's hand was placed on my thigh rubbing soothing patterns calming my nerves down a little.

"Ash." I whispered not daring to speak any louder. The grip he had on the wheel became tighter as his knuckles were turning white. I diverted my eyes from him and looked out of the window again wiping away a stray tear.

"We will get them back, I promise." after that, we didn't say anything else till we had arrived a little further away from where my children were being held.

We all stepped out of the cars and circled around Asher to get our orders.

"Team one and two stay outside and circle the perimeter. Three and four will be on standby and five and six will come in with me, Carter and Paul. Now let's get my kids back. Shoot everyone that gets into your way and capture a few so that we get more info out of them. Priority number one is to get Rose and Damon out of here without a scratch. Break."

Everyone scattered to their posts and Ash and the boys were walking away.

What about me?

"Umm babe?" I questioned waddling over to him.

"Yes, Angel." he huffed running a hand through his lush brown locks.

Focus Everleigh!

"What do I do?"

"Nothing. You are staying in the car where you are safe and you wait till I come back with the kids." he said matter of factly. I scoffed and turned around not wanting to slow down the operations. There is no way I am sitting in the car like a good little girl.

I waited a good ten minutes to make sure the boys were there. I heard the first gunshot that made my heart jump. I quickly speed walked with all my kit in my arms and when to the building that was set about 500 yards away of the building they were in and since it was vacant I set up all my stuff up on the third/ last floor. I placed my rifle on its stand and placed a small sandbag under the barrel to make it steadier. I didn't have to lie down on my belly so that was a plus but I did have to bend over and that was a bit more of a struggle with the balloon I had.

I placed my eye on the lens and directed the gun in direction of the place the kids were held. I hadn't realised how long I had taken to get set up that they were already all over the place shooting left and right. Soon enough I found the small window that Damon had mentioned on the phone call. It was a basement window but it wasn't as deep as I thought it was. I was pretty high up in a basement. I focused the lens on the window and what I saw next nearly left my heart in pieces.

I took in a deep breath and pressed the trigger and prayed my aim was right.

****

Damon:

I was still on the phone with mummy when the scary men from earlier came back. The line was going all weird and I could no longer hear mummy's voice. Ro was crying as the man came closer up to me. He snatched the phone from my hands and grabbed me by the t-shirt.

"Where did you get this!" he yelled in my face as Rose was whimpering a few feet away from me.

"I-I fo-found I-I-it." I stuttered out in fear. He put me down roughly and took out a gun from his back pocket. I stood in fear not quite sure what I had to do. He pulled the thingy down and it made a clicking noise and pointed it straight at me.

"NOOOOOOO!" Rose screamed at the top of her lungs and cried all she could.

"SHUT UP, SHUT UP, SHUT UP!" the guy with the gun yelled over her cries and placed his hands over his ears. I closed my eyes and soon the cries stopped and a thud was what came next.

"ROSE!" I ran up to her limp body on the floor. I turned her over so that she was partly on my lap. Tears were streaming down my eyes as I saw that she was bleeding from her head.

"RORO." I sobbed harder and glared at the man that looked shocked at what he did. The door pulled open and the man with the phone came in.

"What did you do to them? I told you not to come in here! did you just hit her with the gun?" his voice was so low and didn't make me feel any better.

He tried to come up to Rose but I held her close to me and glared and the man.

"Don't touch her." I growled seeing as he wasn't stopping. He came up and tried taking her out of my arms but I didn't let go.

"Take your hands off of my children you sick prick.""I knew that voice. Daddy.

****

Asher Mortimer:

After turning to leave Everleigh, the guys and I walked to

the warehouse the kids were being held at. Soon enough bullets were flying and the house was breached. The people outside knew that we were here but there was still an element of surprise to the ones on the inside.

We longed the walls as we found a set of two staircases. I nodded to the guys to go down one and me the other while my other men took the rest of the house out.

I walked down the stairs as screams resonated through the halls. I walked to where the sound was coming from and then it stopped. I heard footsteps come close to I hid behind a wall as a man walked straight passed me without him seeing me.
The sound of muffled voices could be heard. I walked up closer to the door my gun ready in hand just in case something was to happen.

I peeked my head pasted the door to hear Damon asking the man to not touch Rose but they were blocking my view.

"Take your hands off of my children you sick prick." I growled out. Everleigh would probably kill me if she heard what I said in front of the kids.

I fully stepped in and pointed my loaded gun at the two men, more so the one that was closer to the kids.
They stepped aside and my eyes widened at the sight that was in front of me. My baby girl laid there unconscious with a bleeding gash on her head. My son was there holding her close in his arms attempting to keep her safe and protected. I felt as if this was all my fault.

It all happened to fast. One moment I have the upper hand and the next the second bloke had Damon in a tight grip a gun pointed to his head.

"Get any closer and he takes the blow." my eyes darted all around the room to try and figure out a way to get to them without getting the kids hurt in the process.

There was a 'whoosh' sound and the man that was holding Damon was on the floor with a bullet straight In between his eyes. The shot was so clean that the window didn't even shatter. There was a clean cut hole in the top window. I quickly used that to shoot the other man in the leg and shoulder and called for backup. Carter soon rushed into the room as I had gently cradled Rose in my arms and hugged Damon as he cried into my arms for a bit.

"Let's take you back to mummy." Carter picked up Damon and Paul took care of the rest of the men.

****
Everleigh:

Once the shot was made I packed my things up knowing that Asher would be back soon. I speed waddled back to the car. I came back to the car with just enough time to dump all my things in the back of the car.
Asher came rushing to the car and pushed harder once he saw me.

"Get in the car quick. We need to get Rose to the hospital." I gasped as I saw my little princess limp in my man's arms. Tears pricked my eyes as I brushed the bloodied hair off her forehead.

"NOW EVERLEIGH." he made me jump and rush straight into the driver's side. I buckled myself in as Asher climbed into the back with Carter that had a crying Damon him his arms.

I stepped on the gas and drove like a crazy woman till we finally arrived at the hospital.
We all rushed out of the car and ran to get help.

I had spent the last few hours cradling Damon in my arms, comforting him and to be honest I didn't want to let him go. Ash was taking phone calls getting things set up as we waited for the doctors to come get us after they have run all the tests on Rose.
I was rocking Damo to sleep as the doctor came up to us.

"Rose Mortimer." Asher nodded and I made a sign to him to come closer. Both men sat down in chairs, the doc in front of me and Asher by my side taking my free hand in his.

"Your daughter was very lucky, there isn't any brain damage nor any internal bleeding or brain swelling. The scare she gave us was that the gash on her head was a lot deeper than we had first anticipated. She has stitches and once they are healed it might leave a scar due to the depth of the cut."

I nodded and continued to run my hand over Damo's back as Ash was rubbing the back of my hand.

"You can go and see her now. We have given her medication to ease the pain and once she has woken up we will run further tests and if she is given the all clear you will be free to go back home."

"Thank you very much, doctor." Asher stood up to shake the doctor's hand before letting him leave. He turned to me and picked our son in his arms and help me stand up.

"Let's go see our daughter."

CHAPTER THIRTY-NINE

Everleigh:

It has been a few days since getting the kids back home safe and sound. Rose woke up and after getting the all-clear from the doctors we all went home after all of us got a check-up, Damo and I to be more precise.

My baby is doing fine and growing nicely and kicking like a real football player. Asher has doubled the security and has even set up a few cameras around the house that only he and Carter know where they are. We never let the kids by themselves or out of our site. It's a bit rash but it helps put my mind at ease.

Annie and I have been catching up. I have been giving her tips because it's still her first pregnancy and she was freaking out. Ray has been at her beck and call since she has been experiencing cravings. They were super sweet together and made me wish that Asher had been there for my first pregnancy so that we could learn all this together but it seems like a superior force had other plans...

"Baaaabeeee..." I whined sitting on the sofa. My feet are killing me and I'm starving and on top, on that, I can't move because I have both kids sleeping on me. Rose was straddling my belly, her face was hidden in my neck and Damon had his head on my lap hugging as best he could my belly.

"Yes, Angel." his head peeked out of the kitchen, he was shirtless and only in joggers. I had to swallow hard with the sight in front of me. *Damn hormones!*

"Could you get me something salty like a sandwich with mayo, mustard, sausages, lettuce ... oh radishes maybe add a packet of crisps, salt and vinegar obviously and a chocolate milkshake please?" I gave my best puppy eyes and tried not to talk too loud.

He let out a sexy chuckle and came up to me and kissed my forehead.

"You have some weird culinary tastes I have ever seen and Ray told me that even Annie didn't ask for things as weird as you." he laughed a little more and sat next to me kissing Rose on the side of her head and stroking Damon's head Lovingly.

"When I was expecting Rose all I wanted to eat were bananas covered in chocolate sauce and this type of crab salad with mayonnaise all over it. But with this little guy here it seems that he likes to make me eat all types of weird things."

I smiled down at my belly and rubbed the side of it than Rose's back remembering when she was in my belly. After my very weird meal Asher took me as best he could in his arms with me resting my head on his shoulder.

267

"Ash. What are we going to do?" he turned to me looking confused.

"What do you mean by 'what are we going to do?' " I took a deep breath.

"I think we need a break from here. I feel like everywhere I go someone is going to pop up from the shadows and take the kids away again... The kids wake up with nightmares when they don't sleep in the same bed with us. Louis is finally awake and not saying a word to me nor does he look at me. I just need to be somewhere else, at least for the summer." I felt tears in my eyes. I really don't like the feeling in the air in this house.

"If that's what you want then that is what we will do." I snuggled closer to him as both kids woke up.

"Dada." Rose put her arms out for her father to take.

"Come here princess." he spoke softly to her. Damon took this opportunity to sit up and stretch only to take Rose's place.

A new day and a new day where I don't want to be stuck in this house again. I spend most of my Time in the rose garden that Asher has made for me when we had our first date and when he proposed. I love the memories here and to be surrounded by all these beautiful flowers make me feel at ease. The sun is banging but I don't mind, it sends me to my happy place, far from all the drama that has been going on.

"Angel." his deep voice knocked me out of my daydream admiring the roses.

"Yes?" I turned around with a rose that I had picked. It was lightly faded around the edges.

"What do you think about going to LA for a bit? I have a beach house over there, its summer and like you said we need a break from this house. What do you think? Me, you, the kids?" a huge smile spread on my face as I attempted to run into his arms.

"You are truly the best. When are we going?" I asked eyes full of hope.

"Tomorrow early morning. You might want to start packing." I hopped on my feet and hugged him again and ran inside the house to our room and get things in place and then to the kids' room.

I was so in a rush that I didn't see who was walking in the corridor.

"Louis?" I gasped out of breath.

"E-Everleigh. We need to talk." I nodded unsurely.

"Look I'm sorry. All of this is my fault. I–" he breathed out before continuing "I should have known something was going to happen. I... I'm sorry."

He didn't dare look at me in the eyes. Seeing as I wasn't saying anything he continued.

"I know you probably don't want to forgive me and that I have been acting weird lately but it's because I just can't be in the same room as you, boss or the kids with our feeling terribly guilty and I only wish that you would forgive me."

I placed my hand on his shoulder making him look up at me.

"I forgive you, Louis, sure I was extremely mad when I found out but you were caught off guard. I hate the people that took my kids and made them live through that hell. Not you." I tried reassuring him.

We ended with a hug before we both walked off to finish what we were set off to do.

"Thank you." he whispered before walking off into the darkness of the corridor.

CHAPTER FORTY

Everleigh:

I woke up early with Asher to finish up all the last details. The kids slept with us once again last night. These nightmares really need to stop because:
a) I can't sleep.
b) It kills me to see my kids too scared that they will be taken again.

Damon has been trying to 'man up' a little too quickly. He doesn't let Rose out of his sight too long, it's truly sweet that he takes care of her like that but I want him to enjoy his childhood and not be constantly on guard for danger. Asher does that already and I don't want my 5-year-old to start now like his father.

After getting all the bags and kids in the car we bid our goodbyes to the guys and let Carter and Paul with us on the trip and leaving Ray in charge over here till we arrive in California.

We arrive at the airport in record time, once we passed security and all that jazz Ash lead us to our private jet that I just discovered we had.

"Wow." was all I could muster seeing the plane and same once I saw the inside of it.

There was plenty of room for the kids and us and on top of that, there was a real bathroom and a bedroom with a king size bed. You wouldn't have thought of that when you saw the outside of the plane.

The pilot asked us to buckle ourselves in as the ride was going to be short since the weather was so clement.
The kids had fallen asleep as I laid my head on my future husband's shoulder and let sleep consume me.

"Wake up babe. We are here." his soft voice rang in my ear as he shook me lightly to wake me up.

I opened my eyes to fall upon the familiar blue orbs that he shares with our daughter.

"Hey." I breathed out.

"Hey." he said back kissing the top of my head.

Asher helped me out of my seat then down the plane stairs where at the bottom was waiting for us, a very nice car and the boys each with a child in their arms. I was greeted with the scorching heat of the Californian sun.

"Jesus wept! It's bloody boiling!" I fanned myself with no luck only making matters worse.

I sat in front and sighed in content as the air con hit my face. The car ride was silent as Ash drove us to the beach house.

"We are here kiddos." he exclaimed with a hint of excitement in his voice.

We only had the kids in the car because Paul and Carter came to drop off the bags and check if everything was safe before heading back to Chicago and take care of things over there. This holiday is only going to be us, Asher, Rose, Damon and me. Just us, as a family.

We came into the house as the boys left the bags in the hall and the kids ran around choosing their rooms.

"Welcome home, Angel." Ash came up behind me placing his arms around my waist and resting his hands on my very round belly rubbing small circles.

"Want to head to the beach?" he asked. I nodded my head even if I was really tired after today's travelling but I've been dying to put my toes in the sand.

After putting on a swimsuit and smothering the kids in sun cream we all headed off to the private beach that was just in front of the house when you walk past the two bay windows in the kitchen or living room.
We set our things down in a nice spot and Ash planted an umbrella to create a little shade.

Since we had arrived late afternoon the sun was starting to set so before it got too cold to swim since Rose had already lived by the beach but was too young to remember and I knew that Damo hadn't seen the sea before Ash and I lead them to the sea.

Damo took hold of Rose's hand and I just melted at the sight.

"It's ok Roro. We can go, mummy and Daddy are behind us."

He told Rose to give her a little confidence boost. The sight was just too sweet I needed to snap a picture of that moment. I had on only a bikini bottom and one of Ash's t-shirts not feeling up to go full out this late in the day. I followed both kids in, not too far in but just enough so that the water came up to just below their knees to that they could play in the shallow waters.

I was enjoying the cool breeze and the water at my feet, the children playing when I was cut out of my reverie with the sweet sound of Asher's deep laugh and the sound of a camera snap.

"Asher!" I squealed. He simply laughed harder and looked at his phone.

"You look stunning." he smiled at me showing the picture.

I must admit I looked really nice, so at peace.

"Beautiful." he whispered in my ear. She shared a long kiss before heading back to the house to eat.

We made something simple for dinner and bathed the kids before heading off to bed.

"Asher?" I questioned turning to face him.

"Mmmm" he mumbled half asleep.

"Do you think we will ever see the end of this whole story? The constant fear of the children being taken away? What will happen with the new baby?" my nerves were all over the place.

"I won't let anything or anyone bring any harm to this family as long as I live. I promise." our eyes met and a wave of comfort washed over me.

"I want to get married. Like now." I blurted out. His eyes held as much shock I felt at my words.

"Like the ceremony and all that?" he questioned sitting up straight.

"More like the courthouse, but yeah a wedding ASAP." I clarified. He looked at me and then at the ring on my finger than at me once more.

"If that's what you want then that's what we will do." he kissed my hand like a true gentleman and left a chaste kiss on my lips placing a hand on my belly holding our future child.

"I love you." I called out.

"And I, you." we kissed again and I soon fell into a deep slumber.

CHAPTER FORTY-ONE

Asher Mortimer:

I woke up with my beautiful girl carrying our baby, soundly sleeping in my arms in a very weird position because of the baby bump.

I took my free hand and started caressing her face keeping the fallen hairs out of the way.
She slightly shifted and I was met with those mesmerizing forest green eyes that I can't ever get enough of.

"Morning." I whispered to her. She attempted to stretch like a cat but failed.

"Morning." she smiled back.

That smile gets me every time.

"How are you doing Angel?" I cooed putting my hand away from her face to the baby.

"How's my little man?" I said coming closer to her belly.

"And what makes you think it's a boy?" she giggled as I pulled her top to under her boobs and placed kisses on her belly for my future son.

"I just know it's a boy." I shrugged kissing her tummy again earning a kick from him.

"To be honest I think it's a boy too. I don't carry him the same way I did Rose." she passed a hand through my hair as I continued making small talk with my son.

"What do you think about making a gender reveal at the wedding?" her sweet voice rang out to me.

"I guess we could. Talking about weddings, we need to get things sorted if you want it to be soon. When were you thinking?" I asked sitting up straight.

"Well…" she dragged.

"I was thinking in seven days. We can do it here and have everyone over. So that before we can get a check-up for the baby and get the gender. I don't want anything big. I'll just wear a simple white dress and then you could just have a shirt. No dress code, only comfy clothes. Courthouse, nice dinner and then boom! We live happily ever after." she rambled on, it was quite cute actually.

"If that's what you want then that is what you will have." I smiled down at her. If she would ask for the moon then I would give it to her even if it took me a lifetime.

"Is it what you want?" she nervously tugged at the hem of the shirt that was rolled up.

I took her hand with the diamond ring on in my hand giving it a light squeeze.

"I love you Everleigh and if I get to become your husband today, tomorrow, in a week, or a million years from now then I will not mind when we do it as long as we do. I love you and I will never stop loving you and getting married to you will only show to others that you are mine."

I spoke with every little fiber of love in me for her and I honestly didn't mind when or where we got married as long as I can call her my wife then I'll be the happiest man on earth.
We could get married behind a club, under the rain with Elvis as a priest and us in jeans and t-shirts for all I care.

"Do you really mean that?" tears were glistening in her eyes. I cupped her face and kissed her.

"I really do mean that. I love you, Angel."

"I love you too Asher." she whispered back.

Everleigh:

Today is the day I become Mrs. Everleigh Mortimer and I'm super excited!

All week has been a bit hectic, Annie and Clair flew in the day after our talk with Ash. They have been real gems helping out not only with the little wedding details but with the kids who have been getting their spirit back.

"So we have the dress, the food is set up for later, the boys will be back later they stayed at the hotel, Rose is dressed. All we need is you, darling."

Clair ran other all the details once more. We had booked the courthouse for three pm this afternoon and right now it was lunch so we still had plenty of time.

I picked a simple white dress that stopped mid-thigh and pulled my hair into a low messy bun to really bothered and light makeup.

Rose was in a long summer dress with a salmon coloured top and a sort of chevron pattern and the bottom. Her blond curls were let down.

Clair was in a simple flowy summer dress and simple gold accessories and Annie and her baby bump were in a long black dress that looked absolutely stunning on her.

We were now off the court house in the centre of the town. I was super excited and nervous at once.
I'm getting married to the man I love. I'm actually getting married!

I chanted in my head till the car came to a stop.
I stepped out and went into the building.
Clair had informed me that the boys were already waiting.
The music started as I walked down the makeshift aisle. I was a little sad that my dad and Sergei couldn't come on such a short notice.

Carter stepped in to walk me down the aisle as Ray walked down with Annie on his arm. Clair took care of Rose and Paul stayed as a witness to our wedding. Damon was standing proud, dressed in a clean button-down shirt like his dad.

My eyes ran up and down Asher's body as I was taking every inch of him in.

He's all mine. I smirked to myself.

"I do." I said back.

"By the power vested in me by the state of California. I now pronounce you husband and wife. You may kiss the bride." the judge announced.

And without a minute to waste, his lips were on mine in a core melting kiss.
Cheers erupted in the room as we all walked out with the biggest smiles on our face.

"I love you, Mrs. Mortimer." Asher called out when we were in the car heading back to the house for the after party.

"And I you Mr. Mortimer." we kissed again and arrived at the house.

"Well, isn't it the newlywed!" Paul yelled with a glass of champagne in hand.

Confetti was thrown at us as laughter and congratulations filled the air.
This day couldn't be any more perfect. The best is still to come.

Next is the gender reveal!

CHAPTER FORTY-TWO

Everleigh:

We walked around the house that the girls had set up with decorations. White and pale pink roses were all around and nice white streamers as well as a newlywed sign on the wall. They had set two tables together and put all the food on as an 'all you can eat buffet'.

We ate, danced and laughed. We didn't really respect any of the 'traditional' events that happen at weddings such as the speeches or anything of that sort but I really wanted to do the first dance with my husband. I didn't have a bouquet of flowers so I couldn't throw it to all the single ladies in the room, not that there were any.

"Alright, guys its gender reveal time!" I squealed getting up from my seat and dragging Asher with me.

Paul was the only one to know what the gender was so he blindfolded us and either he would paint Asher's hands in pink for a girl or blue for a boy and the concept was that once his hands were painted he would place them on my white wedding dress and then take his hands off to see the sort of heart-shaped colour his hands would have left behind.

"Are you ready guys?" Paul asked excitement clear in his voice.

"Ready." we said in sync.

"Ok so I'm going to take the blindfolds off and turn you around and at the count of three Boss, you take your hands off. Kay?"

We both gave a 'kay' as I felt Asher hands on my belly as we were turned around.

"ONE, TWO... THREE!" everyone yelled as the blindfolds were taken off at the same time as Asher took his hands off me.

"It's a boy." I whispered in disbelief. I really wanted a boy. I could not help the tears that were streaming down my face.

"We're having a boy." I said a little louder turning around and crushing my lips on Asher's.

"Congrats you guys! A new little boss is on the way." Carter came up to me pulling me into a hug making sure not to touch my still paint wet dress.

 Asher took the time to wash his hands off and go to his mother crying her eyes out just like me. Annie was crying since everyone else was, too many emotions at once.

"We're having a baby boy too." she managed to squeak out drying her tears and cuddled in her man's arms.

I ran, well attempted to run, to her and took her in my arms both our bumps making contact.

"Future best friends?" I giggled as we both broke up in fits of laughter. We pulled away from each other and luckily the paint dries fast if not it would no longer black.

"I WANTED A LITTLE SISTER!" Rose cried tears streaming down her cheeks cradling the new teddy we got for her in her arms.

Asher scooped her into his arms, I let a little giggle out. What? I can't help it her little mad face is super cute.

"Don't cry, princess. It's alright. A baby brother is great fun, you can boss him around. And mummy and I can try giving you a little sister after we have baby brother." Asher reassured her. She sniffed and looked at her daddy. Asher gave me a knowing look full of lust looking me up and down.

"I can?" she asked unsurely. He nodded and let out a small chuckle. Honestly, those two are just the cutest together, like my dad and me at that age.

"What about you Damon? Do you mind having a little brother?" I turned crouching down to his level, he had been very quiet since the announcement.

A tear left his eye as he took me in his little arms holding me closer.

"I am really, really happy." he cried on my shoulder as I

carried him in my arms letting a few tears of my own slip.

"He can help me protect you mummy and Roro." he pulled away holding the simple gold chain I had put around my neck.

What did I do to deserve such a child?

I asked myself holding him close as I could earn a little glare from my husband. He doesn't want me picking and carrying the kids, says I shouldn't be heavy lifting.

I put Damo back on his feet a rubbed the hairs out of his face, lovingly staring at him. He hugged my leg not wanting to let me go.

"How about some cake?" Clair asked as the kids detached themselves from us and ran inside following their grandma for a slice of cake.

"Are we so easily replaced?" Asher walked up to me faking hurt. I laughed at that.

"Wait till she gets a boyfriend and him a girlfriend or vice versa. We won't be their centre of concern when that moment arrives." I sighed imagining my babies with each their other half like me at this moment.

"My princess will never come close to any other man than her brothers, her uncles, grandfather and me. I'll lock her up in her room from all eternity. She will stay my baby girl forever." he pouted but held a look of determination.

"And I won't let my boys fall for a girl that I don't approve of. And I won't let my baby girl get her heart broken by a jerk that wants her for only one thing." I nodded holding the same determination as him. We kissed then headed inside for the cake and to dance a little more.

Our first dance wasn't anything rehearsed, we just played a random song because we hadn't prepared anything.
He just leads me to the makeshift dance floor holding me lovingly whispering sweet nothings in my ear. Soon enough everybody joined us and our solo dance came to a close as we all shared our dance partners.

This day was pure bliss and I wouldn't change it for the world.

CHAPTER FORTY-THREE

Everleigh:

The past few days have been pure bliss. No fights, no threats, no kidnappings no nothing. But sadly all good things must come to an end.
I'm currently with a big part of the family sitting on the beach enjoying the sand and sea. Rose is sitting next to me playing with wet sand as the boys are playing in the water.

I still can't believe that I'm going to have a baby boy and that I have become Mrs. Mortimer. My mother said that all these things would never happen to me. Ha proved her wrong!

"Hey, baby what are you thinking about?" my gorgeous husband sat next to me placing his hand lovingly on my ever so round stomach.

"Just about all this and how grateful I am to have you and all these blessings in my life. That, and I really want a salted caramel ice cream." I honestly spoke having a mini foodgasm thinking about that ice cream.

"You hate caramel." Asher spoke confusedly. I put my hands up in surrender.

"Not my fault. Blame your son's weird food fetishes." I

pointed at my belly getting a little kick in response. His deep chuckle erupted from next to me sending all sorts of butterflies in me.

"Ok then, ice cream it is." he helped me get up as he called all the gang that was composed of Asher, me, Damon, Rose, Carter, Paul and Clair. Ray and Annie had left to visit Ray's extended family that lived an hour away from where we were.

We arrived at the ice cream parlour and I was jumping with excitement when the employee handed me what I had been craving for the past hour.

"Heaven."

I whispered ogling the creamy goodness before devouring it. Us adults sat on a bench in front of this space that had water jets coming from the floor where a lot of kids where playing in. I was scared to death about the kids going there since the last time they were playing in such a public area they got kidnapped but since I need to get over that fear and I don't want to be one of the mums that transmit their fears to their children.

"Go on kids, mummy and daddy will be watching you. Have fun." I knew that the kids really wanted to go and have fun and I wasn't going to stop them.

After about fifteen minutes give or take a few, an ear-piercing scream that I would recognise from anywhere made us all stand in alert.

"Rose." I breathed outstanding up and fast waddling to where the kids where.

She was wrapped up in her brother's arms. I stopped in my tracks analysing the scene as I saw all three boys with guns out on full alert scaring the living daylights out of several people around.

"Rose baby girl what happened?" I questioned ungluing her from her brother.

"I-I thought I- I saw him." she choked out in sobs.

"Who did you see Rose?" I inquired looking a little panicked at Asher and Clair.

"Him." she broke out in more tears before I could ask her anything more. She was clearly still traumatised by all this.

"We are going home. Now." I roared out picking her up fighting against Asher's pleas for him to take her. I grabbed Damo's hand, who was in a sort of daze from his sister crying.

Well, that moment of bliss was short-lived. I sighed to myself once the plane flew off back to New-York.

"You alright?" I turned and asked Asher since he was furiously typing on his laptop with one hand and his phone in the other.

"Honestly Everleigh? I feel like there is somebody after us and the person I am thinking of that may be behind all this is not making me feel any better." he ran a hand over his face in stress.

"Who do you think it is?" I pushed.

"I don't want you to stress about it before I am completely sure that it is really him. Remember what the doctor said, no stress during this pregnancy. You emptied all that when you had the car crash. Now you will do me the favour of resting and dropping the subject and letting me handle things, for the moment there is nothing to worry about."

He kissed my forehead and gave me the look that said 'I am in no mood to discuss this further with you but I still love you' sort of look.
Before I knew it the sandy beaches of California were exchanged for the hustle and bustle of the town. I was glad to be home. I needed that break but nothing can replace the feeling of coming back home.

September soon rolled over and Damo was in school and Rose was going to nursery to socialise three times a week. The memories of the kidnapping were gone like the waves on a beach along with the summer fun. Mine and Annie's baby shower was just around the corner and we would soon finish our collection of baby supplies to last us a lifetime.

"You ready to open your presents girls?" Clair's voice broke me out of my thoughts. She handed Annie and I our first presents each excitement swirling in her blue eyes.

After a million baby grows and other necessities to have a baby, my last present was given to me.

"Open it, mummy!"

It was a gift from Rose and Damon with a little help from Asher. I ripped the paper open to find a wolf grey soft toy that had a blue bow around its neck with a name tag that had ' Dark Snakes' in cursive writing on it.

"I love it, thank you my loves." I kissed them both on the cheeks.

"It's for baby wolf!" Rose squealed out.

She has been calling her baby brother wolf ever since she found out that she can 'boss' him around when he will be older. Why Wolf? I don't know but the name is growing on me but I need just something to complete the name but I haven't found the right match yet.

CHAPTER FORTY-FOUR

A few months later.

Everleigh:

We are now in January, Damo's birthday rolled around fast and my baby boy is now six and has found himself a good set of friends and has been doing really well in school. Rose has been giving puppy eyes to Her Brother's new best friend Kendyn. She gets all cute and cuddly when he is around, it's sweet, really. Christmas came and went will no major problem. I really wanted to spend it in Russia like when I was little but considering that I was eight months pregnant at that time it was a definite no-no to take the plane.

We are now close to the end of January and I have passed my due date by a week now and I still have no baby in my arms.
Joggings and Asher's jumpers have been what I have been living in for the past month. I feel so uncomfortable, I pee every time I breathe and my mood swings have never been worse. It wasn't like that with Rose since she was way too excited to show herself that she came close to two months early and gave me the worst scare in my life.

"I want this baby out!" I whine for the umpteenth time today. Asher, bless, has been really patient like really patient with me.

"I know you do baby but the doctor said that the baby is in the right position and that it is only a matter of days. And you know she said if he doesn't Come by the end of the week she will put you in induced labour." he spoke massaging my swollen feet that I can no longer see.

"But Annie got her baby before me! That's not fair! Ray banged her after me and she gets her son first!" I complained tears leaking from my eyes.

"Why the fuck am I crying? I'm so happy for her and her little Ryder." I cried harder soon finding myself in my husband's warm embrace yet again.

"Baby girl, shhhh." he rocked me rubbing soothing circles on my back easing the horrid pains I had been having recently.

"He will pop up when he feels the time is right. He just hasn't finished cooking yet." he joked early a small smile from me. Gosh, I love this man.

"The kids are in school, I don't have to be in any meetings. It's just me and you today. What do you say about getting all dressed up and going for a lunch date in a fancy restaurant and eat at your heart's content." he suggested.

I looked at him through my lashed and nodded my head like a little child.

"Come on then let's get ready."

As I stood up I felt a little cramp in my stomach.

"Hey angel, you ok there." I gave him a smile and replied a 'fine' before walking off to get ready.

After my shower, I slipped on one of the only pregnancy dress that doesn't make me look like a potato since I'm at the end of the road.

It was a fitted blush pink dress that I paired with a pair of high heel boots where I can still shove my ankles in. I looked myself in the mirror pleased with the way I looked.

Mama still got it!

My inner voice high fived herself. I decided to take a picture of how I looked because I feel good so every opportunity to take a pic if good in my book.
Asher even came to join me. He wore something more simple and comfortable but still looked well dressed.

We were about to walk out the door when I felt a sharp pain that had me bent over.

"Angel?" Asher's voice called out. I put my left hand up to stop him as the other was holding my stomach.

"Shit." I cursed out.

"Baby, tell me where it hurts." the light panic in his voice was starting to rise.

"My water just broke." I looked to see him frozen in his spot.

"Well don't just stand there do something!" I yelled at him breaking him out of his state. A goofy smile was plastered on his face when he walked out with me to the car, hospital bag in hand.

"I'm going to be a dad!" he called out not quite believing what was happening.

"You are going to be a dad before we arrive at the hospital if you don't start that fucking car!" I snapped at him feeling a new contraction coming.

We were coming close to the hospital and my contractions were fifteen minutes apart.

"Breathe Angel. Like this." he was more panting than breathing.

"Asher. If you tell me once more to fucking breathe I swear to god I will strangle you then tell you to bloody breathe." I glared at him which made him stop straight.

He got me out of the car and as soon as I stepped foot in that hospital I was taken care of. My contractions had become closer and closer together and I was screaming bloody murder after a few hours had past.

"Get me the drugs Asher or so help me god I won't ever let

you touch me." I seethed out grabbing him by the collar. He visibly gulped and nodded. As he was getting out the door when the doctor in charge of me walked in.

"I'm afraid Everleigh there won't be the time for the drugs." she went between my legs.

"Like I thought, you are fully detailed. Now, my dear, you will have to start pushing for me. When you feel a contraction coming on I want you to push do you understand Everleigh?"

She asked and I just nodded letting out a little whimper feeling the contraction coming.

"And push!" by that time two midwives and a nurse were in the room.

Asher had called everybody to the hospital yelling in the phone "SHIT IS GOING DOWN."

My breathing was erratic and sweat was dripping from my forehead as I was squeezing the hell out of Ash's hand, so much that it was turning purple. He was my rock and not once did he complain that I was screaming too loud or that I was holding his hand too tight.

"The baby is crowning! Would you like to see?" the doctor called out to Asher. He let go of my hand and took a step towards my feet to seek a peek. His face turned pale and he wobbled a bit.

"Are you feeling alright Mr. Mortimer?" the nurse asked.

"I feel a little light-headed." he admitted. I pushed again with all my might feeling like I might tear something.

"DON'T. YOU. *SCREAM* DARE. GO. SOFT. ON. ME. NOW. MORTIMER!" I screamed out pushing at the same time listening to what the doctor was asking me.

He nodded his head not wanting to upset me further.

That's right! Submit to me! I'm the one pushing a fucking little person that YOU implanted in me out of my vagina and I'm doing it like a boss!

My inner voice spoke up once more.

"Last one and you will be able to hold this little man in your arms. On Three. ONE. TWO and THREE. PUSH!"

I let out one last scream and was close to head-butting Asher unconscious till I heard that melodic sound.

"Congratulations! You have a beautiful baby boy!" the doctor said over the cries. Tears left my eyes, I feel too tired but I'm so glad that he is out and in good health. Asher cut the cord and came up to me.

"You did it Angel. He is finally here." Asher kissed the top of my head pushing the sweaty hairs off my face.

"Does mommy want to have the first cuddle with her baby?"

The midwife asked handing me my baby boy.

"He's so perfect." I sobbed out stroking his face and planting a kiss on his head.

"Just like his mother." Asher and I shared a long kiss full of love.

The midwife took him to clean him up and finish with all the necessary tests, giving me time to make myself a little more presentable and rest.

A few minutes later she steps back in with a baby cot and placed it next to my bed in the new room that they took me to.

"So what is the name of this little man?" she questioned looking at Asher and I. He nodded to me as I cradled my son in my arms.

"Wolfgang Oliver James Mortimer." I smiled down at him.

"Lovely. I'll leave you to meet your son." she smiled back at me and closed the door behind her.

Asher took a photo of me and Wolf to 'reenact' when he was first in my arms in the delivery room, me kissing our son's head holding him to my chest.

"Little Wolfgang Mortimer." Asher spoke so softly next to his son's ear. It was strange to see something so fragile and little in the buff arms of my gang leader.

I can't wait to show him off to everybody. My heart has been filled a little more with unconditional love.

CHAPTER FORTY-FIVE

Asher Mortimer:

It has been a few hours since my son had been born. I still cannot believe that he is here. Everleigh did absolutely amazing. I have no idea how women can do that, I mean to give birth. Leigh was like Wonder Woman with superhuman strength. I felt like she was going to break my hand because she was holding it so tight but that was the small pain I had to endure for all the pain she was in.

When I heard those first cries resonated in the room I felt as if I was a little more complete inside. After our first cuddle, I left Everleigh to sleep as the midwife from earlier took Wolf where the rest of the newborns were whilst Everleigh got her well-deserved rest.

I had called my mother and she was on the first flight over, Carter had gone to get Damon once his lessons were over, Paul was left in charge of the gang and would be over later, Louis was out on a mission and so I Asked Ray to bring Rose over when he had a minute since with his newborn son at home things were complicated.

I went out in the waiting area outside Everleigh's room to call her dad and Sergei.

"Hello." Sean picked up after three rings.

"Sean, its Asher."

"Is Everleigh ok? Are the kids ok? Has something happened?" he frantically asked over the phone.

"No, no. All if fine. Never better actually. I called to tell you that you are now the grandfather of a new grandson." I couldn't stop the smile that graced my lips as the line went silent.

"She gave birth?" he questioned shock laced his voice.

"Yes, A few hours ago. Both mother and child are doing well and I thought you would like to know." I turned around and saw that Ray had arrived with Rose tugging him along rushing towards me.

"I have to leave you Sean and congratulations." I called out once more.

"Congratulations to you my boy. I'm glad my daughter has found someone like you. Send my love, I'll be down at some point to meet my new grandson." after that the line went dead and a little bundle of blond curls came hurtling into my arms.

"Hello, my princess." I twirled her around and kissed the top of her head setting her down once more.

"Hey, you alright mate?" Ray can to me and gave me one of them Bro hugs.

"I can't believe he is finally here, he took his sweet time." I joked as he patted me on the back.

"I know what you mean. I still can't believe that I'm a dad now, me? Who would have thought?"

We both let out a laugh, out of all of us we thought it would have been Carter to be a father first but I was so that proved that theory wrong.

"How are Annie and Ryder doing?" I asked as we made our way to were the newborn babies were as we stood in front of the glass window, my eyes searching for my son.

"They are doing just fine. Annie is scared every time I take him in my arms says she's scared I'm going to drop him." I could definitely see Annie panic over that.

"Yeah I can imagine, I'm honestly scared too."

We both snapped out of our thoughts when I felt a tugging at my jeans to see the little girl that shared my eyes.

"Daddy? Uncle Ray said baby brother was here. I want to see him." she inquired making grabby hands for me to take her in my arms.

I picked her up and pointed to the baby in the third row with a baby blue beanie and cover.

"That's baby brother." I whispered in her ear.

She squealed and clapped her hands. Ray and I both laughed at her cuteness before a nurse came here to tell me that Everleigh had woken up and call calling for me, the nurse then stepped into the baby filled room to get my son and bring him to the room so that we could introduce him to family members visiting.

We all stepped into the room as Rose wiggled her way out of my arms and straight into her mother's.

"Hello, my sweet." the nurse left us and I bent over the cot and picked up our son making sure his head was well held and offered Ray to hold him. He cooed at the baby rocking him back and forth. He makes a great dad.

"So what did you name him in the end?" he turned to me seeing as the girls were engrossed in a conversation about Barbie dolls.

"Wolfgang Oliver James Mortimer." I stated proudly getting my son back into my arms cradling him to my chest. He left out a little whimper before falling back to sleep.

"Why that name?" Ray spoke.

"Wolves are great leaders when they are in a pack, well more like the Alpha is the leader and my son will become the leader and 'gang' means 'path' or 'journey'. Besides the holders of that name have been successful in their careers such as Mozart. That and Rose kept calling him Wolf when he was in the womb so it kind of stuck." I smiled at the memory.

"'A leader's path' nice, holds strength and meaning behind the name. We didn't think more than that on Ryder's name. Annie just blurted it out once he was set on her chest. I didn't have a say in his name picking at all even though we had discussed this many times. We had settled for Finn but she just changed her mind seeing him. And I must admit Ryder suits him better."

I nodded and handed Wolf over to his mother so that Rose could see him. She stayed calm as I placed her against Leigh and brought the baby down on her lap so that Everleigh could help Rose hold him correctly.

Soon after the rest of the family came into the room with balloon, gifts and flowers congratulating us on our new son. It was a waltz of different people coming in to greet the baby, many of my men had stopped me to congratulate us. At this moment I felt proud of all the things I had accomplished looking towards my family, my two sons, my daughter and my beautiful wife.
I am one hell of a lucky bastard.

****

Unknown pov:

"The child is born sir. Both are well and should be home tomorrow." my undercover spy spoke to me as I took the other puff of my cigar.

"What is your next move?" he asked not daring to look me

in the eye.

"We wait until the time is right, I am in no rush to get to him just yet. I want to play with his mind a little more to make things later on more... fun." I raised my cigar and took one last puff before sitting it down in the ashtray.

"You may leave now Louis." I waved my hand dismissively at him motioning him to leave my office.

"I got to him twice, I will get to him a third." I spoke my thoughts out loud. I turned to look at the single picture Frame that was sat on my desk.

I traced my finger over the woman I once loved and the child with the brightest blue eyes his mother and I gave him remembering all the memories they held in one single photograph. Smiles gracing their faces as the still young boy was standing held in his mother's arms.

Don't worry my son. Daddy will be home soon, very soon...

CHAPTER FORTY-SIX

Everleigh:

Coming home with this newborn baby was one hell of an adventure. I had to teach Asher all there was to know about taking care of a newborn child and I must say it was very funny the faces he pulled when changing our child's nappies after he did a number two.

But we have successfully managed to keep this little human alive for a full five months and going strong. Rose's birthday flew by as well as Asher's. I can't believe my baby girl is now four years old! She will be starting school in September. Damon and Rose no longer have nightmares and have been absolutely adorable with Wolf.

Damon is taking his big brother role very seriously and has been guarding Wolf's room when he sleeps and won't let people come too close.

I was glad that Asher took a break from the gang when the baby was born because I do not think I could have done it by myself a second time, especially with two more kids then when I had Rose. Clair stayed a little after his birth because I was super sore down under and I was on bed rest for two weeks and Asher still had to sort out details with the gang at that time.

I spend most of my days with Annie as we have constant play dates with both of our new baby boys and both of them have grown so much, it's crazy.

Wolf looks just like his dad but with my blond curly hair and my green eyes. He's a very smiley baby and has just started doing his nights and I thank the lord for that because he wasn't doing them until recently and I needed the sleep.

"Hello, my baby." I cooed walking into his nursery seeing as he had woken up from his nap. I took him in my arms and placed him on my hip bending down to retrieve the soft toy that I got from my big kids at the baby shower.

I changed his nappy and sat on the rocking chair by his window and started breastfeeding him slowly rocking back and forth.

"What a sight. It never gets old." I looked up and smiled at Asher who had just stepped into the room leaning against the door frame.

"Well, I see that Daddy has also woken up from his nap." I giggle looking at my famished son.

"I wish I was in his spot." Asher spoke in a husky voice stalking towards me like I were his pray.

"Mmm I'm sure you do but no touching me for the moment so you will have to keep it in your pants, Mr. Mortimer." I told him out of breath as he started kissing my neck.

"I have a baby in my arms." I spoke softly as his kisses went down to my exposed breast.

He kissed the top of Wolf's head then kissed my lips grabbing a chair and placing it next to me.

"I actually came to talk to you about something." I hummed in response burping our son that had finished eating.

"I know that our wedding wasn't what you had dreamed of." I was shocked by his statement.

"It was all I could hope for, I got to marry you and if I remember correctly I asked to get married in such a rush." he took my hand that wasn't holding our son and kissed my knuckles.

"I know, but I know that it's not the wedding you had dreamed of. The December wedding under the Australian summer sun."

"H-how do you know about that?" I asked bewildered.

"I overheard you and Annie talk about it the other day." he rubbed the back of his neck.

I stood up and placed Wolf on his play mat for a bit of tummy time before taking a seat on the floor by him soon followed by Asher sitting behind me.

"Where are you going with this Ash?"

"Well I might of, I don't know, made 'save the date' as well as invitations for our proper wedding that will be on your birthday In December like you wished for and of course back in Australia." he gave me a cheeky grin.

"No, you didn't! You didn't! Tell me this is a joke, Asher!" I poked his chest my voice getting higher pitched.

He just nodded showing me the piece of paper he had hidden in his back pocket. My eyes scanned the invitation placed in my hands.

It was a simple card paper with gold embellishments around the edges and the calligraphy was gorgeous.

You are cordially invited to the union of
Asher Mortimer and Everleigh Graham in holy matrimony.
The 19th of December of this year.
At a venue in Sydney Australia.

I squealed and jumped into his arms resulting in knocking him down on the floor and me attacking him in kisses all over his face.

"I love you so much but you didn't have to do that." I exclaimed pulling the both of us back into a sitting position. He just shrugged.

"I just want this to be perfect and you have the wedding of your dreams fits into that. Everything is up to you, go nuts the sky's the limit." he pointed his hand at the ceiling to prove his point.

"You really don't have to do all that to make me happy you know. I have more than enough in my life to be happy. Just having you by my side and my kids are all I need to feel complete. You really don't have to organise my dream wedding." I intertwined our hands together getting lost in that ocean of blue that were his eyes.

"You know what they say 'happy wife happy life'." he joked.

"Besides, I already sent the invites so it's too late to stop now." I scoffed and hit his chest.

"Asher!" he simply laughed at me and kissed me once more before standing up and heading to the door.

"Might want to get started, you have a dress shopping appointment this afternoon and after that, we have one with the baker to pick out the cake. Only another five months before the big day!" with that he left me stunned in my spot on the floor, the only noises were the gurgling sounds of our son happily discovering how to roll on his side.

That man will be the death of me.

CHAPTER FORTY-SEVEN

Everleigh:

Those five months have flown by in the blink of an eye. I can't believe that in a few hours I will wed the man I have fallen madly in love with for the second time. Our 'first' wedding anniversary came and went and we spent it just the two of us in a hotel for a whole weekend, no kids, no work, nobody to come disturb us. It was pure bliss. And well let's say that we were very busy with each other during that time *cough, cough*.

Anyway I'm currently sitting in a bathrobe as Annie went to fetch my wedding dress down in her room because she is my maid of honour and I didn't want Asher stumbling across my wedding dress so in the meantime I'm just playing with Rose and our hair curlers sitting by the vanity whilst my bridal cortege get their hair and makeup done since I was the first one to be placed in their magical hands, what was left was my dress and get the curlers out.

"I have the dress!" Annie entered holding the bag with today's outfit. She hung the dress on the bathroom door and asked me to get out of my silk robe. After having Wolf I sort of got my post baby body back which I was pleased about.

She took the dress out and held it as I slipped into it. A few gasps and 'wow' travelled around the room. I stepped in front of the mirror taking in my image running my hands down the smooth fabric of my skirt.

It was a 'V' neck centred at the waist with a transparent lace back with lace details all along the bottom of the skirt. The fabric was light because of the heat outside and the fact that we were having a beach wedding.

"You look stunning my dear." Clair came up behind me tears glistening in her eyes.

"Thank you." I turned to hug her. Once we pulled away she handed me a red velvet box that seemed a bit old.

"What's this?" I asked opening the box. I gasped placing a hand over my mouth then taking the fragile piece of jewellery out of its box.

"It's beautiful." I whispered admiring its beauty. It was a simple pendant placed on a silver chain. The pendant in itself-was a silver heart with a deep blue sapphire in the centre and on the back was engraved 'love always.'

"It was my great-great grandmother's necklace. She wore it for her wedding and her daughter after her, and her daughter after her till it came to me and I wore it to my wedding but since – as you know– I had a son I want you to wear it. You are my daughter now." I let a tear escape my eye as she told me the story behind the necklace. She took it from my hands.

"Here allow me." she placed the delicate jewels on my neck

and closed the clasp when she was done then placing my hair over the back.

"You needed something old, borrowed and blue. So here it is." I played with the pendent placing it nicely on my chest.

"Thank you, Clair." I hugged her again.

"Alright, ladies! Gather round to take your flowers it's showtime!" Annie exclaimed directing everybody down the stairs, out of the hotel and down the beach.

I took one last look at all my bridesmaids who were in a light pink flowing bridesmaid dress with a top in lace to remind my dress. The colours were blush/ light pink.

Rose was in a dress of the same colour with a flower crown and a little bouquet in her hands. Her dress had a little more going on, she chose it and I liked it so that's what she is having after many temper tantrums, tears and screams.

The boys all had matching pink ties with white or pink roses on their boutonnieres, white shirts, suspenders and light brown suit pants giving them a vintage type look.
My dad walked up to me as the rest started walking in front of me when the music started.

"You ready princess?" he asked pulling away from our hug and taking my arm under his.

"Never been more ready in my life." we stood out from behind the bridal car and walked towards the beach where there was a white carpet rolled out for me to walk on.

All that was running in my mind was don't trip, don't trip. But when I saw the look that Asher had and the smile that graced his lips as I walked down I knew that I made the right choice by choosing him in my life. My dad gave me away giving me a kiss on my cheek before taking his seat next to Asher's mum.

"Dearly beloved. We are gathered here today—" I tuned out the priest that was marrying us as just stared into my husband's eyes. So many emotions were running in them as were mine and the more prominent one was love.

"You may kiss the bride." after we exchanged our vows and rings once again Asher literally swooped me off my feet in an amazing kiss. Just like the first time, cheers erupted all around us as a new song played when we walked back up the aisle rose petals being thrown over us.

We all met up at our dinner venue that had a great view, it was in a luxurious hotel. We put the little ones for a nap in one of the hotel rooms and hired a nanny for the event to watch them once the wedding pictures were over.
During one of the shots, Asher leaned down to whisper in my ear.

"So does this match the dreams you had about our wedding?"

"It's even better than my dreams. I love you." he said it back before we got knocked back to reality by the photographer yelling 'next'.

CHAPTER FORTY-EIGHT

Everleigh:

This day couldn't get any better. I finally got my dream wedding, marrying the man I love not once but twice. Granted the first time I wore a dress out of Target and there was only very close relatives. Now I have the great big wedding in my country under the Australian summer sun. The ceremony was breathtaking and now we were all sat around the table for the evening meal.

To my right was my handsome husband and next to him was Clair. To my left was my dad. Sergei was at a table in the front row. The kids were on a separate table with the hired nanny. Next to my dad was Annie and Ray. Next to Clair was Carter and Paul.

We had arrived at the last dish. The never leaving smile that graced my lips was soon replaced by a look of panic. Gunshots rang in the air as I saw all my "none gang-related" guests, as well as the staff, take shelter under the tables around the room. I'm glad I'm the daughter and wife of Gang leaders as well as the goddaughter of a Mafioso because at least we were armed.

All Asher's men, as well as my dad's and Sergei's that were invited or on duty, pulled out their guns.

Clair, Annie and I rushed to the children followed by Ray who ran to us taking the kids to a safe place. I shoved my shoes off and pulled the skirt of my dress up.

I knew I did right putting a handgun in my garter.

I went back into the room making sure no one was there to point a gun at my head. I rushed to my husband's side nodding to tell him that the kids were safe. Bullets were flying across the room as is a symphony was playing.

"Where the hell did they come from?" I yelled over the fires.

"I don't know angel but they are shooting left and right. Some went down." he stood up from behind the turned tables to shoot some more.

"Hey, Ash? How many ammo do you have left?" Carter asked.

"Half a strip left, you?"

"One bullet left." Carter said back.

I rolled my eyes. *Men! Never prepared.*

I shoved my hand down my cleavage and pulled out three strips full and gave one to each one of us, then I lifted my skirt I got another strip out and threw it to Paul that was further down the row of tables.

"Have you boys got enough?" both of them looked at me their faces full of shock before Asher's turned into a smirk.

317

"That's why I married you." he kissed me before adding:

"If I would have known you hid them there you could have asked me to get them out of there." he gave me a cocky smile and ran his eyes up and down my body.

There was a loud bang.

Did something just explode? As in a bomb? Screams followed as well as more gunshots and sure enough, there was now a sky view at the opposite end of the room where there wasn't one before.

"We need to move. NOW!" Asher roared taking me by the hand and dragging me. But in the process Asher's great-great-great-great grandmother's necklace fell off, landing on the ground when we arrived in the corridor.

"Asher stop." I stopped and let go of his hand placing it on my chest where the pendant once laid.

"The necklace." I dropped to my knees in search of it.

"Leigh. We need to go right now. Leave it." he tried getting me off the ground but I didn't budge.

"No. It means a lot to me and more importantly to your mother. It's a family heirloom and I'd be damned to be the one who loses it. So I'm not leaving before I get it back." I stubbornly said.
The gunshots were coming closer.

"Got it!" I exclaimed running off again.

"Well, well, well. What do we have here?"

Asher and I bumped into a very familiar looking man. He was a man advanced in age, to say the least, grey hair and a light beard. He had a gun pointed at us just as Asher did to him.
I had dropped my gun in all the commotion. This man had bright blue eyes. Blue staring into blue.

"What do you want dad?" Asher growled out.

And that's when it clicked. The man seemed familiar because he and my husband shared the same facial features and those eyes.

"I just wanted to meet my daughter in law but apparently I wasn't invited to the wedding. So I took matters into my own hands."

Neither of them put their guns down. I stayed behind Ash not wanting to get in the middle of a family feud.

"Don't you like the little gift I got you? It's as close as I got to fireworks." Asher's dad piped up. He never spoke of his father and now I know why the hell why. This guy is crazy.

Something in me snapped after his words.

"You did this? What kind of sick freak does something like this on someone's wedding day especially when it's your son's"'' by that point, I was no longer behind Ash but coming straight up to his dad.

"Angel, get behind me." Asher called out gently not breaking eye contact with his father.

This, however, got me distracted and gave the opportunity for his father to grab me and put me in a headlock pointing his gun to my temple.

"Quite a feisty little thing you have there. Your mother was much more obedient." I tried taking his arm away from my neck with no luck. Asher cocked his gun and took a step forward.

"Ah, ah, ah. It would be a shame to stain this lovely white gown." Asher stopped straight in his tracks understanding what his father meant by that.

"What makes you think that I'm not going to shoot you?" Asher cocked his eyebrow matching his father's look.

Not the time to be comparing the two of them! My brain yelled at me.

Asher pulled the trigger but no bullet came out, he was dry.

"Seems like you lose once again son." before he could do anything a shot rang out and I swear you could see the bullet fly next to my head in slow motion like in action movies.

"Sergei." I breathed out. Ash's dad lost his balance giving me the chance to get out of his grip and back into my husband's arms.

"Go you two, I got him." Sergei's thick accent rang in my ears as Ash and I ran in the opposite direction.

I know I shouldn't have turned my head when I heard the gunshots but I couldn't help it.
There I saw, Sergei on the ground blood quickly oozing out of his body.
Things seemed to have stopped in time. I didn't even hear my own screams, they seemed like distant echoes. I rushed back to his side. Asher's dad had made a run for it as more of my dad's men had come to help.

"Papa." tears were streaming down my cheeks as I put his head on my lap trying to stop the blood flowing out of his bullet wounds getting my hands covered in his blood not caring that my immaculate white dress was getting stained too.

"You can't leave me. I still need you with me." I said to him. Sergei's response was giving me a smile I haven't seen since I was just a little girl playing with his daughter.

He cupped my cheek with his bloodied hand. Tears at the corner of his eyes.

Never had I ever seen this man cry.

"I'm so very proud of you my snowdrop. I always will be. Take care of that little princess of yours and those princes. I love you." I smiled as he whipped my tears away, nodding at his demands. Asher just stood there not quite knowing what to do.

"Don't be sad for me, little one. I will soon be with my beautiful wife and daughter. Galiana and Victoria. It's yours now." he reached in for his left hand and took off his Russian mafia signet ring and placed it in the palm of my hand before folding my fingers over it.

"I'm glad I could save you. And I'm glad that you are the one to take my place." he coughed up blood a little more before exhaling one last time.

"Sergei? Sergei?!" I called out until his breathing stopped for good.

My world just crumbled to pieces.

"NOOOOOOOOO!" I yelled shaking him by the shoulders. I continued yelling till I felt a presence behind me.

"Everleigh, angel. Stop. It's over, he's gone." Asher shut Sergei's eyes before engulfing me in a hug.

I shook my head in disbelief before the dam broke and I let grief take over.

CHAPTER FORTY-NINE

Everleigh:

I stood under the snow in the cold. Holding my son on my hip holding the hand of my other son as my husband has our daughter in his arms. The funeral car started as we followed. I was leading the crowd that had come for his funeral. I was in a black dress, black tights with a long black coat and a black veil to crown my hair that was in a simple low bun at the base of my neck.

The walk to the graveyard was long and the cold of the Russian winter was getting the best of all of us. Once we had arrived at cemetery all of Sergei's men that were now under my command scattered around and made sure all was safe before we stepped on the grounds.

"You alright Angel?" Asher's deep voice rang out next to my ear. I nodded readjusting Wolf on my hip not looking into his eyes and thank god he didn't push further.

We all sat down in our allocated seats, my kids, Asher, my dad and myself were in the first row as the rest were filled in by other people close to my godfather.

The priest started the ceremony and poor guy looked like we were about to shit himself looking around all the men in black fully armed that surrounded him.

Soon enough the body was brought to the ground as there were a few weeps from his ex-wives and other mistresses. I placed my son on my father's lap before stepping forward to start with the mud-dumping that you do at funerals over the casket once it is brought to the ground.

As I took the shovel, the ring he gave me before he took his last breath stood out on my hand. The bulky ring with his initials engraved on it took its toll on me, it didn't fit right.

"I can't do it."

I had kept a brave face on all week, all the fucking week were I had to organise his funeral, be introduced as the new leader, go back to god damn Russia, a place I haven't step foot since I was thirteen!

"He can't be gone I don't allow it!" I yelled letting the tears I was holding in slip from my eyes.

Asher stood up from his chair and made his way towards me and stood me up wrapping his coat around my shoulders. I hadn't even realised that I was sat in the cold wet snow.

"Shhh Angel, I'm here. I'm here." he held me closer in his arms.

"Let me help you."

He whispered in my ear letting his warm breath fan my neck. I nodded as he turned us around to pick the shovel back up. Asher placed his hands over mine keeping his face cold in front of all these gang leaders.

Once I did the first scoop of dirt Asher lead me back to my seat shielding me from the distasteful looks I received from the other men.

"Weak." one of them muttered making me pull my face further into my husband's chest.

Once everyone took their turns we headed off to Sergei's place on the outskirts of Moscow. My father informed the guests that there would be a buffet at the house with refreshments.

Once I stepped foot into the house I took Wolf back into my arms and went straight to the room where the kids were sleeping for the past couple of days. I put him in the travel cot for his nap after feeding him and changing him.

I watched my son fall asleep in the blink of an eye.

"Angel?" his voice was so soft as if, if he spoke any louder he could break me.

I turned to Asher and walked out of the room closing the door gently behind me.

"The guests are downstairs. We are waiting for you to start things off." he brushed a stray hair out of my face, cupping my cheek.

The day dragged on and tomorrow all his will be behind me.

I can't let this grief be my downfall I have to be strong not only for my kids, for Sergei, for this mafia but most importantly I need to be strong for me.

No more harmless Everleigh, Gang leader Everleigh needs to take the lead.

A new week went by and we are still in Russia, Christmas is this weekend and I just couldn't leave right now I had too many things to handle.

I had passed the stage of denial and depression, I was full of anger. I was so angry with everything and everyone. I was angry with Sergei, I was angry with Asher's dad, I was angry with myself, I was angry at the universe for everything bad that has ever happened to me. Ben and Victoria's death, Sergei's death, having the devils spawn as a mother all my life, dating Dan and letting my daughter be in that environment. And the only way I could let off some steam was sex and I was more than happy to oblige to my husband's every need and desire.

After our last round, I turned to see the time.

"Shit!" I mumble under my breath.

"What is it, babe?"

Damn Asher's morning voice is super sexy.

"I have a meeting with Sergei's alliances in about an hour." I groaned rolling back under the covers.

"We still have time for one more round don't we?" Asher started kissing up my arm across my collarbone and back down my exposed chest not stopping until he reached what he wanted down south.

"Mm Asher we need to stop, this meeting is important."

"Ok fine quickly." I caved to my man's touch.

Once I managed to get out of my husband's grip I shoved a tight black dress, my signature heels and blood red lipstick.

"Hello, gentlemen." I greeted once I stepped into the conference room where all around the table where the most influential and most wanted men of the world were seated.

"You are late." one of them spoke up. I smirked and looked his way.

"Until proven wrong, this is my territory now and you are simple trespassers. I'm directing this meeting, therefore, I am not late, I'm just on time." he grumbled under his breath something along the lines of 'bitch' but I didn't want to make my move just yet.

"Let's start shall we?" I leaned back in my chair making deals with other leaders, signing contracts and so on till it was time for me to make a deal with the same man that told me I was late.

"I'm not making a contract with you Ms. Graham."

"It's Mrs. Mortimer." I snapped.

"And why so?"

I enquired leaning back into my seat playing with the blade of the knife Sergei gave me the day he told me I was his successor.

"You are weak and a pathetic excuse of a leader. Women shouldn't be assigned this post and you will bring this mafia to its destruction it's only a matter of time." he spoke with so much venom in his voice pointing in my direction.

"Well then that means that you want war Mr. Romwe, and well I'll be more than glad to give it to you. And lord only knows that I never lose."

My voice was dangerously low as I glared at him. The rest of the men around the table we holding their breaths as the man that was standing up against me spoke up.

"I don't think you will." he cockily added.

"Well, that's where you are wrong. You see I wasn't chosen at random to be in the seat I am today. Mr. Romanov didn't just pick me for my pretty face and my reputation. I am the daughter of Sean Graham, the wife of Asher Mortimer. And if those men don't ring a bell you might also know me as Shadow. Need I to go on?" the more information I was throwing his way the more he seemed to back down in his seat.

" I don't like to be underestimated by some arrogant fuck boy that was handed his spot by daddy dearest." before he could say anything else I threw my knife and it landed right between his two eyes.

Mama still got it! My brain cheered. Seems like I haven't lost my touch.

"Now." I laced my fingers together sitting forward.

"Anybody else, want to add something?" silence filled the room, I smiled at that.

"Good. Someone clean this mess I don't want to stain the carpets."

Shadow is back and she is not getting pushed around anymore.

CHAPTER FIFTY

Asher Mortimer:

Since we have been back from Russia my mind has been all over the place. So many things have happened in the last few weeks and it's like nothing ever stops.
The wedding, Sergei's death, my father coming back, Sergei's funeral, Everleigh becoming the new head of the Russian mafia, Christmas, Wolf's first birthday and now all the added stress that comes with coming back home and handling gang matters that I set aside for the darn wedding and all the events that followed.

I don't begrudge having my wedding with the woman I love in her home country but I was away for two months and that is not something that goes unnoticed in our world. A new gang has set up and is starting to get a little cocky and intruding on my territory. Everleigh has been having mood swings. One minute she is loving, the next she is crying or extremely mad and wants to rip all of our heads off.

Her way of grieving is:
 1: having wild sex (not that I mind)
 2: is to spend her time, when we aren't in bed, working.
As in gang work or taking care of the kids. The last few weeks I have been spending more time at the warehouse office then at home and I feel as if Everleigh needs the space and I need it too.

"Hey, boss. Some of the guys and I are heading to the club for a few drinks to cool off after the mission. You want to come?" one of my men came into my office after knocking.

A beer or two wouldn't hurt, besides if it's to come back to an angry wife might as well drink some liquid courage so that I can make it to the next day.

"Sure. Let me finish this up and we can head off." I typed on my laptop and signed a few more papers making sure that all as in order before we head out.

One at the club and my second beer my phone rang. I looked at the caller ID and I saw that it was Leigh.

"Hey, man tonight no phones." one of my gunmen called out handing me a new beer. I ignored the call and took a swig of my beer looking at the time. Eleven pm. I shrugged it off and continued the night relaxing.

The drinks continued to be handed my way and the more they came the stronger they became and next thing you know I was drinking shots off the stomach of some random chick that had arrived to drink with us.

"Hey man, I think you have had enough. Might want to go home now." Carter, of course, had to be a buzzkill and pulled me away from the girl.

"Naahhhh mate! I'm fine! I want to drink some more." I slurred on a few words but the disappointed look on Carter's face was clear.

"Ash I think it's time for you to stop." he sternly said, which got me mad.

"I'm the boss here." I snapped and then there was a hand placed on my shoulder.

"Hey, Carter leave him. He's a grown ass man and if he wants to still drink then let him." Louis came to my rescue and now that I think about it he was the one to pass me my drinks.

"Fine but you make sure he gets home safe and remember we have a meeting tomorrow and it's already two am so you all might want to head home now." Carter was a good friend, a little too good but I do what the fuck I want.

Louis pulled me back to the bar and so the night went on.

****

Everleigh:

I was glad to be back home, back in my bed, my house surrounded by familiar things. I've been doing better since we came back but I haven't seen a lot of my husband. I've been taking care of my kids and the house and of other little details all while making sure that my right-hand man was following my orders back in Russia.

I had just put the kids to bed. And Asher still hasn't home which was a little weird because it was our belated

Valentine's day and he said that he would be back in time to put the kids to bed. Rose was in tears when she saw that her daddy still hasn't come home yet and it just broke my heart.

I remember when I was her age I always wanted my dad to be there to wish me a goodnight and read me a bedtime story. We are daddy's girls we can't help it.

I rang his office. *No answer.*

I rang his phone. *No answer.*

I tried several times and left a few messages, but still nothing.
My heart started racing and my mind just went loopy.

Was he dead?

Was he hurt?

Did he just run out of battery?

Was he busy with work that he didn't hear his phone?

Was he cheating on me?

Or was he simply ignoring me?

Rational and irrational thoughts were jumping back and forth and none of them were putting me at ease. I waited for a little as I thought he might have been driving home or something but still nothing.

Midnight struck and my nerves were still on edge. The dinner that I had prepared for our Valentine's dinner was long cold and at this moment I was just praying that he was alright. I had called Paul but he told me that he was on a trade so that meant that he didn't know.

I called Carter and he told me that he was going to go search for him.

My phone rang making me jump and answer it.

"Asher?" I called with hope in my voice.

"It's Carter." I sat back down and couldn't help but frown.

"Oh, it's you. Sorry, I thought that he was calling me." my voice broke at the end. I heard him sigh on the other end.

"I know where he is but he is drunk and is hell-bent on staying at the club and Louis isn't helping matters here." I ran a hand over my face.

"Thank you, Carter, at least I know that he isn't dead in a ditch somewhere."

"Yeah. Right good night."

"Night."

After that, I hung up and sat looking into space.

Why is he at the club drinking? Not that I mind him having a little fun now and then but he could of at least called me and tell me that he was fine and just out with friends.

I have lost enough loved ones, I can't lose him too.

I didn't realise that I had fallen asleep on the sofa till I heard the jingle of keys in the lock. I sat up and glanced at the clock.
I waited till he stepped in and turned the lights on startling him.

"Where were you?" I asked crossing my arms over my chest. He froze then turned.

"You still up?"

"Yes, I'm still up when your husband doesn't have the decency to call you to tell you where he is and just waltz in at three in the morning like nothing has happened!" I stood up flinging my arms in the air.

"Do you know how worried I was Asher? I thought something bad had happened to you. I- I thought you were dead." I whispered the last part for only for myself to hear.

"Well I'm here now aren't I so drop it. I'm going to bed." he tried to walk past me but failed.

"Not until you tell me where the fuck you were and why you didn't tell me." He looked pissed but he owed me at least that.

"You don't need to know now leave me the fuck alone!" he roared sending me a few steps back. Tears pricked my eyes. He had never raised his voice at me ever.

"You want to know why I didn't tell you where I was. Well, I just wanted a fucking break from you, from this house. You have been all up my arse lately and I have had enough! I have enough shit to deal with and I don't need you and your fucking temper added on top of that."

I was shocked by his words. Am I really that annoying that he needs to be away from me?

"That still doesn't tell me where you were." I know I'm pushing and that I should tell him to talk to me about his feeling but I know that he won't do that.

"I was at the office." he said nonchalantly.

"You have the nerve to lie to me and just shrug it off like it was nothing? I know you were at the bar drinking."

"Then why the fuck are you asking me where I was if you knew?" his voice got louder and I was scared that he was going to wake the kids up.

"Because I wanted to see if you were going, to be honest with me and clearly I was wrong. I've been waiting for you to come back home for eight hours! Eight bloody hours and I had no news, no way of contact with you and you don't even seem to be fazed by it." I said flabbergasted.

"Rose was crying her eyes out calling for her daddy to be back because he had promised her to come back and you couldn't even hold your promise to a four-year-old. Does that mean that the promises we made on our wedding day are just lies too?" I know I took things further than they needed to be but I can't help but think that.

Tears were falling from my eyes. I locked my gaze on his and saw hurt, guilt and anger flash in his eyes. In a flash, I was pinned to the wall by my neck by Asher.

My eyes widened at his action.

"Don't you ever say that I was lying about my vows. I don't lie about things like that!" He growled holding my neck tighter.

"A-Asher let go. I- can't – breathe." I could feel myself go as I got less and less oxygen flowing through me.

"Daddy?" a sweet little voice called out in the silent room. *Rose.*

I can't let her see me like this, much less her father being the one doing this to me. He realised what he was doing and let go of his hold lending me to fall to the ground in a coughing fit.

I looked up to see Asher walking up to Rose, but too late she saw and tears were in her eyes.

"Hey princess what are you doing out of bed?" he cooed.

Bipolar much?

She backed away from him in fear clutching her teddy closer to her chest. Even if Asher's back was to me I could only imagine the look of hurt in his crystal blue eyes.
She ran up the stairs screaming waking up her baby brother on the way. Asher knelt down next to me.

"Baby I'm so, so sorry. Are you alright? I'm so sorry. I don't know what came over me, I–" I put my hand out to stop him talking any further and to keep some space between us.

At this moment I knew what I had to do.

 I need to take my kids far from here for a while, because if he is capable of doing that to me then I don't want my kids to be in the way of his wrath. At least until he calms down and maybe leaving him by himself will teach him a lesson.

I stood up and headed to our room. I grabbed a bag and started shoving clothes in it for me.

"Baby what are you doing?" he called out panicked at the door but I just ignored him, shaking off the sound of brokenness in his voice.

I zipped that bag up and went off to Damon's room softly waking him up and getting a bag for him as well as a couple toys. I did the same for all my kids and went downstairs to find a very broken down Ash on the sofa hunched over and running his hands through his hair.

Baby on my hip, bags in hand I asked Damo to grab the car keys and start to get in and take a very tired and sad Rose with him.

"Everleigh Angel, don't leave please don't leave. I'm sorry. I'm so sorry. I'm drunk, I couldn't control my actions. It won't ever happen again, I promise. I love you don't leave me." Asher was holding gently on my hips bringing me closer to his body and placed his forehead on mine.

"Please." he breathed out but the stench of alcohol was still there reminding me why I'm leaving in the first place.

"I can't. I love you but I can't stay with you like that. Goodbye Asher." I detached myself from him and headed to the car after strapping all the kids in and myself.

As I drove off I gave one last look at the house seeing Asher on his knees, and what appeared to me as tears running down his face matching mine.

I glanced at the mirror to see my kids sound asleep once more and I knew that I had made the right decision in leaving.

CHAPTER FIFTY-ONE

Everleigh:

I drove straight to the place where I know that I can stay and be safe from Asher but not super far away either. I had stopped crying and started to focus on the task before I was to drive safely till I arrived at my destination.

I stopped the car in their driveway and I was sure that when I sent her the message that she would go and kill him but I just really needed a friend right now. I stepped out the car locking the sleeping kids in as I marched to the front door. Before I could knock it was ripped open by none other than Annie.
I opened and closed my mouth like a goldfish before she swooped me into her arms and I just broke down once more.

"Sshhhh... Leigh shhh. It's alright. I'm sure he didn't mean it. Let me get Ray and we will bring the kids and your bags up, mmm kay?" she ran her hand through my hair soothingly as she spoke in a calming voice.

I nodded in her chest then pulled away and went to the car grabbing two bags and Rose. Soon after Ray and Annie appeared again and Annie took another bag and Wolf as Ray took Damon. After setting the kids in one of the many guest rooms they have in their big but not too big house, we headed downstairs for a little talk.

"Tell me exactly what happened babe." both Annie and I sat with my legs under me on the big sofa as Ray sat behind Annie.

"Yeah so that I can beat the shit out of him when I see him." Ray pointed out letting a small laugh escape my lips.

"Before I start I want to thank the both of you. I know it's really late and uncalled for but I just... I just needed to get away and I didn't know where else to go." I single tear left my eye. I felt really blessed to have friends like them in my life.

"I'm glad you came to us. And remember our door is always open for you. Now tell us what happened."

Annie's voice was very soft and caring, not wanting to shake me up too much. I took a deep breath and told them what happened in fine detail, well as best as I could and I was surprised they got half of it because of my constant hiccups and cries.
By the time I was finished I was cradled in Annie's arms as Ray was saying that he was going to kill Asher for what he did to me.

"Don't be daft Ray." Annie commented seeing her boyfriend pace around the room plotting the murder in his mind, silently maybe too silently.

"What are you thinking about Rayray?" I inquired knowing the nickname would tick him off.

"I can't tell you." he simply said.

"Why not?" I questioned.

"Simple, I can't plan a murder out loud." he shrugged his shoulder earning a smile from me. The happy couple returned that smile making me miss the feeling of being happy with them.

"Well, we might as well get some sleep now folks before the kids wake up and run around like they are high on something." we all let out a chuckle before heading our separate ways.

I woke up the next morning in a cold unfamiliar bed. I turned to the side to look at the time. I decided it was time to wake up and face the day and see what it had in store for me.

I stepped into the connected bathroom and wincing at the sight that greeted me in the mirror. I gasped seeing the prominent bruises on my neck, you could clearly make out the hand print. I let the tears roll down my face as I sat on the cold tiled floor.

The harder I cried the more I felt nauseous, and sure enough I spilt my guts out, luckily I sat down next to the toilets so I didn't make a mess of myself. After that, I stood up, took a shower, got dressed in some joggings and one of Ash's hoodies that I stole when leaving, brushed my teeth and sorted out my hair and face leaving it bare, with my hair in a

French braid.

I walked down the stairs still feeling a little light headed and I put that on the fact that I had hardly slept and that I threw up first thing this morning and probably as well that I didn't eat since four o'clock the day before.
I was greeted with the smell of something good cooking and the noises of chatter coming from the kitchen.

"Mummy!" Damon yelled and ran straight into my arms giving me a hug that I gladly gave back.

"Good morning my love. Sleep well?" I brushed the messy boy's hair looking lovingly into his chocolate brown eyes thinking back to the day I had saved him.

"Very good mummy and you?" Such a sweet boy, I smiled.

"It was ok." he nodded before heading back to his seat at the table as I kissed my children's heads as well as Ryder, Annie and Ray's son.

"Morning babes!" Annie hugged me followed by Ray moments later.

I sat down drinking my cup of tea still feeling a little sick. The kids soon finished eating and went to the living room with Ray to watch a morning cartoon before getting ready to play. I loved these relaxed mornings when nobody is in a rush and you can just snuggle up with the kids.

"How are you feeling this morning?" Annie shook me out of

my dreams talking a seat in front of me at the table, she too sipping on her cup.

"Honestly?" I sighed.

"I feel like shit, I look like shit. Even threw up this morning and I still feel sick to my stomach." I pulled the hoodie neck down to show her the bruises.

"I even have those." she gave me the same reaction as I did this morning.

"Ohh Everleigh... I'm so sorry. I'm going to go rip his balls and torture him till he begs for forgiveness." she spoke softly at first but her evil side turned up at the end.

"I think I just need a few days to cool off and think things through, you know? And we both need our space to think. I mean I lost my godfather and became head of a mafia overnight and his dad is back. I know he never spoke of his father as I never poke about my mother and now I can see why but I don't want to push it. I love him and I can't see myself without him. I just can't." I sighed once more whipping away the stray tears that left my eyes.

"I understand and we will–" but Annie couldn't finish her sentence as yells were heard by the front door. We looked at each other before seeing what all the commotion was about.

"Leave this fucking house Asher you are not welcome here, not after what you did to my sister!"

Ray yelled at a very beaten up Asher. I took a good look at my husband. His skin didn't have the glow it once had, his eyes carried bags under them and he lost that sparkle that once lived in his crystal blue orbs that were now all red and puffy.

"Please, I need to see her. I need to talk to her. I want her back." he pleaded. I had never seen him like this, so, so... broken.
Ray was about to speak again when I cut him placing my hand on his shoulder letting him know I was there.

"Go home, Asher." I said I voice blank of any emotion. His eyes met mine for a brief moment and they lit up seeing me but soon became full of sadness seeing the way I looked.

"Angel."

He breathed out like I was the water he needed in the desert. He was about to come and hug me but I stopped him not letting him get any closer because I would just forgive him straight away and melt in his embrace, he needed to learn his lesson as much as it killed me.

"Just go home." I said again.

"No Angel, I need you back. I regret everything. My actions, my words, my choices that night. I wish I could turn back the clock and choose differently. I love you baby and I can't live without you or the kids." I was doing my best to hold back the tears that were threatening to escape.

"I can't do this right Now Ash... I really can't. I need time to think and I think you do too. We both need a break from each other. I love you, I really do but you need to learn from your mistakes and for that, you need to focus on getting the stress out of the way, that being gang business then we can work on our relationship. Not before." my voice was so low I was surprised that he could hear me as I found it hard to hear me myself.

He gulped and I saw his fists clench and unclench.

"You need to work on the anger issues and the drinking. You never drank that much and I think it might have had an impact on what happened." I spoke again not daring to meet his eyes.

"Okay." he whispered. I lock eyes with him before he continued.

"I will do what you said. I will leave you your space, and you mine. I will go to rehab and anger management classes if that's what it takes. I want you back and I will prove to you that when we spoke our vows that I meant them, I will prove you that I am the best father I can be for my children and future children to come, I will prove to you that I am worthy of you and my children. I love you more than life itself and I would walk a thousand miles, run through a brick wall, burn in the flames or drown in the sea If it meant that I could get back to you."

I let my tears fall a little but I was quick to make them disappear. He bent down to pick up something off the floor.

He handed it over to me and to my surprise it was a white rose with the tip of its petals in a faded pink. I took the flower from his hand, our hands touching for a brief moment before they were no longer. I already miss the warmth of them.

"It's a rose from the garden. I picked it this morning as I know you love to smell them and pick out your favourite. That one was my favourite because it's unique beauty reminded me of you." I inspected the rose letting its petals glisten in the morning sun.

Before I could thank him he was off and the only sound heard was one of a car driving off down the streets. I closed the door leaning against it smelling the flower before I dropped to my knees crying clutching the flower to my chest. Ray picked me up and gave me a much needed brotherly hug to make me feel better.

"It's going to be alright. It's going to be alright." he repeated in my ear, Annie had left to tend to the kids.

But was it really going to be alright?

CHAPTER FIFTY-TWO

Everleigh:

It's been a week since Asher came to the house to talk to me. And since then every day I have been receiving a rose and a letter with one sentence that he said during his vows the two times we got married and every time I fall back in love with him all over again.

It's been really hard on the kids too especially Rose. She loves her dad and not having him around to push him about and get anything she wants out of him is hard on her because she doesn't understand the situation so I'm been just saying that we are on a little holiday out of the house. She's a real daddy's girl. Damon misses the games he played with his father and Wolf just calls out 'dada' because Ryder does the same so he just copies but I can't help but feel guilty that Asher isn't here so see him grow and miss his first word.

I've been thinking very hard about going back home. I think that I have overstepped my boundaries staying a week and a few days here, even though Annie says that it's fine I know that it's time to leave and I think it's also time for Asher and me to really talk things out.

A new day begun, I woke up to the laughter of my children that can walk, jumping on my bed as if it was the greatest game in the world. But unfortunately for me, it gives me sea sickness. I sit up feeling dizzy as I attempted to stand up and make my way to the bathroom while the kids are still jumping and yelling in the room. I make it just about to the toilet before chucking up my guts.

A felt a presence behind me as the white noise of the children played in the background. My hair is pulled back as a hand rubbed my back in circles till I finish. I turn around tears in my eyes and I'm greeted with the familiar brown ones of Annie. I wipe the tears away and Stand up to rinse my mouth, Annie stood too and closed the toilet lid, flushed it then took a seat on the rim of the bathtub.

"Leigh, it's been a week since you have been chucking up like it's going out of fashion. I know you and Asher are always at it like rabbits so it's not like it's just a one off. When was the last time you had your monthly?" I drank in her words holding on the side of the sink to keep me steady. I think my face mirrored my thoughts of utter panic.

I started counting on my fingers the last time I had my period. I looked up at her and just spoke those dreadful words.

"I'm late." tears poured out of my eyes as Annie took me back in her arms to comfort me.

"Get yourself dressed and we will get some tests just to put your mind at ease yeah? Ray will be off at the warehouse and I'm pretty sure he took Rose and Damon to school. Now, babes, I'm going to check on the boys." I nodded and waited for her to step out so that I could have a shower and relax before facing the rest of the day.

"Is it time yet?" Annie tapped her foot impatiently like a five-year-old while bouncing a fussy Ryder on her knee. Wolf is on the play matt on the floor that we have moved to the bedroom.

"Still two minutes." I called out from the bathroom. My phone rang indicating the end of the timer.

I took a breath and grabbed the stick that held a life-changing answer. I stepped out of the bathroom.

"So?" Annie enquired a pinch of excitement in her voice. I looked down at the stick in my hand, the two pink lines staring back at me.

"Positive." I couldn't help the smile that came on my face as Annie jumped up putting Ryder on the floor with Wolf.

I was crying tears of joy and Annie and I jumped up and down like teenagers. This in one of the first times that I'm really happy to be pregnant even if Asher and I are on a rocky road.

"When are you going to tell Asher?" she spoke after our high. I sobered up looking at my son that is the spitting image of his father.

"I don't know. His birthday is coming up so maybe then but we have to talk first."

****

Asher Mortimer:

This break has been pure torture, that's what it felt like. Weeks without my Angel in my arms, the screams and laughter of my children around the house. The 'firsts' of my youngest child, first words, first steps...

Talking about first steppes Annie sent me a video of Wolf's first steps with a little help for Everleigh. I have been playing it on replay every opportunity I have.

"Annie look! Are you filming?" her sweet voice rang out of the device.

"Yeah, I am! Look at him go!"

"Good boy come to mummy! That's it! One more step! Yay!"

Wolf had taken two steps and landed in his mother's waiting arms. She picked him up and swung him in the air making his giggles erupt in the room making my lips tilt up to the sound of two of my loves laughing and looking so happy.

The video came to an end and I only wish it would last longer. Anger surged through me again I stood up and slipped all the things that were on my desk sending them to the floor with one swipe. I heard the sound of glass shattering and bent down to see that I have knocked over one of the photo frames that graced my desk.

I picked it up running my thumb over the rim of the wooden frame keeping clear of the shattered glass making the picture look broken. It was the picture of Everleigh and I the day of our first wedding. Her belly was round and she was glowing in the white dress she wore that day. We were outside the courthouse and were surrounded by our friends in the background, you couldn't really see them though because we were right in front but we look so at peace and happy. Our eyes spoke for ourselves and it is honestly one of my favourite pictures.

A knock on the door brought me out of my state of trance fixed on the photography in my hands.

"Enter." I grumbled loud enough for the person to hear me. My back stood to the door as I started placing things back on my desk.

"Ash?" I turn around to see Carter standing there with paper in his hands.

"Can I come in?" he asked again. I wave my hand indicating him to come in. After he closes the door he takes cautious steps towards me.

"What happened in here?" I roll my eyes and continue picking things up.

"These need to be signed, it's related to the deal with Barry Mancuso." I grabbed the papers scanning then through before signing them and handing them over again.

"Anything else?"

"Yes actually, how have you been holding up? I know that Leigh is trying to keep herself busy with Wolf but Ray tells me she has been sick recently. Told me she lost that little spark in her eyes." I sighed sitting down in my chair not wanting to meet Carter's gaze.

"Honestly? I'm broken. I need her, I need the kids. I want them back and I did all the things that I promised to do. I went them fucking anger management classes, I stopped drinking like I used to and I know it's been just a few weeks but shit man, it's been weeks of pure hell. I want to cradle her in my arms and tell her everything will be alright. I want to be there for the kids because god only knows that I had a shit father, and there is no way I will let my kids live through that too. I even missed my son's first steps!" I finished off my rant to see a smirking Carter.

I really wanted to shoot him.

"What? Why are you smiling like an idiot?" I was starting to lose my nerves then and there.

"You are truly whipped man. It's a different side to you that is starting to grow on me." he laughed out. I leaned over to throw him a punch in the shoulder.

"But in all seriousness what you did is unforgivable, especially considering her previous relationship. But you guys are meant to be! In fact, you guys happen to bump into each other one day and a few months later turns out she was the girl you couldn't forget that one night which resulted in you having a child. If that's not a sign that you were meant to find each other then I don't know what is." he put his hands up in surrender standing up, heading back to the door opening it and saying half way through it

"Go home and fix yourself." after that, he left.

That house is not a home without them in it.

I thought to myself listening to Carter's advice and heading back to my now empty house.

CHAPTER FIFTY-THREE

Asher Mortimer:

I drove back home and walked up to an empty house. The weather was nice today for the last week of February. I fiddled with the keys and opened the door. I headed upstairs to take a shower.
Once that was done, I changed into a pair of grey sweats staying shirtless because the house was warm. As I headed back into the living room with my laptop I saw the familiar scene of chaos I haven't seen for what feels like forever. Toys were scattered around the living room, bags were sat by the stairs.

Her bags.

She's back.

I ran around the house like a child at Christmas. I know she isn't upstairs I would have heard her. I went into the kitchen hoping to find her there giving a snack to the kids. But the window leading to the garden caught my attention.

Of course, she is in the rose garden!

I rushed out not caring about the cold breeze that was nipping at my skin. I saw here there like she always was, smelling the roses. Wolf was in a pram sleeping, as Rose and Damon were running around in the bushes.

"Careful little ones, roses have thorns." I love her voice.

I ran up to her sweeping off her feet. A surprised squeal escaped her lips as I held her bridal style smiling like the Cheshire Cat. Her body against mine gave me the boost of energy I was seeking all this time she was gone.

"Ash put me down!" she giggled. I missed that laugh.

I set her down but held her at her waist so that she can retrieve her balance.

"Hey." she breathed out before my lips came crashing on hers in a kiss long overdue.

"Hey." I replied once we finally pulled away from each other still staying at arm's length. Soon the pitter patter of small feet came to my attention as both of my little mini-me's came crashing into my legs earning a 'humpf' noise from me.

"Daddy!" I crouched down to their level taken them both in my arms in a strong hug.

"I missed you. All of you." I spoke up looking straight into Everleigh's forest green eyes.

After playing a little with the children it started getting late so for a little treat since they didn't have school tomorrow we decided to allow them to watch a movie before bedtime. Everleigh doesn't like them to be addicted to the TV so movies were always a treat for them. That left us the time to put Wolf to sleep after dinner and for us adults to talk.

Everleigh was tinkering around the kitchen, the kettle boiling and the clinks of tea cups and spoons. I just stood there watching her move about with such grace, closing the drawer with her hip. She poured the burning hot liquid into a cup taking a spoon and adding a spoon of sugar.

"Oh! You scared me, I didn't see you there." she sat down on one of the bar stools as I did taking the one in front of her.

"What are you drinking?" I needed to start the conversation somewhere. Since she came back we haven't really talked to each other apart if it was kid related.

"Mint tea, I have had terrible heart burns, it helps a lot." she ran her finger around the rim of her cup not daring to make eye contact.

"Carter told me you haven't been feeling well recently. That you have been sick. Is that true?" she sighed and nodded her head.

"Yeah, I've been a little under the weather recently but nothing to worry about." she tried reassuring me but I could see in her eyes that it was only half of the truth.

"I'm fine honestly Ash. It's just a pacing phase, a bug or something." she tried shrugging it off but I know her and she is hiding something. But I know she doesn't want to talk about it any further.

"I'm sorry I didn't ask you if you wanted anything. I can fix something up for you if you wish." she stood up getting herself prepared in case I wanted anything but I just sat there smiling admiring her.

She had her hair up in a loose ponytail and she wasn't wearing any makeup, accentuating her natural beauty. She had a pair of light blue ripped jeans and a big knitted sweater that covered up her slim waist leaving it all to my imagination to figure out what was underneath.

"Yoo-hoo! Asher? I asked you a question. Would you like something to drink?" I snapped out of my daydream and shook my head from side to side.

"Nah thanks, babe I'm fine, sit down." she followed what I told her as she took her cup with both her hands blowing on it before taking a sip.

"I know I've said it a thousand times Everleigh but I am truly sorry. I-I don't know what came over me and I truly regret what I have done and I know it's unforgivable and–" she put her cup down and took my hand in hers cutting me off in my rambling.

"I forgave you a long time ago. But I needed time and I needed you to have the time to think things over, to get your head straight. You needed to learn from your mistakes and staying away and cutting all contact was the only way I thought to punish you." a single tear left her eye.

"I didn't know what to do to give you a 'shock' strong

enough to make you realise that you can lose us in a blink of an eye if you continue like that." she cried and I couldn't help but feel the tug at my heart at every tear that left her eyes.

I stood up and walked to her taking her hands in mine and lifting her off her seat and taking her in my arms.

"I'm so sorry. I know it doesn't change what happened but I regret the actions I've done and the words I've said. I know you did right in what you did and I've learnt my lesson. Not having you in my arms was like an eternity of torture." I held her tighter in my arms loving how her body fits perfectly in mine.

"Let's go to bed Angel. It's been a long day." she complies and we head upstairs grabbing each a sleeping child and putting them in their respective rooms after changing them into their pyjamas.

I followed the familiar path to our room and slipped under the bed sheets waiting for my wife to resurface from the bathroom.
Once she came out she was sporting a pair of shorts and one of my tops, her hair now let loose.

"I love you, Asher. I truly missed you." I pulled her into my arms never wanting to let her go ever again.

"I love you more than life itself." I kissed the top of her head before we both fell into a deep slumber.

CHAPTER FIFTY-FOUR

Everleigh:

I woke up in the arms of my husband and I was more than happy. I know that what he did should have been something that makes me leave for good but I just can't. I know that I should and I did, for a while but we both needed time apart, after all, that happened.

I shifted to look at the time and saw that it was still early so I decided to put my plan into action because today it's Asher's birthday. I slipped out of bed as quietly as I could and headed downstairs and prepare for his birthday.

I started with making his favourite breakfast humming along to the radio. The baby monitor started making noise so I placed the hash browns in the oven then headed back upstairs to find all the children awake. Wolf on my hip, I descended the stairs. Rose and Damon insisting in helping me out with their daddy's presents so I set them at the dining table with paper, pens and other arts and crafts supplies so that they can make things to their hearts contents.

I joined them making the 'classic' father's birthday presents gifts such as the handprints from the kids and the other little children orientated handmade gifts.
I hanged the painted pictures to dry in the sun. I washed the

kids and managed to keep the bile from rising.
After cleaning all three kids up I sent the two eldest to wake
their father up.

"Hello, Angel." his groggy morning voice couldn't be
anymore butterfly activating in my belly. He came to me and
kissed the side of my head as I finished dishing the food.

We sat the kids at the table eating in relative silence till we
finished.

"Kids it's time for presents!" I said excitement lacing my
voice.

Damon dashed to where the now dry paintings were placed
and came rushing back followed by Rose. Wolf was clapping
his hands seeing Asher smile and thank the kids swinging
them in the air.

"My turn now." I smiled and walked out of the room to
retrieve his gift.

I resurfaced a moment later with a gift-wrapped box and
handed it over to Asher.

"Happy birthday"" I kissed him sitting back into my seat.
I watched him open it giving me a skeptical look with a
smile at the corner of his lips.

The moment he opened the box and started reading the
cards his eyes held shock and one he lifted up the baby grow
he was smiling wide looking at me for confirmation.

"Is this for real?' his voice took a higher pitch holding the papers in his hands. I met his smile and nodded my head like a crazy person. He ran to me and picked me up in his arms twirling me around.

Once he set me back down on my feet I couldn't help the giggled that escaped my lips.

I have my loving husband back.

"You are really pregnant. Like for real. There is a baby in there." he pointed at my belly covered by his t-shirt.

"Yes, that's our baby." I smiled softly at him as he knelt down in front of me putting his head on my flat belly.

"Our baby."

"Our baby." I confirmed.

"Baby number four. I think we are on a roll here" I joked running my hand through his hair.

"This is the best birthday present I've ever received." he lovingly stared back at me placing one last kiss on my now exposed belly, before standing up and kissing the living daylights out of me.

Announcing to the children that there will be a new baby

was funnier than I thought it would be. Damon ran straight to his room and started sorting out all his toys for the new baby and in doing so made Rose cry because she didn't want to share her toys. And she was finding all sorts of silly arguments and then she ended up packing a small bag and sat on the porch for a good thirty minutes saying that she didn't want to share her toys nor did she want to be moved from her room.

I couldn't help but laugh at her state, to which she just pouted even more. Sometimes I wonder where she gets that character from because she certainly didn't get it from me.

Looks up in no particular direction, whistling.

Ok, maybe she got this stubbornness from me. But she came back in the end because she was getting hungry. I can't imagine what could be running in that little mind of hers. Now I'm coming up to my fifth month, my belly is a little smaller than my two previous pregnancies but the doctor says that all is fine and that baby number three is doing great and growing good.

Asher and I's relationship is going strong but I know that he hasn't got any leads on his father's whereabouts and that is worrying me and him. If he is capable of trying to kill his own daughter in law and my godfather in cold blood just out of spite for his son, god only knows what else he is capable of and Asher knows that full on. So he has assigned Carter to 'protect' me since Ash has been busy with all this going on and I like Carter's company in all honesty.

But I can't help but feel as if something bad is going to happen soon and I just know that whatever is going to happen won't end well...

CHAPTER FIFTY-FIVE

Everleigh:

Asher and I just came back from the eighth-month doctor's appointment. He and I decided to keep the gender a secret because for the previous pregnancies I always asked but I want it to be different for this baby.

"I'll drop you back at the house, I need to head back to the office. My dad has sent a message and I need to look more into it." Asher spoke up on the drive back to the house.

He pulled up the driveway and helped me step into the house before heading back to the car and leaving. Rose and Damon were at school and I started putting Wolf in a playgroup two times a week. Annie has been taking him and Ryder now since it's getting more difficult for me to bend down and sit on the floor with my huge belly and besides Asher wants me to rest because this pregnancy has been a little difficult. I got a case of Braxton hicks that scared the living daylight out of everyone when I got them. The doctor told me to take it easy for the rest of the pregnancy.

I set my bag down and called Clair up to give her an update on the pregnancy. I made myself a cup of tea and sat down on the sofa catching up with 'how to get away with murder' because I never got the chance to start season two with everything going on.

I was snacking on a bowl of grapes when the front door opened letting in a familiar built.

"Hey, Carter!" I smiled trying to get off the sofa with a little struggle.

"Hey, mama." he pulled me into a hug making sure not to put too much pressure on my stomach.

He has been calling me mama since we told him that I was having another baby and even if at first, it pissed me off, but I got used to the nickname.

"Get your lovely self-ready I am treating you to lunch, courtesy of your husband who wants you to relax."

I smiled widely and waddled my way to change into something a little more comfortable which consisted of a flip flops, a black short dress that hugs my curves and threw on one of Asher's grey old t-shirts to which I tied a knot too over my belly, leaving my blond hair in its natural curls.

"Ready to go, mama?" Carter asked taking my hand and leading me to the door then helping me to the car.

"Where are you taking me, my good sir? the excitement building up.

"It's a surprise mama sit tight and just enjoy the ride." we sat in relative silence, the music of the radio playing in the background.

"It's super cute!" I clapped my hands waddling over to the restaurant doors.

I stepped into the small little sixties style dinner and was greeted by the smell of fries and burgers. I walked over to a booth and took a seat as Carter took his in front of me. It was pretty empty but I didn't think more about it since we are in the middle of the week and most people work at this time of day since we were having a late lunch.

"Hello there, my name is Betty what can I get you today?" a sweet looking old lady came up to us with notepad and pen in hand.

"I'll take a double cheeseburger with extra pickles, no mayo, a large portion of fries, a chocolate milkshake, a jug of water and some strips of bacon on the side please." I smiled sweetly at her finishing up my order.

"Alright, then my dear." she turned to Carter who ordered a simple burger, a salad and fries and we would share the jug of water.

The food came along a little later and I just dug in moaning as my taste buds came into contact with this heavenly food.

"So Carter, how long have you known Ash?" I asked sipping on my drink.

"We have known ourselves since we were about six years

old I think. Then Paul showed up in high school, a year later it was Ray but he only truly joined three years ago and Louis came up in college." he munched on a piece of lettuce.

"Mmm, I see. And would you say that Asher has changed over the years?" I inquired interestedly.

"Yeah, since you showed up he is becoming like his old self again, like when we were kids. The other guys have never seen his old personality, they only know the ruthless gang leader persona. And it's good to get my old mate back again. You and those kids bring something out of him that his mom and I missed." he confessed.

"We are like brothers and it feels good to have your brother back you know?" I have never seen Carter open up so much in all the time I have known him.

"Yeah, I can imagine." I was going to ask him a new question but the sound of his phone rang into the oddly quiet dinner. The old lady hadn't made her appearance and it has been a little while since we had finished and we were the only clients there.

"Mmm, yeah. Ok." he hung up the phone taking my hand and dragging me out of the booth.

"What are you doing Carter? I haven't had dessert yet and they have this incredible brownie-" he pulled me out of the restaurant looking left and right keeping his other hand on his holster.

"We need to leave Leigh. That call was from Paul and he said that we have been followed by an unknown car. It's not safe here anymore."

"Carter, stop I forgot my bag, we need to go back." he huffed but we headed back inside. I waddled back to where we sat and grabbed my bag but walking back to the door where Carter was waiting I saw a sight that I wasn't expecting to see.

"Carter come here." I stood there shocked not knowing what to do.

There on the ground behind the counter was the lovely old lady that served us, surrounded by her own pool of blood.

"Leigh we need to leave now!" he growled.

I looked out the big restaurant windows that covered the walls and I saw six black vans park up front.

"We need to go by the back door before they get to us."

Carter dragged me once more and we went as fast as I could go considering I was huge.
We arrived at the back but the door was stuck. I could hear the other men walk into the restaurant but then something struck me.

"Carter." I whispered.

"Who killed the old lady when no one but us was in the

restaurant?" he turned to me and stopped trying to pry the door open. His look mirrored mine as the information I had just said sank in.

But we couldn't do anything about it, before we knew it Carter was knocked at the back of his head falling straight to the ground a gasp escaping my lips. My hands placed themselves protectively over my stomach as I backed away slowly from the man that was stalking towards me.
My back bumped into a firm surface as a hand clamped itself over my mouth to prevent me from screaming. I yelp of shock attempted to escape my lips but the firm hand muffled the noise. My watery eyes looked down at an unconscious carter that was been dragged out by two men that I assumed came from the black vans.

"Shhhh calm down Everleigh. We need that baby fine and well. And your panicking isn't helping my dear."

That voice. I know it but from where?

Next thing I know, I feel a pinch in my neck as the hand that was held over my mouth loosened. My vision became blurry and I felt my body being laid gently on the floor. Before I slipped into complete blackness my eyes met with a familiar face.

"Louis?"

Black dots started taking over most of my vision by this point and soon my eyes closed but my hearing was still working.

"Please forgive me Everleigh."

And then I was locked up into complete nothingness.

CHAPTER FIFTY-SIX

Everleigh:

"Place her on the bed, gently then cuff her to it. We don't want any runaways, not that she could in her state."
I felt myself be placed on a semi-hard surface, I suppose it was the 'bed' that the voice his ordering I be put on. I tried opening my eyes but they are just so heavy and I'm not sure I want to face whatever is coming right now.

"What about the other guy?" a new voice called out.

"Tie him to the bottom of the bed, we never know what can happen when we are not here and he would be the first to help her and I need her and that baby to be ok." the first voice confirmed.

The sound of the door closing caught my attention. I tried opening my eyes again with no luck. I heard a shuffling sound and then a warm hand take mine.

"Leigh. Princess, you need to wake up for me. Mama please, open those eyes. I need to know that you are alright."

That voice... *Carter!*

I strained my eyes and focused on opening them.

"That's it, Leigh. Continue like that." his voice brought me a sense of peace. I soon felt my eyes flutter and I was met with deep grey eyes.

"Carter?" I winced trying to sit up with carter's help.

"Take it easy love." once I was sat, I started crying.

"Shhh it's alright Leigh, I'm here." he tried taking me in his arms but with him cuffed it was more of a one-armed hug.

"I'm sorry... it's just I don't understand what is going on." I whimpered.

He sighed and took my hand giving it a reassuring squeeze.

"Asher won't take long to find us, I'm sure of it." I nodded not quite believing him. I believe he will but I'm scared he won't find us in time. Something just doesn't sit right.

"How long do you think we were out for?" I ask after I had calmed down.

I took a look around this room we were held in. It was a grey and dismal room, there was a table in the far end and next to it was a door that was left ajar and I could just make out the shape of a sink, so I assumed it was the bathroom. I was sat on a bed that was on the wall opposite of a big door which I think must be the one that leads to the rest of the place.

Carter was sat on the floor next to me patting himself down.

"I'm not sure. I woke up during the car ride and I couldn't

figure out what time it was, they blindfolded me. They took my gun, phone and everything." he puffed out a breath bringing his hand down to his side.

I put my hand on my belly feeling the baby kick, I let out a breath of relief. The baby was fine at the moment but I felt really uncomfortable.

"You alright Leigh?" he asked again seeing me fidget in my spot. I nodded then the events of the past hour ran in my mind once more.

"Oh my god your head!" I screeched taking his head in my hands inspecting it. Sure enough, there was a lump where he was hit and there was a little bleeding cut from where he hit his head.

"I'm fine, I've been through worse, trust me." I shook my head holding my hand to my mouth.

"Louis. He was there. He's in on it he–" the door creaked open letting in two very familiar faces.

Louis and Asher's father came into the room followed by two other scary looking men.

"Ahh, sleeping beauty is awake!" Asher's father exclaimed. I was just left speechless.

"What do you want Darnel?" Carter growled out to which Darnel simply laughed coming closer to him and game him a good punch making me gasp at the violence.

"I didn't talk to you now did I little boy." Carter shut his mouth but game a burning glare towards Asher's father.

Louis just stood there not daring to meet our gaze.

"What are we doing here?" I whispered out.

"What you are doing here? You are one funny girl. Well to get back at that no good of a son of mine."

"Why?" I said a little louder than intended.

"Why? What makes you think you will win out of this? Why are you doing this to us?" my voice was getting louder and louder by the second.

"What sick game are you playing keeping a heavily pregnant woman captive? Huh! Explain." he came up to me and I braced myself for the hit but he only caressed my cheek. I jumped from his touch, cold and hard.

'Now, now darling. I think you should calm down, we don't want anything happening to that precious bundle of joy of yours now do we?" his voice held a secret promise, sending shivers down my spine but not the good ones.

"Don't touch me you sick fucker." I gritted out feeling my confidence picking up again. I heard the sound before I felt the sting.

He had just slapped me. Like really. The tears pricked the

corners of my eyes.

"Hey! Keep your hands off of her! If you want someone to hit, hit me! Not her!" Carter yelled out trying to place himself protectively in front of me.

Darnel let out a sickening smile and knocked Carter back on the floor and started throwing punch after punch until his face was bleeding.

"STOP! PLEASE STOP!" I screamed from the top of my lungs, tears freely streaming down my cheeks.

Darnel stood up as Carter rolled to his side groaning in pain. Asher's dad sported a proud smile as if he had just created a masterpiece. He turned around and gestured to the little crew that had followed him in to follow him back out.

One the door closed again and I couldn't help the sobs that racked through my body.

Oh, Asher, I hope you find us and put this nightmare to an end.

CHAPTER FIFTY-SEVEN

Everleigh:

The day dragged along and every time that Carter would try and protect me or if I spoke up a little too harshly Carter would get the beating of a lifetime because for some unknown reason they would not dare to touch me, apart from when Darnel slapped me but that was the only time. We haven't seen him since, nor did we see Louis.

I still wonder what and more importantly why is Louis siding with this monster? I just don't get it I thought he was friends with Ash, that he was loyal. He was so nice to me and Rose at the beginning and since I had my car accident and the kids kidnapping he has been distant, acting odd... and know I can't help but think he had a role to play in all that happened.

The door pulled open again, one of Darnel's goons came in with a tray of food and placed it at the end of the bed but not too far so that I could still reach with my big belly in the way.

"Eat." he commanded and I don't like to be told what I need to do.

"What makes you think I will? For all, I know this could be poisoned and how do I know if what is in this won't harm my baby?" I nearly growled out.

The man came closer to me in a dangerous manor and even if Carter was in a really bad state, I suspect a few broken ribs and a dislocated arm, he still came in front of me to stop the other man from coming too close.

"That's enough Fred, step away from them." Louis' voice rang out in the almost empty room.

The man, now known as Fred, stepped back and glared at Carter, me and then to Louis before walking off.

"You need to eat Everleigh, you have the baby to think about." he sighed as started walking over to me.

"Don't you dare take on more step forward you traitor." Carter spat out at him. Louis stopped in his tracks putting his head down in shame.

"I know how this looks like but you don't understand." he pleaded.

"Then tell us, explain, let us understand what is the purpose of all this nonsense." I sat up better getting myself a little more comfortable by leaning against the cold concrete sending shivers all over my body making me wrap my arms around myself.

"Let me get you a blanket then I will talk." Before I could protest he walked off.

****

Louis:

After stopping Fred from nearly beating the crap out of
Carter for the umpteenth time today I walked back out of the
cell making sure it was locked behind me before getting
some blankets for Everleigh. The last thing we need is
getting her ill, the boss would kill me even if I am his son.

I stepped back into the room to see that Leigh hadn't moved
from her spot nor did she touch the food we had given her.
Mother says it has all she needs for the baby but I
understand that she doesn't trust us anymore.

Carter was looking in such pain and I did feel bad for him
but we can't let him be strong or in good condition because
we can't give them the possibility for them to run away, even
though I am sure that Asher is looking everywhere to get his
angel back and I almost want to put everything aside and
drop it and let them both leave but then it would be my life
on the line and I can't let that happen.

"Here." I dropped the first blanket over her lap and placed
the second one by the end of the bed, purposely avoiding
Carter and his murderous glare.

"Stop stalling and tell us what the freak is going on."

Everleigh's voice was void of emotion and that reminded me
of the time she tortured that guy in the cellars when Asher
was ambushed.

I sighed and took the chair that was by the table on the opposite wall and placed it at a safe distance from them locking the door and double checking to see that no one else was there to listen in.

"Darnel is my dad." I breathed out not wanting to look at their faces and only earning a small gasp from Everleigh.

"B-but you look nothing like Asher or him." Everleigh pointed out.

"You are brothers?" Carter was next to add.

"Half-brothers actually, I would have much preferred if Clair was my mother but I wasn't so lucky." I ran a hand in my hair debating if I should tell them the full story.

"Darnel had an affair with my mother when Asher was just born and nine months later I popped up in the picture. Darnel left my mother to turn back to Clair because in his eyes Asher was a better fit than me to succeed him in his place as the gang leader." I took another breath, taking a peek at their confused faces before continuing.

"My mother fell into depression and started taking all sorts of stuff the get over the pain all while neglecting me. Needless to say that my childhood wasn't all butterflies and rainbows. When I turned sixteen, he came back into my life saying that Asher was no good and that he had challenged his own father for the authority and kicked him out of his own gang. I was young and gullible, I only wanted to have my dad around and when he came back my mother was paying a lot more attention to me and I felt like I had the perfect little family.

Ohh but I was wrong. My father prepped me to infiltrate Asher's gang and I joined you guys in college. It was hard at first because you were a close closed group and you let nobody in. But when I finally got their trust I thought everything was over. Meaning that I had finished what my father wanted and all I needed to do was give him updates. But when you showed up Everleigh, things took a drastic turn for the worst. I didn't know he would do the things he did and I am really sorry for everything."

"What do you mean, 'everything he did'? What else did he do other than crash my wedding and kidnap me when I am 8 months pregnant?" Everleigh spoke up after the short silence that followed my statement. Carter just glared at me the whole way through and clenched his jaw balling his good hand into a fist.

"He was the reason you were in that car accident, he was the reason the children got kidnapped. And I was just a pawn in his game to get to Asher by every means possible which were you and the kids." her face held shock then anger came surging in her eyes.

"YOU DID THIS? YOU LET THIS HAPPEN? YOU KNEW ALL ALONG AND YOU DIDN'T DEEM RIGHT TO TELL US, TO TELL ME! I COULD HAVE DIED, OR LOST MY UNBORN BABY, MY CHILDREN!" she screamed at me, to which I flinched in response.

"Does that mean he is going to do that now... kill two birds with one stone, the wife and the unborn child. Is that what he is going to do next? Is that his plan? Put me at ease, build my trust and kill me?" her voice suddenly went calm, fear was lacing her voice while she placed her hands protectively over her growing stomach as if she was protecting it from any harm.

"Tell me now Louis so that I can prepare myself... please." she begged. Her green eyes were full of tears and I almost broke me seeing her like that, but I didn't know what his plans were.

"I don't know what his plans are. We won't tell me, guess he figured that I would talk sooner or later." I could see that Carter was doing everything In his power not to fucking lose it and to control his anger because he was sure in no state to fight and It was clear that he wasn't ready to lose this battle and protect Everleigh and that baby till the end.

My phone vibrated in my pocket. I took it out seeing it was a message from Darnel, that he wanted me in his office.

"I need to go but I'll be back later with more food, and till then I want you to eat what is on that plate. Am I understood?" I stood up to leave placing the chair back in its previous place.

"What? You can't leave now, I'm sure there are more things you are hiding." she spoke once more but I chose to ignore her calls.

"LOUIS!" she screamed before I closed the cell door behind me locking it before heading to see what my father wants from me.

CHAPTER FIFTY-EIGHT

Asher Mortimer:

They have been gone for about twelve hours now. I don't know where they are, in what state they are in, as the hours go past I get more and more worried as to what condition my angel is in.

I knew that Carter was taking my wife out for lunch because I wanted her to relax but now I regret my choice, she should've stayed home, where it was safe, I should've stayed by her side, make sure she was safe and that no harm could come to her, but I failed.

I failed her again...

I had come home to an empty house. Annie had taken Wolf back to her house so that Everleigh could have a peaceful day without the kids running and screaming about the house and the two eldest were out at school and would head out for ice cream with Paul when he would go and pick them up.

"Everleigh? Angel? Are you home?" I called out, no answer. I shrugged it off and went up to our room, maybe she was sleeping. To my surprise, she wasn't there. I rang her cell and went straight to voicemail, same for Carter.

I started to get worried, Carter always picks up. So I took my keys and rang up one of the technology guys and asked him to pull up the GPS signal on Carter's car. The technology guy sent me the address and I headed in that direction.

I cut the engine and stepped out of the car. I walked up to the little diner.

I'm not surprised Carter brought Leigh here, she loves cozy little diners. I thought to myself when I stepped in.

"Hello? Is anyone here?" the place was very quiet. A little too quiet. But the odd thing is that it seemed closed but the door was still open.

I walked further into the restaurant until my eyes fell on Everleigh's bag that was placed on top of the counter by the cash register.

How odd.

I took a step further and that's when I saw the body of an old lady, I'm guessing the owner, lying on the ground, lifeless in a pool of her own blood.

If she was in that state I can't imagine how my loved one and best friend might be in. I called for backup and made my way to the back to see if there was anything that would indicate me to what happened here. I came to the back door to find it locked when in reality it should have been open because it was an emergency exit.

I heard the car of my men pull over in the parking, so I

headed back into the main room to give them my orders.

"Clear this place up, find out if this woman has any family and organise a funeral. I want all security footage and I demand to know what happened here. Am I clear?" they all responded with a 'yes boss' before doing what I told them to do.

I came back to the office and called every person that was with my children back at the house because I can't risk having something happen to them too. Killian the tech guy came into my office handing me a tablet.

"I think you should see this." I played the video on the device and saw that Carter and Everleigh were taken by none other than Louis and my father. I paused the video that showed clearly both of their faces and I was so close to smashing the tablet in two and trash this office if I were not interrupted by a little voice.

"Daddy? Where is Mummy?" Rose came skipping into the room and I picked her up placing her on my lap and gave her a hug that I really needed.

"She is just off for a walk with Uncle Carter, she won't be long." I dismissed Killian before ordering him to find a way to track them down.

Paul rushed into the office out of breath.

"There you are, Rose! Didn't I tell you not to run off like that!" he scowled making a pointy finger towards her.

"I sowy Uncle Paul." a little frown formed on her face and my heart clenched at the sight.

Man does she have me wrapped around her little finger.

"I wanted to see daddy to sing him the song I learnt." she wiped away a fake tear that had fallen. I knew her tactics now but they were still quite effective.

"It's ok, but next time you have to tell us where you go." I told her.

"Have you found a way to trace them yet?" Paul asked walking in closer and leaning against the wall.

"Nah... And that's what worries me, not finding them in time."

"Are you listening, daddy?" Rose snapped my attention back to her as I saw excitement bubbling in her. I smiled softly and nodded.

"Ruby ring, Ruby ring, where are you?" she started in her little baby voice before putting her hand in front of me and waving her fingers in my face.

"Here I am, here I am, how do you do?" she continued singing and then it came to me.

"Sowy daddy I only know that finger." she looked down but I kissed her head and pulled her closer to me.

"Princess that was great, you helped daddy a lot." I looked at Paul giving him a nod and he ran out of the room to pop up again with his laptop in hand, he was my best tracker.

"Her ring. Her engagement ring. There is a GPS tracker in one of the diamonds. I put it in for the insurance just in case we lost it or if it was stolen so that I could get it back. It should do the trick."

Paul started typing away like a maniac on his laptop for what felt like ages while Rose was talking about her day, she is so much like her mother it's uncanny.

"Found it."

******

Carter Bellantuono:

Everleigh had finished crying soon after Louis left. I tried telling her that everything was going to be alright and that seemed to have helped a little but I knew the fear was still there.

She hadn't touched the food and tried giving me some but I declined because there might be truth in the fact that they may have put something in it.

"Oh yeah right. I forgot." she pulled the blanket that Louis gave her closer to her chest. The silence filled back the room till there was a hiss coming from her.

"You alright?" I asked alarmed remembering that last time she was holding herself like that she ended up in the hospital.

"Yeah, I'm fine. The baby is just deciding that it's the right time to start jumping about and it's just really painful especially that sitting on this bed without moving isn't helping either." she confessed.

By the look on her face, I knew that something was wrong she was holding her stomach and wincing in pain. I was just praying that she wasn't in labour because that would be a fucking mess!

The sound of the lock on the door interrupted my thoughts as I saw Louis resurface. His eyes landed on Everleigh after he closed the door behind him.

"Is she alright?" he came rushing to her side but she stopped him with her hand.

"Does she look fine to you?" I snapped back making him give me an irritated look.

"Guys I'm fine I just need to walk about for a bit. I promise Louis I won't try anything I just need to walk and it should pass." Louis gave a skeptical look but Leigh gave out another hiss and held her belly.

He took out a set of keys and un-cuffed her from the bed and helped her stand up, slowly making her take little steps. I was fuming at that point. I can't let him touch her after all that he has confessed to doing to this family, to my family. Leigh is like a little sister to me and nobody dares to harm MY family.

"Get off me!" Everleigh's voice spoke up as I saw her trying to shove Louis off of her.

"I can walk by myself thank you very much." she sassed pulling her grip away from his, but he tried holding her again.

"She said to let her go, and I would advise you do as told." I defended.

Louis took a step away from her and came in my direction.

"Oh yeah? And why would I listen to you? You have been nothing but a pain, a barrier between my brother and I."

"HALF brother." I cut him off, emphasising on 'half'.

"Oh you think you're so smart don't you Carter well let me tell you-" he couldn't finish his sentence before Everleigh's spoke over his.

"Umm Guys...." both our heads snapped in her direction to see a puddle of what looks to be water, surround her feet.

"We have a situation." our eyes darted to the puddle on the floor then back to her eyes.

"My water just broke."

Oh shit.

CHAPTER FIFTY-NINE

Everleigh:

"My water just broke." I said in panic. Both boys were looking from me to each other.

"Well don't just stand there do something!" I yelled, gosh I feel like I'm back with Asher when I was in labour with Wolf.

ASHER! Ohh no no no!! I can't deliver this baby here without him! Heck, I shouldn't even have it here in this cell.

"Louis I can't have this baby here. I can't let my baby be born in a cell, I can't." I choked out crying my eyes out holding my belly as another contraction passed through me again.

"Shit man! What do we do she is right." Louis looked back at me running his hands in his hair pacing back and forth.

"They can't know what is going on here. It won't end up pretty."

"Ok, this is what we are going to do." Carter's voice was very calm and soothing my nerves a little, Louis was having a mini panic attack in the corner.

"Louis dude, you have to work with me on this one, for the

sake of the baby and Everleigh." Louis nodded and stopped pacing.

"Start off by un-cuffing me, we are going to need all hands on deck." once that was done Carter stood up with a little struggle before limping to me taking my hand and wrapped the other around my waist so that I could lean on him as he started making me walk around the room telling me to breathe in and out.

"Next, Louis you need to find a way of getting clean towels and hot water and sterilised shoelaces and the sharpest scissors you can find."

"Shoelaces? Are you planning to play MacGyver with my baby?" I joked through a new contraction.

"The shoe laces are to section off the umbilical cord without cutting it or harming you or the baby."

We continued walking around the room to get my cervix a little more dilated, and before you ask nor did Carter nor Louis put their hand down there. I did, it's my third kid I know what I'm looking for.

"I've got what you have asked for." Louis rolled in with all sorts of things.

I sat down on the bed taking in deep breaths feeling the pains come in closer and closer to each other. I think that I was walking about for thirty minutes and another ten to get things ready.

"Carter I think it's time, I can't hold this baby in any longer." I called sweat running down my forehead.

"Ok, now Leigh you have to relax ok. We want this to go as smoothly as possible. Louis is going to act as your backrest, use his hands to hold when you push to that you don't slip too much." he took my legs and placed a foot on each of this shoulders so that he had better access.

I really wish Asher was by my side and that I was delivering in a sanitised hospital rather than in his crap hole.

"When you feel a contraction I want you to push Leigh."

"There is one now!" I screamed my lungs on the first push.

"You're doing great love now when you are ready, do that again." I could see the stress on Carter's face and I knew he wasn't exactly comfortable with the situation and I knew he wasn't a doctor but he was doing a hell of a good job.

After a few more pushes that drained all my energy out the baby was finally crowning.

"I can't do it. I can't do it anymore. I give up. The baby is here too early!" I breathed out letting go of Louis' hands, I nearly forgot he was there in the room.

"You can do this Everleigh. You have done it twice before. You are nearly there." Carter encouraged.

"The last two times I was in a freaking hospital, not here in this dump where I could die any minute and risk my baby's life." I sobbed.

"You have to finish this love because the more you wait, the more it gets dangerous for you and that baby boy of yours." I dropped my head forward to look into his warm brown eyes that he shared with his sister.

"Boy?" I asked.

"Yeah Paul and I made a bet, he says it's a girl, I bet on a boy and I'm pretty sure I'm going to win." he grinned cheekily at me. I just rolled my eyes leaning my head against Louis feeling a new contraction building up.

"PUSH!" both men yelled at me, I screamed in pain once again before the heavenly cries of a newborn resonated in the room.

I relaxed as my body went numb. Carter wrapped the baby in a towel to clean it off a little before handing me the baby.

"I guess Paul will need to pay up. It's a boy." I let a few tears leave my eyes looking down at my crying angel.

Louis helped me to go deeper in the bed and place me under the blanket. I cleaned my baby boy off and Carter handed me a new towel to wrap him up in and then I swaddled him in another blanket. I was so concentrated with my new baby I didn't even hear the door open.

"Ahh hello my dear! I see you got that thing out of you! Finally, that serum took its sweet time to get you into labour."

I looked ups from my now asleep baby coming face to face with the woman I despise the most in my life.

"You are in on it?" I questioned in disbelief holding my baby closer to my chest. I saw that Carter was being held by two men in black and Louis was sporting a guilty look on his face.

"You knew?" I turned my attention to Louis who didn't dare speak back but I knew the answer that's why he managed to find all those things we needed without raising suspicions.

"B- But how?" I spoke in a whisper not wanting to wake the baby. Carter was trying to get out of the hold he was in and it didn't seem to work.

"How do you think we managed to knock you out? There wasn't only a sedative in that syringe." she laughed darkly at me.

"Why?" I asked tired of all the past events.

"Because we need you to suffer, I want you to know how it feels the loss of a child." something unknown flashed across her eyes. I didn't think she could do something so cruel.

She walked over to me putting her hands out, I knew that

announced nothing good so I tried ignoring the blasting pain in all my lower abdomen and scoot as far away from her holding my son closer to my chest protectively.

"Hand me over the baby Everleigh. NOW!" I shook my head tears threatening to fall. I was so vulnerable I knew that I wouldn't win.

She leaned over and snatched my baby out of my arms holding him carefully in her arms.

"NOOOOOOO!" I screamed once he left my arms causing him to start crying.

Tears of anger and frustration ran from my eyes as I tried getting out of the bed but I was held back by a third man that was in the room. I tried getting away from his grip, with the little strength I had left I tried, in vain. I was screaming, I was so distraught I didn't even see the events that happened right in front of me.

Carter had head-butted both of the guys that were holding him, kicking one and punching the other sending them to the ground as he limped to my mother who was approaching the door baby in hand.

"Give that baby back!" he roared.

He was nearly there I had a glimmer of hope, Louis did nothing to stop him and I knew that it was a way to say that he was helping out, or so I thought.

My mother turned around and there was the sound of gunshots, a thump and the continuous cries of my baby. My eyes darted to Carter who had fallen to the floor, I was reliving Sergei's death all over again in slow motion. I was finding it difficult to breathe. I jumped out of the bed to stop my mother to make her pay for the things she has done my legs gave out under my weight after all the efforts I did delivering my baby.

She simply turned around and smirked at what she had accomplished and locked the door again behind her. I crawled to Carter, my knees scraping the concrete floor, my elbows and forearms doing the same. I reached Carter's body laid limply, his breathing was shallow and by the blood leaving his mouth when he coughed I knew a lung was hit.

"Carter I'm so sorry. This is all my fault. Why did she have to be my mother? This is all my fault." I sobbed.

I saw that Carter was attempting to talk but blood was only coming out of his mouth. There was so much blood I didn't even see where he was hit exactly. He was coughing so much and the rest of his blood was just oozing out of him, I felt so lost in what to do.

Soon his coughs stopped and I no longer saw his chest rising and falling. My body was a little further from him as I was flat on the floor. He turned his head to me before his eyes closed. The last time I would ever see those soft brown eyes of a brother I would no longer see that did everything in his power to save me.

Soon I felt my eyes become heavy, the lack of food and the fatigue was catching up with me. I was soon welcomed by a familiar darkness, gunshots ringing in the distance.

CHAPTER SIXTY

Asher Mortimer:

It was a two-hour drive out of the city. I felt like it was taking an eternity to get there and my nerves were skyrocketing. Deep down I knew that something wasn't right and the scenarios I was thinking about didn't help to ease my stress.

The car stopped near an abandoned building. I gave the order to the snipers and the rest of us just charged in. There were shots flying everywhere and I was nearly hit a few times, with a couple scratches here and there.

I walked into a dark looking corridor and over the bullets, I could hear the sound of a baby crying. The noise peaked my interest so I followed the sound of it, keeping my gun. I came up to a door which was left a little bit ajar. Light shone through the big windows that were in the room. The baby was still crying and I could just about see it laid in a crib a woman waving her hands in the air yelling at it.

I frowned once I saw who it was. Everleigh's mother was pacing in the room yelling at the child for it to stop crying.

"Darnel, I can't stand this brat crying! Why do you want to keep it? The bitch gave birth and I killed the other one. What do you plan on doing next? They are here shooting about left and right!" she yelled at my father that I supposed was somewhere in the room with her.

Was she talking about Everleigh? Who is the other one? Is she talking about Carter? Who does this baby belong to?

So many questions were running wild in my mind. I couldn't let them get away with any of this. I called for backup and told them in a whisper where about in the house I was at. For some reason, I lost my balance and ended up stumbling on the door.

"YOU!" I picked up my posture and pointed my gun at the both of them taking them by surprise.

This is not exactly how I had imagined confronting them.

"Where is my wife?" I growled looking at my father a glass of brandy in hand.

"I don't know what you are talking about son. You could at least knock next time" he scolded

"Where is she?" I called again.

"Wouldn't you like to meet your son first?" I looked at him in disbelief and glanced towards the crying baby in the cot.

"That's impossible." I breathed out not once letting my eyes leave the baby.

I guess he took that opportunity to disarm me and turn the

gun to my direction. Everleigh's mother ran, hiding behind my dad for protection.

"The tables have turned son, now say your last goodbyes. I win." I looked at the baby and I had the overwhelming feeling to protect him or her.

I bent down to take him gently in my arms and ran to a corner of the room holding him close to my chest to block him out of any shot that could come our way. The baby's cries were the only thing resonating in the room after a first gunshot followed by another. I looked up and saw that Ray was now standing by the door and both my father and Leigh's mother were on the floor in a pool of their own blood.

I stepped closer to them still holding onto the baby protectively. Ray had done a good shot, Everleigh's mother had a bullet lodged between her eyes. I knew that Ray didn't kill my father on purpose, he knew I wanted to finish him off for all that he has done in my life.

"S-son…" he choked out.

"Where are Everleigh and Carter?" I asked again sending my foot into his ribs making him cry out in pain.

He smiled his teeth full of blood, coughing up before speaking up.

"You're too late." that was enough for me to pick up my discarded gun off the floor and putting a bullet between his eyes to match the woman laid beside him.

"Asher, we need to go and get that wife of yours back. Hand me the baby I will take care of him." I hadn't even realised that I started rocking the baby back and forth in my arms.

He looked so tiny in my big muscular arms, a little too small.
I nodded and handed him the couple hours old baby telling him to get it straight to a doctor for a checkup because if my father was right and that was my baby, it was in need of some serious medical attention.

Knowing my father, I knew that there was some sort of basement area in this huge house and after a couple of tries I finally found it. I shot the lock on the door, then pushed it open.

"Everleigh. Carter." I stated in shock seeing the both of them covered in blood.

A single tear left my eye, I walked up to them then kneeled down beside both of their bodies. I checked Carter's pulse to find it nonexistent. I hit the concrete ground with my fist so hard my knuckles started to bleed. I held onto his shirt and let the tears of anger ripple through me, grieving the loss of my best friend, my wingman, my second in command, *my brother*.

Once I pulled myself together I dragged myself to my wife, a breath of relief left me when I saw her chest rise and fall but the amount of blood that was on the lower half of her body and the missing baby bump was what was worrying me. The room looked like a battlefield, bloodied towels where spawn across the room.

She gave birth here. She had to go through that I this hell hole and I couldn't even protect her nor my unborn child. I scooped her into my arms carefully and made my way to the door again. On the way back up everything was relatively quiet, I had sucked my tears in not wanting to appear week in front of my men. But I knew my red puffy eyes would give away the fact that I cried.

"Where's Carter?" Paul asked from the front seat of the car. I looked him in the eyes, lying Everleigh on my lap.

"He's–" I couldn't finish, I shook my head to stop the tears from leaving my eyes. I looked up and Paul once more seeing his image reflect mine.

He started the car, no words were exchanged between us. I drifted my attention the beautiful creature laid on me. I ran my hand in her tangled hair.

"Please baby, wake up. I'm here now. It's all over. I love you." I kissed the top of her head sweeping all the matted hair stuck to her forehead away before so.

"My baby... I need my son." her eyes fluttered open again as she battled to keep her eyes open.

"He's taken care of. I got him. I got our baby safe." I managed to say before her eyes fluttered closed once more.

I have been waiting in the hospital for the last couple of hours. Since I have my own private doctors when these sort of confrontation happen we were all taken care of right away. They assessed all our injuries and now we play the waiting game.

The doctor that was taking care of my son told me that for a premature baby born in the conditions he did was a very strong and relatively healthy baby and that we were very lucky for that to be the case.

I thanked the doctor once he told me that he had to stay the night so that they could keep an eye on him but other than that he would make it. Everleigh, on the other hand, was a little bit of a different story. I, fortunately, got to her in time but she lost a lot of blood during the birth and all the stress that was inflicted on her body only made matters worse. In short her body went into lockdown.

"Angel, I know you can hear me and I want you to know that I am here. Our son is a strong little thing and that he will pull through. I just need you back here with me, with us. The other little ones are at home waiting for you to come back. They miss you terribly, as do we. I miss you, Leigh, I need you back. Please... I love you. I can't lose you too."

I poured my heart to her placing my head on her chest to hear the beating heart. It was the only thing that calmed me down after everything that has happened the last 48 hours.

I didn't realise that I had fallen asleep to the sound of her heartbeats until I was woken up by a soft touch running in my hair. I shot up straight in my seat, eye to eye with a pair of deep forest green eyes that I love so much.

"Angel." I called out not quite believing that she was there, awake and looking well.

She smiled that bright smile but there was a dullness in her eyes and I think mine mirrored the same.

"I'm sorry." was the first thing she said before breaking up in tears. I immediately took her in my arms sitting beside her on the hospital bed.

"You should not be sorry."

"He's dead. He's dead." she repeated as I rocked her back and forth pulling her impossibly closer to my chest.

"I know baby. I know." I cooed, but this was hard on me.

"He wanted to save me, to save the baby but he- he–" a loud sob erupted from her mouth.

"She took him away. She did it. She took both of them away." she cried again, I just listened I knew she needed to tell me even if it hurt me to find out how my best friend died and seeing the state that put her in.

She pulled away from my chest but still staying in my arms.

"I want to call our son Carter, I want him to have the name of the man that helped me bring him into this world, the man that tried to save him not thinking about the consequences to his life. I want our son to grow up and know all that. To hold the name of a brave man, that did everything in his power to protect the ones he loves. I want our baby Carter to know all that and be proud of his name."

Her speech brought tears to my eyes. She is the love of my life and I know that isn't the name we had settled for if we had a boy. We planned on calling him Benjamin in honour of her brother and she was willing to change his name to remember the man I saw as a brother in my eyes. I kissed her with passion letting my tears fall and mix with hers. We let our love and grief for the ones we lost in that kiss and in those tears.

"Our baby Carter." I confirmed pulling her close into my arms once more.

EPILOGUE

Five years later.

Everleigh:

I was woken up by the sun shining past the gaps between the curtains and the window. I stretched only to be pulled back to a hard and warm chest. I smiled in content turning around to see the sleeping face of my handsome husband.

Asher and I have come so far during the years and I wouldn't have changed them for the world. There were a lot of tough times, tears, fights but also happy moments, full of love and new cherished memories. Carter's death left us all stunned and he is still missed dearly to this day. There is never a moment we don't all think of him and little Carter is so much like him in the way he acts. It's like that saying when they say that when someone dies its spirit seeks refuge into a newborn baby and reborn, well I think that's the case with both the Carter's. Louis managed to run for it and nobody has seen nor heard of him in the last few years.

"Morning Angel." Asher's sexy morning voice knocked me out of my day dream. I gave him a quick peck on the lips and pulled back.

"That's not how you say good morning." before I could utter another word, his lips came crashing on mine in an intense but loving kiss that turned out in a full make out session making me all hot and bothered.

But all good things must come to an end... all the kids ran straight into the room and jumped on our bed screaming at an ungodly hour of the morning.

Our sweet moment was cut short as the girls went straight to their father and the boys straight to me.

You must be wondering, girls? Well I fell pregnant again when Carter was two and well it turned out to be twin girls much to my surprise but Asher was over the moon with having two new daughters and I was happy that the numbers equaled out.

So now Damon is eleven years old, Rose is nine, Wolf is six, Carter is five and Amelia and Annora are both three. All six of them were taking up all the space between my husband and I and I did miss the warmth coming from him but I love my babies too and I love the cuddles.

"We are stopping at six." Asher confirmed looking at me with a determined look.

I smiled at him sheepishly.

"It's a little too late for that I'm afraid..." I turned from his confused face to get something in my nightstand drawer, turning back and handing it over to him.

"What is this?" he cocked his eyebrow taking a look at the

positive pregnancy test in one hand holding Amelia to his chest to stop her from falling with the other.

"Surprise!" I gave him a nervous chuckle waiting for his reaction. When I saw a huge smile grace his lips and seeing his attempt at shuffling over to me I knew he was happy deep inside.

"Happy father's day." I said once he managed to get closer to me without knocking any of the kids off the bed.

"I love you." he kissed the tip of my nose with a little struggle.

"I love you more." I said back.

"Impossible!" he faked shock and we both laughed. But between the silence, we heard a few tummy rumbling.

"I hungry mama." Annora pouted looking at her tummy and her sister copying her actions.

"Me too." Rose added in sync with the rest of the boys.

We all pulled ourselves out of the bed and let the kids go first to head down the kitchen. I was about to pass the door when I was held back by strong arms that soon placed themselves on the little bump that started to form.

"Baby number seven. I wonder what we will have this time." I whispered to myself-seeing as Asher was just enjoying rubbing circles on my belly with his thumbs, keeping me close to his chest his head in the crook of my neck placing small kisses up and down it.

"As long as you stay healthy and the baby is healthy and all is well I don't care what we have as long as we have this adventure together."

He placed one last kiss on my cheek before taking my hand and dragging out of the room and into the chaos that is my life with six soon to be seven kids and a gang leader for a husband.

EVERLEIGH'S STORY

On Wattpad, the platform I had first published this book on, I received a lot of comments regarding the following questions and so I had decided to address them in a separate part at the end and here are the answers that you may or may not be wanting to know about Evereleigh and other characters of story details you didn't quite grasp:

"But if she can fight why didn't she just leave Dan? Why didn't she fight back? Why has she been taking all the abuse? Why didn't she leave before? If she is the daughter of a gang leader...." And much more. And I will also address the numerous comments about Asher, Everleigh and Rose's fast-growing relationship.

So to start off: EVERLEIGH IS NOT TRAINED IN HAND TO HAND COMBAT! Thus making her defenseless against Dan.
Furthermore, she used to be in love with Dan, I haven't mentioned it in the story but he was there for her all through her second half of pregnancy with Rose after Ben and Victoria died.

She moved back to England and that's where she met Ben. In her life in England, she ended up staying with a lady that was renting a room in her house since when Leigh left Australia she refused to take part in anything involving her family much less their money. The lady where she was staying had a son, and you guessed it, it was Dan.

They started off as good friends but as the relationship grew so did their love, she hates bringing up that part of her life because it was a hard one. After she moved with him to the USA to build his company when Rose was two, that's where he became aggressive because of the stress and the failure of his company that he ultimately blamed on Leigh. He never knew of her past and nor did she want him to know because we still have to remember that Everleigh had Rose when she was twenty-one and she still is very young when she meets Dan and she is transitioning into adulthood and still who hates her parents and basically ran away from all her problems. She couldn't go and live with Sergei because of the embarrassment it was for her to get pregnant so young and his daughter just died and it was hard for him to be around his dead daughter's best friend.

When she lived with her parents, her father only prepared her to be a leader and in his mind, it was only the political side of things since he always surrounded her with guards and she constantly had her brother around her that was fully trained to protect her. The only things he taught her was to handle weapons since the major thing they do in their gang is a gun trade.

In addition, she never left Dan because she thought deep down that he would get over it and get help, you can't just abandon someone you love for the sake of them being in a bad phase, at least that's what she thought until a certain point where she no longer loved him like she did. And besides, she couldn't just leave and go somewhere else, she needed the money, she needed a place to stay and somewhere as safe as she could for Rose even if Dan was abusing Everleigh. She couldn't just live her life in hotels and hope for the best, not when she had a child at charge. Also, if I break things down by a timeline time order. We'll start off at the gang meeting when Ash and Everleigh first met.

As explained in one of the chapters, Everleigh gets in a fight with her dad about her mother and about other things that she didn't like during the meetings because she always felt as if she was incapable of doing things and living up to the standards that her parents fixed for her. Her father wanted to protect her and not put her in harm's way by showing her off as the new leader in fear of her getting hurt, and her mother just simply didn't like her as much as her brother and wanted him to take over even if he was younger.

After the fight she goes and gets drunk, meets Ash, they talk for hours getting to know each other, have sex and never see each other again. Well, that's what they are led to believe. Asher after never forgetting his night with her but not remembering her, started looking for her by any means possible, he has been looking for that woman for years and after a while stopped since he had lost hope and he had other issues to deal with other than finding that one-night stand.

The day they meet up again isn't the first time they see each other obviously but it is the first time that they actually remember each other without really remembering if you see what I mean. "I feel like I have seen her before." Was what runs in Ash's mind whenever he sees her. But since his mind was focusing on other tasks at hand it didn't click.

When Everleigh finally gets the courage to leave the hell hole she is in after realising that it wasn't healthy and it has gone too far and she decides to leave even if it meant to sleep in the streets then so be it. She happens to come across Dan getting beaten by Ash and the boys to get their money back. Of course, she isn't going to feel comfortable with these sort of men around her daughter and like some of you guys said she should have run away from him but why?

They had given her no real reason to flee. Without their tips at each lunch she would have never left, thanks to them Dan was no longer an issue, a man she barely knew defended her against her monster. And even if she did try to run, they would have got to her and there could have been a possibility of Rose getting hurt so that was a big no-no. She left with them because it was like coming home, or at least to the feeling of home because she knew that they were in a gang, that was the obvious part and she knew it. She left with them because even if at first she didn't think she would stay long, at least that night she had a safe place to stay until she could figure something out in the morning the next day.

Asher was very touchy feely and giving out sweet nicknames right off the bat because he felt comfortable enough to do so. Some people are just very comfortable with people they have just met and the thing with Asher also is that deep down he has always wanted a family and the fact that Everleigh seemed so familiar just made him connect with her even more. Sure they have been living under the same roof for a little three months, yeah I know it's a short period of time but why leave when you have protection, a roof over your head, food on the table, a man that treats you and your daughter the way you deserve and has shown you no reason as to why you should fear him and leave. She grew up in the gang life and sure she ran away from it and never wanted to associate herself with that sort of lifestyle but it has always been in her, she just needed that other half, that someone to show her that she can actually do it, to help her with her daughter. And that person was Ash.

When she goes to get Asher back in the first few chapters when he is held in a cell, the only thing she does is shoot at people and throws knives at the guy that is torturing Asher. In times of need, that killer/ gang leader side of her shows up. And in others, like when she was with Dan, it disappears and acts as if it was never there, to begin with.

And I know you all hate me for killing Carter and I'm sorry but I had too, he had to die... I still grieve for him and I think I will never stop but it was his time.

So there it is! I hope that you get a little more why she acts like she does and why that couple started off so fast.

Mortimer series:

His, Hers, Ours (book one)
Guns and Roses (book two)

Wolfgang (book three)

Her Damon (book four)

The Lost One (book five)

Trouble and Law (book six)

More books from this series may follow.

ABOUT THE AUTHOR

French and British eighteen year old living in the UK. She started writing the Mortimer series when she was sixteen and received an incredible response from her readers, so here we are! Currently studying History and Philosophy at the University of Kent, she is an animal lover, book reader, foodie, cinema enthusiast and with a love for music.

Follow the author for updates on all the books from the Mortimer series and other books on Instagram :

@mayacrosbyemery
@repunzel_0313

Or on Wattpad :

@repunzel0313

Or on twitter:

@may_crosby

Printed in Poland
by Amazon Fulfillment
Poland Sp. z o.o., Wrocław

57537272R00247